ONE WICKED MOMENT

This was the second time she had found him being cautious in his drinking. He would ruin his reputation as a dissolute man-about-town if he was not careful, she thought with a twist of the lips.

"Tsk, my lord! People have assured me you are very steeped in immoral ways, yet I never get to see you being wicked."

A slow smiled pulled at his lips. "Immoral? I could demand that you give me another kiss. Would that do?"

"A kiss is not immoral," she murmured.

His peacock-blue eyes danced. "It is if you do it properly."

Her lips parted as though she meant to speak.

"Charlotte?"

The blood tripped through her veins, making her breathe more rapidly than she ought. It did not take much soul-searching to realize that the attraction she'd experienced earlier in the night had been no accident.

"Yes?"

"I know I have disrupted your life," he said. He lowered his gaze, looking down to his hands holding his hat. "I would like to make up for it in some way, if you will let me. . . ."

The Reluctant Smuggler

Teresa DesJardien

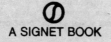

A SIGNET BOOK

SIGNET
Published by New American Library, a division of
Penguin Putnam Inc., 375 Hudson Street,
New York, New York 10014, U.S.A.
Penguin Books Ltd, 27 Wrights Lane,
London W8 5TZ, England
Penguin Books Australia Ltd, Ringwood,
Victoria, Australia
Penguin Books Canada Ltd, 10 Alcorn Avenue,
Toronto, Ontario, Canada M4V 3B2
Penguin Books (N.Z.) Ltd, 182–190 Wairau Road,
Auckland 10, New Zealand

Penguin Books Ltd, Registered Offices:
Harmondsworth, Middlesex, England

First published by Signet, an imprint of New American Library,
a division of Penguin Putnam Inc.

First Printing, February 2001
10 9 8 7 6 5 4 3 2 1

 REGISTERED TRADEMARK—MARCA REGISTRADA

Printed in the United States of America

PUBLISHER'S NOTE
This is a work of fiction. Names, characters, places, and incidents either are
the product of the author's imagination or are used fictitiously, and any
resemblance to actual persons, living or dead, business establishments, events,
or locales is entirely coincidental.

For Rich, Lorraine, Pete, Elizabeth,
and Tara DesJardien.
May the miles never divide us.

Chapter 1

The young, widowed Mrs. Charlotte Deems startled awake, realizing almost at once that a gust of wind had slammed open her front door.

"Oscar?" she muttered, sitting up, searching her bedchamber with one quick glance as she pushed her hair out of her eyes. She'd blown out the lamp, but the fire on the grate was enough to light even the corners of the small room. "Oscar?" she called again, louder, more alarmed. No answer came, no childish giggle.

Charlotte rose so swiftly and suddenly to her feet that the motion left her dizzy for several seconds—but the sensation passed, leaving in its wake a horrible feeling of pending disaster. Where was Oscar? Charlotte's gaze moved to her bedchamber door and beyond, to the wide open door of the front room.

She moved quickly, making a frantic search of the two other rooms the small cottage possessed, the kitchen and the front room. She looked in the portmanteau she had brought with her here, and in the basket for dirtied clothing, and under her bed. Her two-year-old son was not in the cottage.

I fell asleep, she accused herself even as she turned to run to the open cottage door. *While Oscar was awake, I fell asleep.* It did not matter that she'd been awake for almost two whole days, tending the boy's fever day and night. *Oscar was awake, but I was not. There was no one watching over him.* I *was not watching over him.*

Charlotte flew out of the isolated cottage, twisting right then left to search the immediate area. "Oscar!" she cried, hearing the fear in her own voice before the wind carried it away. There was no sign of her son, no gleam of white nightshift against the darkness that pressed upon her like a chilled hand.

The cliffs! her heart cried out, and Charlotte began to run, calling her son's name again and again. What if she were too late? No, she could not be! It could not be too late for him to hear her call. She would find him. He would be all right. The words wound through her mind, a prayer of sorts, as her gaze scoured the dark landscape for any sign as she hurried toward the treacherous cliffs above the Severn River.

There was no rain, thank God for that, but neither was there lightning, which might have provided at least a flash by which to spy her toddler. *He's scarcely two years old,* Charlotte thought, ruthlessly stifling a sob. Crying could do no good; it would only blur her vision. That was of no use, not when there was only the light of the moon, already made fickle by the clouds the blustering wind blew across its face.

"Oscar!" Charlotte screamed, knowing it was useless, that the wind carried the sound away—away from the cliffs.

She stumbled toward the cliffs, fear making her stiff, her gaze flitting from trembling branch to stirring leaf. She searched for movement, for a shade that was out of place, and her ears strained to hear a small cry over the wailing of the wind.

There, on the very edge of the cliff, she saw something. It was not right, it did not belong—but it was not a little boy standing there, Charlotte knew that in a moment. Instead of frightening her, the oddness made her move forward more quickly—was it an outgrowth of rock? Where she had never seen rock before? She thought she knew these cliffs overlooking the river, but in her dread had she wandered farther afield than she thought? Or did the night play tricks, making the familiar seem strange . . . ? Her steps slowed as she tried to understand what she saw. She was nearly at the edge of the cliffs— if Oscar was here, she did not want to startle him, did not want him to tumble over the precipice to a battered, watery death below.

The unfamiliar shape proved it was not a flight of her fancy, however, for of a sudden it bent. Charlotte gasped in surprise until she suddenly made out that it was a man, now on his knees. He was dressed all in dark clothing, with not even a hint of white linen at wrist or neck. His hair was covered by a dark, large, floppy hat.

"Smuggler!" she cried to herself in the slightest whisper. Her dread doubled, freezing her in place as she tried to sort in her mind how a smuggler came to be here, and if his presence had anything to do with Oscar.

The man's crouch altered again. Now he was lying flat on the earth. He looked like a shadow cast against the ground, and she thought she could easily have missed seeing him at all had he not moved. What was he doing?

His head disappeared from view, as if it had been severed from his length—and Charlotte had to bite back a scream just before she realized that the man had lowered his head and half his torso over the edge of the cliff. By all that was holy, was he there to commit suicide, and so strangely? She half-turned to leave, to find Oscar and let the madman do as he wished—but then a prickling on her neck stopped her, and she wondered if she had heard a small sound, a toddler's babble, carried by the wind to her ears.

She hurried to peer over the cliff's edge, mindful of the killing drop a misplaced step would bring, her heart pounding in a weird combination of hope and dread. She leaned forward, peering out and down.

At first all she saw was the dizzying, dark abyss just inches from her feet. But a flash of white trained her eye to the right spot—and there was Oscar, sitting on a tiny ledge that overlooked the river. Vertically, he was only two feet down, but from where Charlotte stood he was more than ten feet away. Charlotte's heart did a flip, reacting to a strange mingling of joy and dread. Oscar was found! In the very next instant, though, she knew he was far from safe. His thumb was in his mouth—causing Charlotte's heart now to sink; Oscar comforted

himself by sucking his thumb. It was a clear sign that he
felt some distress, some awareness of the precariousness
of his situation. His eyes, staring up at the man above
him, were wide and sober.

The man entirely garbed in black lay just above Oscar's position, and Charlotte could see now that he was
carefully stretching down his arm, reaching toward where
Oscar sat.

She took a step toward the man, the dark-clothed
stranger whose outstretched hand could rescue Oscar—
or push him to his death.

"Madam, do not move. He has not seen you yet. And
do not speak, I beg you," the man spoke low, but with
authority. "Do nothing to cause him to move."

Even as Charlotte wondered if she could leave her
child's fate in the hands of this man who clearly was on
the cliffs for no lawful purpose, he managed to gather a
handful of nightshirt in a black-gloved hand. In one swift
motion he pulled the nightshirt tight against Oscar's
form, and then lifted her son with a grunt. Charlotte gave
a strangled cry as her son dangled at arm's length, his
little feet kicking against the surprise of being hoisted
into the air, but then the man rolled onto his back at the
same time as he sat up. And there was Oscar, cradled
to the stranger's chest, both of them safe atop the
cliff's edge.

Oscar spied his mother at once and took his thumb
from his mouth to twist violently toward her, his small
arms uplifted in silent demand. Charlotte snatched her
son from the man's arms, took one step back, and then
fell to her quaking knees, unable to remain standing.
"You saved him," she said to the man, her voice quaver-
ing with relief. "You saved him. Thank you."

He must have heard her ragged words despite the
wind, for he nodded from where he sat. It was then that
the clouds parted for a long moment, allowing moonlight
to touch them both. His hand sprang to his face, discovering in an instant what had already been revealed to
Charlotte: that his black kerchief had slipped to pool

around his neck. His face was fully exposed to her, recognizable at once, as was his profession.

"Lord Sebastian Whitbury!" she said on a gasp. "By God, sir, you are a smuggler."

She regretted the words as soon as they burst from her lips. She should have pretended she did not recognize him, did not guess his purpose at waiting on the cliffs in all dark clothing.

He gave her a steady gaze; if there was any alarm in him, it did not show. "I presume I have now met the Widow Deems?" he said in return. His voice was firm and clear, not shaky and unnerved like hers.

He rose to his feet, and Charlotte desperately wished she had the ability to do the same, but it was all she could do to keep her trembling hands from dropping Oscar. For with the overwhelming relief she felt at holding her son once more in her arms, a new alarm mingled. This man had every reason to regret that she had seen his face.

"You do not need to kill us," Charlotte began at once, her voice steadier than her hands. He had just saved Oscar—surely he would not now choose to murder them both? Oscar could hardly identify him to the authorities—but Charlotte could. "I will swear not to tell anyone what I saw tonight!" she said, having to speak a bit louder to be heard over the restless wind. "I . . . I will move away from here—"

"I shan't harm you." Lord Sebastian shook his head and gave a puzzled smile.

A smile? It was the last thing she had expected.

"To what purpose?" he continued. "To keep you mum, is that the idea? But to achieve that end, madam, it would be more likely that I would marry you."

Charlotte parted her lips, but she knew no sound would come forth. What—? Marry her? Could he—?

"I was jesting, Mrs. Deems," Lord Sebastian said, his voice gentle, his mouth quirked in wry amusement. "Although I confess I am wounded to my very soul that the idea of death at my hand kept you speaking with me, whereas the very idea of marrying me made you turn absolutely mute." He extended his hand, supposedly a gentlemanly offer to help her to her feet.

Charlotte gripped Oscar more tightly with her left hand, slipping her right into Lord Sebastian's. His kid leather gloves were soft, expensive, and dark-colored in order to hide his hands. How absurd to give her hand to him, he who was plainly a smuggler. . . . But he had just saved her child—and she knew from her own past that not all smugglers were desperate men capable of murder.

No knife sprang from his sleeve, no movement revealed a pistol beneath his coat—all he did was help her to her feet, his other hand encompassing her elbow for a long moment, no doubt because he saw her teeter.

"I will tell no one," she said again, unsure what else to say.

"Do not look so terrified. Can you be so sure I am a smuggler, up to something nefarious?"

She eyed his attire, the kerchief now made pointless, and his large floppy hat. "You are no gentleman out for a leisurely stroll," she said, but despite the proof of her own eyes, of a long and deep dislike of smuggling, she felt her fears retreating. He had passed up too many opportunities in which he could have easily silenced her forever.

"Perhaps dark colors are all the rage in London these days?" Lord Sebastian suggested. He still sounded amused, sounded as if he had nothing to fear, perhaps to his folly. She could ruin him, by giving his name to the authorities . . . well, perhaps not. He *was* the son of a marquess. It would be his word against hers, and she was nobody. Perhaps he indeed had nothing to fear from her.

"I have recently come from London"—she served him back some of his own oddly inappropriate humor—"and I can tell you that white linen is all the mode."

He laughed, making a chill chase up her spine at the unexpected sound, but it was not a chill created from fear. His laugh was . . . pleasing, even under these peculiar circumstances.

"So you will not believe my fairy story?" He smiled,

and then a gust of wind swept over them, making the hair that had fallen from the knot pinned at the crown of Charlotte's head to whip about her face.

She saw that the wind did the same to him—and he doffed his hat and reached behind his head, dragging forward a length of hair half-fallen from the ribbon meant to bind it. His hair was as long as hers, past his shoulders, a fact she knew from having seen him out riding or walking the commons, even though they had never been introduced. He pulled the black ribbon from his hair, and the length of it cascaded around his shoulders, the only paleness about his person besides the oval of his face. In daylight his hair was a rich, deep, golden blond, just a few shades shy of brown, but even here in the moonlight it was easy to see it was some manner of honeyed color. It was the hair of a pirate, she found herself thinking.

She shook her head, blinking herself free of the long stare she realized she'd just given him. "I must go. Oscar—my son—has been unwell—"

"So he *is* a boy. I thought he looked like one. I am sorry to hear he has been ill." He hesitated. "But, Mrs. Deems, how can I let you go when you know my mission here, as well as my face?"

A chill of dread returned, doubled—she had been wrong to think he would not harm them. Charlotte half-turned away, shielding Oscar against her chest in case a blow should fall. The boy murmured around his thumb in protest.

"I will not tell anyone what I have seen," she assured him one more time.

"Promise," demanded the black-clad Lord Sebastian. He sounded firm—not cruel, but decisive, like a man used to being obeyed. But was there also something else there—more humor? Empathy? No matter. She would give this man his promise, if that was what he wanted.

She parted her lips to speak, but was momentarily struck dumb when her gaze touched his: he had oddly colored eyes, marked even in moonlight—she would guess they were blue, but a deep, rich blue. Her own eyes were blue—a nice, normal, sort of baby bunting blue, which she'd often been told was pretty with her brown hair. But his color of blue was . . . unusual, even arresting. More important, she would swear there was a dancing light of amusement in those eyes. Was he . . . could he be jesting with her? Even . . . flirting?

"I promise," she said at once.

He shook his head. "More fully than that. Say 'I will not tell anyone, ever, that I saw Lord Sebastian Whitbury, dressed in smuggler's clothing, standing atop the cliffs, not this night nor on any other before or since.' "

"I will not tell anyone, ever, that I saw Lord Sebastian Whitbury . . ." She paused, having lost the words in the muddle of caution and agitation that filled her. She wet her lips, struggling to recall his words.

"Not on this night nor on any other before or since," he prompted.

"You . . . you will use my property again, then?" she asked, then could have bit off her tongue for the foolishness of the question. But she had to know what he was making her vow to. Clearly, part of that vow was that she must turn a blind eye, must never bear witness against him for his act on this night or nights yet to come.

"Since you have seen me, yes, that is my intention. I will stand here every night until my task is complete. You, Mrs. Deems, have made your property a haven for me." He hesitated, then added, "That is the price you pay me for having saved your son."

Charlotte put her hand protectively over Oscar's head. "Did you put him on the ledge, just so you could rescue him?"

All humor faded from his face. "No," he said with cold finality.

She had insulted him! It seemed odd to be able to insult a smuggler—and, more oddly yet, to believe what he claimed.

"All I want is your word, Mrs. Deems." He turned his gaze back to hers. "I do not know you, so I can only trust that your word is of value. Give me that word, and then you may return to your cottage."

"Agreed," she said at once. "You have my word. I will tell no one, ever, of your presence here."

"Good." He nodded, gazed into her eyes, then tilted his head in the general direction of her cottage. "Then go."

She turned at once, and took four strides before she thought to glance in fear over her shoulder. He did not come after her, was not behind her with a raised cudgel or garrote—he only gazed out to sea, with his oddly long hair whipping about his shoulders.

She stopped, surprising herself—but the moment was unfinished. Devil, madman, deliverer from harm—whatever he was, she owed him at least one small thing. "Thank you. For saving my son."

"And probably yourself as well, Mrs. Deems." He nodded without looking at her. "The ledge had a narrow path down to it, that was how your lad got there—but I doubt either you or I would have fared so well upon it."

A vision flashed before her eyes, as chilling as the wind that snatched at her clothing. She saw herself teetering on a thin path, and then a small loose rock under her slipper making her lose her balance . . . her fall forward, sweeping Oscar with her to a death on the rocks below the cliff. . . .

"Wait," Lord Sebastian said just as she turned again to go. Now he did turn to face her, crossing at once to her side. "I have one last request of you, this one for saving your life."

What could he want? She shook her head. "I have no money—"

"I wish to seal our agreement."

"I gave you my word."

He shook his head. "It's not enough. I want your kiss as well."

"A kiss?" She stared into his face—belatedly realizing he was handsome. Peculiar that the fact should strike her now, at this moment.

He did not wait for her to answer or sort through her thoughts—he gently nudged Oscar to one side, so that she settled her son onto her hip, and then he took her

face in his hands. He kissed her full on the mouth, but
not roughly. It was an intimate kiss in many ways— de-
manding, warm, unrestrained. She felt an impulse to
close her eyes, but she merely blinked, and watched as
the wind caught his hair, sending it to flutter in tendrils
around both their faces to tangle with her own hair. Then
her gaze met his over their kiss, and that shock was more
intimate in some ways than the kiss itself.

With just as little ceremony, he stepped back, his hands
dropping, his warm mouth gone from hers, leaving her
own mouth tingling with awareness.

Was that really all he had wanted, a kiss? A shiver
chased through her, making her frown, for his kiss had
not been utterly unpleasant. It was difficult to believe
that he would not demand more, not charge that old
payment that scoundrels always demanded of lone females, that she bed with him. If that was what he wanted,
then she would beg, plead on her knees if she had to,
that she be allowed to go back to her cottage, that she
could place Oscar in another room. . . .

He made no suggestion, however, nor did she discover
it in his steady gaze.

"But why?" she whispered, questioning the kiss.

He smiled, ever so slightly. "Some bargains are best
sealed by a hand clasp, or by the spilling of blood—" He
took a step closer, looking down into her face, undoubtedly seeing her questions, her resistance. "The bargain
of marriage is sealed by the sex act," he added, his gaze
tripping over her mouth. "But," he went on, perhaps his
smile growing a fraction wider, "our bargain has been
sealed by the oldest method of all, by a kiss. A woman
may forget many a word, Mrs. Deems, but she always
remembers a kiss. You will remember the pledge we
made here tonight."

"Yes." She nodded reluctantly, not wanting to agree,
but knowing he was right. He had meant to fix their
bargain in her mind—and he had achieved his goal. She
could not deny that, not with her lips tingling yet.

"Go," he said then, not unkindly, and turned away
himself. His long black great coat swept behind him like

a cape, his unbound hair forming another small cape upon his shoulders. He did not look back, only stopping long enough to fetch up something—the merest glimmer of light made her think it must be a sheltered lantern—and then he faded into the darkness of the night as easily as a wraith.

Charlotte stared after him, a little in awe of how quickly the night had swallowed any sign of him. She then looked down at her son, only to find him staring up at her, his thumb now neglected. Oscar was already once again content, not looking anywhere near as stunned as his mother felt.

She realized with a shiver—this one of relief—that her son was whole in her arms, and the fever that had dulled his eyes for two nights was now broken. While she'd slipped into unintended slumber, he'd tossed off his fever and grown eager to play, to try his luck at opening a door by himself.

"Oh, Oscar!" she said, lifting up the front of her skirt to wrap it around his shoulders in a vaguely capelike fashion, feeling the night's chill creep through her petticoats. She turned toward her cottage, walking with limbs made curiously light by release from the double dread she'd experienced this night. "This, everything that happened tonight, would never have occurred if I had remarried," she said to her son on a sigh. The bane of her thoughts: remarriage. She should, she should, she knew she ought to remarry. Oscar deserved security, and he deserved a father, regardless of her own desires.

Her own desires made her turn away from the very thought of remarrying.

"What if I married Lord Sebastian Whitbury?" she said to Oscar, feeling a bit giddy from the wash of emotions that had coursed through her this night. "And what if trout learn to fly?" She swirled around, making Oscar chortle.

"Well, I think perhaps 'no' on marrying My Lord Smuggler," she said, swirling a second time so she could join her son in relieved laughter. "Still, at the very least," she said, kissing her son's head as she turned to stride toward her cottage, "from now on, I will hire a minder to watch you when I *have* to sleep, imp. And I will use the latch on the door," she vowed, even though only yesterday she'd vowed to take it off entirely. It was a reminder that her cottage had once been used by smugglers—men perhaps more cruel than Lord Sebastian—men who made decent folk want latches on their doors.

Now she felt that need as well, as she shut the door behind her and ran the bolt home in order to keep her son inside . . . and, it was to be hoped, keep dark-suited strangers outside.

Chapter 2

Oscar sat on Mrs. Hyatt's hip as Charlotte waved farewell to him, but Oscar's attention was already focused on the clearly intriguing three little Hyatt girls. His fascination made both ladies smile across the distance that separated them before Charlotte turned away.

Well satisfied that Oscar would be content, Charlotte moved through the woman's front gate, a little dazzled by the bright sunlight that crept around the edges of her bonnet. Had it only been last night that the wind had blown so—and when a smuggler had taken a kiss from her in the dark? It was almost impossible to believe what had transpired, so different was day from night. But the dirt on her dress's hem this morning had convinced Charlotte it had not all been a bizarre dream, that she had almost lost her son over the cliffs—if not for the intervention of the unlikeliest of all rescuers.

Well, Oscar would never again have the chance to wander out of the house unminded. The bolt would be thrown every night from now on. And the nearest neighbor—whose "nearness" was a quarter mile distance from Charlotte's cottage—had just agreed to mind Oscar when the occasional need arose, in exchange for Charlotte minding Mrs. Hyatt's children in return.

Oscar had brightened at once upon discovering Mrs. Hyatt not only had ginger cake to offer, but three little girls of an age to gain his rapt attention. Charlotte would have to make a point of bringing him to Mrs. Hyatt's, for a lad must have playmates, and Oscar had gone two months with only his mama for company as they'd settled into their new life.

He would have had many a playmate in London—but there was no point in worrying that old bone, for they had been unable to remain in London. They lived in Severn's Well now, in a small cottage on the cliffs above the River Severn, because no place else offered the combination of affordability and invisibility, both of which Charlotte needed now.

She shook her head, dismissing old thoughts, pleased Oscar had agreed to stay with Mrs. Hyatt—or, to judge more correctly from his open-mouthed stare, with Mrs. Hyatt's six year old daughter, Evie, and Evie's two littler sisters.

"I will be back soon, after I take a stroll," Charlotte had told Mrs. Hyatt. "Perhaps to the common."

"The common? Then you will see the match there," Mrs. Hyatt said with a pleased nod.

"Is there a cricket match today?" Charlotte had asked, smiling with real pleasure when the other lady nodded. What an unexpected treat, for the sport was Charlotte's favorite to watch. In fact, she would have taken a leisurely stroll toward the common but she found her pace picking up, as though to echo the thrill that swept through her at the familiar sound of cricketers calling to one another.

"Back, Maddock, else he'll send it behind!" a male voice called out.

The sound carried on the air, making Charlotte envision the game she could not see because of the shielding trees that marked this side of the common. She knew just beyond the trees was an expanse of lawn, trimmed haphazardly by the local cattle that had the right to graze there.

She adored the game of cricket, without quite understanding why. She ought to resent it, for her father had gambled away much of the family income by betting on sporting matches. Of course it had seldom been cricket, mostly it was cockfights or prizefights or horse races. The urge to wager had been woven into Papa's very nature; Charlotte had even been grateful that he knew a certain stopping point, that he made sure the estate was tended and a roof kept over their heads. That had been a naïve notion, she knew that now; when Papa had passed on, so had his income and his estate, except for a small jointure for Mama.

It had been a terrible strain, moving out of the family home so that Uncle Gerald, the new lord of the manor, could move in. They hadn't known it then but dementia had already begun to claim him, and he'd made it clear he felt no obligation to house his brother's wife and daughter.

Before, due to Papa's wagering they'd not had many servants nor new clothes—but once he was buried they had none. Sometimes dinner was only a thin soup. And Mama had fretted constantly about the cost of coal when the weather turned cold. One winter of near-poverty had convinced mother and daughter to look about for marriage, and both had been relieved when the Reverend Jarvis Deems had offered for Charlotte.

Still, even if cricket and its like had siphoned away the money that would have given Charlotte some choices in life, even though its loss had propelled her into a hasty, unfortunate marriage, she could not resent the game itself. Some of her fondest memories were of sitting at her father's side, cheering on the local lads. She would not forget the good times just because bad times had followed.

Jarvis, on the other hand, had thought of cricket as nothing more than a waste of God-given time. Sometimes Charlotte wondered if his objection to the game was the very thing that had kept her interested despite everything . . . ?

But, no, her interest in the game had endured for years now. She could sit and watch cricket for hours on end, reveling in the skill of the bowler and the power in the batsman's swing. Her father had taught her the finer points of the game, and they had shared a special bond in its appreciation. Papa had passed on to his reward three years ago, yet even with the revelations his death had brought, Charlotte's love of the game had not died with him.

And what had Jarvis and I ever shared that I yet love? Charlotte asked herself, already knowing there was but one answer: Oscar. Their child had been the only thing that Jarvis had left her. The Reverend Jarvis Deems— her husband, now nearly six months deceased.

He'd been seven years older than Charlotte, and a bit bombastic even off the pulpit—more than a bit, in fact. He'd made up his mind it was time for a helpmeet in conducting the busy duties of his vicarage shortly before he'd met Charlotte, and once she had counted herself lucky for meeting him at such an opportune moment in time. Unfortunately, his fatal flaw—an impractical nature—had not been evident until after their hasty marriage was made. Indeed, its extent had startled Charlotte terribly when Jarvis had passed on and the extent of his folly had been revealed.

It was for her husband that she still wore black— although for two months she'd been allowing bits of white to show here at her collar or there at a ruched hem. She *did* mourn his passing, for he had not been so much an awful man as a foolish one—but nothing would keep her in black one day longer than the normal six months of mourning required. She would be glad for the lavenders and browns and grays of half-mourning, and gladder yet when she could once again don any color she liked. It was not even the lack of choice that bothered her—it was having to make an outward show of grief that she did not feel in the depths of her heart.

She had tried to love him, at least as much as he'd allowed her to, and he had tried to make a home for her, even if he could not love her. He had never truly liked the person Charlotte was, she knew that now. It had not been that Jarvis was unkind—but simply that he did not share her humor or her aspirations. Their marriage had been a misalliance, and he had at some level realized it first. What a burden she must have been to him, trying to make roses bloom on sterile ground, for that was what their marriage had become.

His passing had been a shock, not least because a part of her had still been hoping against hope that familiarity might one day make things right between them . . . but one day was not to be.

Today, however, was too bright and clear a day for mourning. Today was one of those crisp spring mornings that lifted the heart and made one wish to think of the future, not dwell on the past. It was a perfect day for settling on the common, watching handsome, well-to-do young men play on a team against another made of their butlers or valets, and letting old cares melt away in the promise of summer sun to come.

Charlotte stepped through the barrier made by the trees, smiling at once at the sight of men in their shirt-sleeves and waistcoats. Their coats were cast aside into a pile, their concentration utterly given over to the moment between the bowler and the batsman, the latter intent on defending the wicket while the former attempted to send the bails flying. It would be pleasant to watch the game for a little while, to let her cares be forgotten as she enjoyed the play of the ball across the rich green field.

There ahead was a perfectly placed oak, just right for a back rest from which to observe the cricketers. Charlotte settled beneath the tree, spreading her skirts over her outstretched legs, but had no more than reclined against the tree trunk when she sat straight up again in surprise.

The batsman was none other than Lord Sebastian Whitbury—the smuggler from last night. His long honey blond hair was pulled back in an orderly queue. He had shed his coat like everyone else, revealing a waistcoat of gray and white stripes atop gray breeches and white stockings. There were, in fact, no dark tones about his person today at all, quite unlike last evening.

"One garb for night and one for day," Charlotte said to herself, and it was almost as if he might have heard her, for at that very moment he glanced her way. He dropped out of his stance, staring at her over his bat, clearly surprised to see her there. Then he howled in outrage as the ball bounced up from the dirt and knocked his wicket apart with a dramatic scattering of stumps and bails.

"Sir, that is an out!" declared the nearest umpire, who was also the local baker.

Lord Sebastian's teammates called out in jocular derision, as teammates ever do when one has made a foolish play. "You could have had that one, Whitbury!" a tall young gentleman hooted.

"He was fouled," the blatant untruth was offered, carrying clearly across the field.

"What's the first rule, Whitbury? 'Watch the ball!' That's what you tell me constantly, ain't it?" taunted the man who came out to take his place as the field shifted to defend the second wicket.

To his credit, Charlotte saw that Lord Sebastian grinned. "Glad to know you listen, Hainesbury," she heard his reply.

Lord Sebastian handed Hainesbury his bat, and then hastened off the field of play. To Charlotte's surprise, he did not move to join his teammates yet waiting to bat, but came directly toward her.

He gave her a nod as he drew abreast of her, then without ceremony threw himself down on the grass beside her, balancing his weight on his elbows, his long legs stretched out before him. He was still coatless, nor did he sport either hat or gloves.

He clearly had determined for himself that his presence would be welcome—but Charlotte did not expect better manners of him. She had not been in Severn's Well more than a day before she'd first heard tell of the wicked and wild third son of the old Marquess of Greyleigh.

"A real cares-for-nobody," was the general consensus. "And with a devilish smile that makes you forget you're cross or cautious around him," said half the women who spoke of him.

Charlotte had been told a dozen eyebrow-lifting tales to support the claims, from live trout he'd placed in the punch bowl at the wedding breakfast of a former sweetheart, to midnight picnics in the churchyard with a gaggle of doxies. While these were things that might be excused as youthful flippancy, then again they were enough to show Sebastian Whitbury had a wayward side, a disturbing tendency to seek out trouble.

Yet this was the man who had saved Oscar. Curious, to find both generosity and vice in the same man. Her husband, Jarvis, had been upright sometimes to the point of blandness, Charlotte thought and not for the first time. Lord Sebastian was clearly not of the same ilk.

"Good morning, Mrs. Deems," Lord Sebastian said now, shaking her from her observations as he glanced at her from the corner of his eye. He was no more than an arm's length from her side, yet there was something in his manner that suggested he would not stay if he remained uninvited. So perhaps he had some limited sense of manners—when he chose to exercise it.

"Good morning, Lord Sebastian," she answered in a cool but marginally friendly voice, thereby granting him the privilege of her company.

He settled back onto his elbows; if he'd been right beside her, his head could have rested on one of the large roots of the tree against which she reclined.

He turned his head to glance at her as he grinned. "You cost me that wicket, you know."

"I do know. I saw you startle."

"I did not startle!" He seemed offended, but then she saw that his grin had not faltered. "Well, not much anyway. It is simply that the moment I spied you it had me remembering last night."

She blushed, recalling their kiss even while she knew a shock of surprise that he had mentioned their encounter. She would have thought he'd prefer to pretend his nocturnal activity had never occurred.

"I must thank you again for rescuing Oscar," she said, wondering if a repeat of her thanks was what had drawn him to her side.

"Oscar? Is that your lad's name? I do not think you said last night."

"I had . . . other concerns on my mind."

"You were shaking like one of the leaves in the wind. I could see that even though it was dark."

She considered him for one long moment, noting that

daylight did nothing to change her opinion that he was handsome. It was said that of the three Whitbury sons, Lord Sebastian was the most attractive—handsome as the very devil and about half as wicked, some said. She wondered why he wore his hair so unfashionably long, although she had to admit it suited him, especially when it flowed around his shoulders as it had last night. In daylight it was easy to see she'd been right, his eyes were a rich blue—a unique color that demanded a closer inspection. Not that she had any intention of ever being closer to him than she was at the moment.

"You speak so openly. Are you not concerned?" she asked.

"Of what?" he countered, rolling over onto his stomach, now a foot closer to her, unknowingly defying the distance she'd hoped to keep between them. She could reach out and brush the hair from his forehead, if she desired.

He placed his chin in his hand and gazed, unblinking, up at Charlotte in her elevated sitting position. She could now see clearly that his eyes were almost like the blue of a peacock's tail, a blue made deeper by a hint of green. She'd seen sky blue, and robin's egg blue, and ocean-depths blue eyes—but never this particular shade, like the summer sky after dusk but just before night stole away all color.

She shook her head, belatedly recalling he'd asked her a question. What would he have to be concerned about? "That I will tell your secrets," she said.

"But, Mrs. Deems, you promised not to, and sealed that promise with a kiss." He grinned. "A nice kiss, if I may say so."

He looks very like a cat, Charlotte thought around a strange flip-flop sensation in the pit of her stomach, *a poorly behaved cat that* enjoys *being poorly behaved.* If only he had a tail to twitch.

"A kiss that was forced upon me," she stated.

He rolled once more onto his elbows to face the game, clearly unconcerned about whether he might stain or muss his well-fitted clothing, and gave a laugh. "Hardly forced."

Charlotte felt a blush bloom in her cheeks. The cursed thing of it was that she could not argue the point with him—she had not been forced to kiss him, not really.

The crack of wood against leather made her join him in observing the game, and out of the corner of her eye Charlotte saw Lord Sebastian's fist clench in a sign of satisfaction as the cricket ball soared into the sky, only to fall to earth between two of the fielders. "Go, Clarence! Go, Derrick!" he called out to his fellow batsmen.

When the two batsmen had both safely crossed the crease twice, achieving two runs, Lord Sebastian turned his gaze back to Charlotte. His eyes were like blue flames, plainly reflecting his satisfaction with the play. She wondered fleetingly if she had anything like this look about her when she got caught up in the game of cricket, and frowned a little to think she might. His delight at his team's success was too . . . too *immediate*. Frank. Even raw. Jarvis would have taken an immediate dislike of Lord Sebastian, she knew, for the simple sin of showing too much pleasure in a mere game's results.

Since his gaze was so candid, she decided to be frank as well. "But I truly am curious. Why did you come over to visit with me, just now?"

He glanced at her out of the corner of his eye again, not quite grinning. "Perhaps I crave another kiss from your lips."

"Pshaw."

"Pshaw? I did not know anyone under the age of forty ever said 'pshaw.' You are a constant surprise, Mrs. Deems."

"No less so than you, Lord Sebastian. But, come, tell me the real reason you chose to share my company."

He crossed his legs at the ankle, a man of leisure—at least during the day. "You are new to Severn's Well," he said, his words perhaps still laced a bit with amusement, but honest enough, not mocking her. "You have been here only a few weeks. No one knows much about you, although the general feeling is that you are an honest sort, not given to gossiping, and you tend to keep to yourself. I came over to judge you, in a way I could not last night. You must agree it was a difficult circumstance under which to make a quick judgment of your nature."

"You mean, you wondered if come the morning, despite my promise, I would tell what I had seen?"

"That is exactly what I mean, Mrs. Deems." He sat up, wrapping his arms around one leg as he turned more toward her. He grinned, but the smile did not reach his eyes, which watched her own closely. The image of a cat—leisurely one moment, but with focused attention the next—sprang to mind again.

"I do my best not to break a vow," Charlotte told him.

He gave a small grunt, then nodded. "I heard how you hedged that, you know. 'Do my best.' In the past you've had to break a vow, have you not? Perhaps even though you did not like to do it?"

"Or could it have been simply an awkward phrase," she offered, "not meant to hide anything at all?"

He stared at her, considering. "Possibly," he conceded, but she did not think he really believed it. She must have given herself away somehow, for the truth was she *had* broken a vow, even if not by choice. In the end she'd been unable to honor her husband as she'd promised she would, as she'd said she would in her marriage vow.

Whether Lord Sebastian believed her or not, his grin now spread up into his eyes, making them sparkle like exotic gems in the morning sunlight. "Well then, ma'am, please do your best by your vow to *me,* will you? But for now, let us find a new topic. As a newcomer to Severn's Well, I value your opinion. What do you think of the plan the aldermen have for building a set of assembly rooms . . ." But the question was never finished, for Lord Sebastian's whole attention had been captured by a new sight.

Charlotte twisted where she sat, to gaze in the same direction as he. She saw at once what had robbed the man of both his words and attentiveness: Miss Natalie Talbot, promenading on the arm of her father, approaching the common.

Miss Talbot and Charlotte had met twice before, their acquaintance consisting of one quick introduction, followed a week or so later by their mutual attendance at a meeting for the ladies who arranged flowers for the church. It had not taken any more time than that, however, for Charlotte to be aware that Miss Talbot was the sort to turn male heads, for even their married vicar was at once enchanted by the woman's company.

It was not that Miss Talbot was a great beauty, although she had a pleasant visage, even pretty. Her black hair was always artfully arranged under her bonnet, but it was not glossy nor lustrously thick. It did, however, show to advantage her creamy white complexion.

Yet there was something in her demeanor that caught one's attention, a way of holding her head and shoulders that made her seem prettier than she was, and a manner that made her seem polished. Miss Talbot would never laugh too loud, but all the same she could be free with her smiles. She came from a good family, but did not stand upon ceremony when it did not suit the occasion. She would be gracious until one crossed her, then her faintly injured frown was enough to make you desire to repent whatever sin had offended her.

It was difficult to find a fault to pin upon Miss Talbot. Which, Charlotte reflected with a wry twist of her mouth, made Miss Talbot the most annoying creature on the face of the earth, at least to every other female.

Now the male of the species . . . Well, Charlotte could hardly blame Lord Sebastian if he was attracted to the perfection that was Miss Talbot.

"Mrs. Deems, do please excuse me," Lord Sebastian said as he leaped to his feet.

"Certainly," Charlotte replied, but he had already begun to walk toward Miss Talbot before Charlotte could get the word out completely. Instead of taking umbrage, Charlotte smiled to herself. He did not even pretend at indifference toward the woman who now captured all his attention; he did not realize how much—or else did not care—that his infatuation with Miss Talbot was there for all to see.

Chapter 3

Charlotte shook her head, but not at Lord Sebastian Whitbury. At herself. She must be, what? Two years older than him? Still, at the grand old age of four-and-twenty she felt in spirit a dozen years his senior. She doubted she'd ever had such stars in her eyes—no, not even when she had first agreed to marry Jarvis. That had been an utterly practical decision, with no pretense at love, only the hope of it.

She'd prayed for affection's growing touch, had tried for a long while to pretend she felt it spreading between them. She'd thought that a bit of determination could bring forth an infatuation for her husband, one that could have bloomed into love—but willing a thing and actually having it turned out to be two utterly different things. They'd formed a tolerance, yes, but never affection.

So, truth be told, it was not love that had aged and wounded her heart, but a *lack* of love. It had been Jarvis's on-going coolness toward her that had made her emotions feel constantly pummeled, that had aged her soul beyond her meager years. It was a *lack* that had left her heart unable to foolishly tumble into the kind of instant and fragile attraction that milord so obviously had developed for Miss Talbot.

Mouth pursed by the pain of old memories, Charlotte lingered a while longer watching the cricketers. The game, as always, served as a distraction and a balm. She found herself cheering equally for both teams, both for the Gentlemen and for the valets and grooms who made up the Players. It was the skill she celebrated, not caring if a good play was made by a man of better birth, or

lowly. She saw out of the corner of her eye that Miss
Talbot, the woman's father, and Lord Sebastian only ap-
plauded for the Gentlemen's good fortune—as might be
expected, since Lord Sebastian batted for the Gentlemen.
However, for herself Charlotte enjoyed a good play no
matter who made it, aristocrat or servant, and she
cheered and clapped equally to let them know it.

The sun had risen about as high as it would on this
spring day, proving it was time for luncheon and to retrieve Oscar. When Charlotte rose and walked away
from the game, she had to pass the very group she'd
glanced toward several times. Miss Talbot gave her a
cool nod—all that was proper, if not exactly friendly—
but the woman's father the baron, Lord Lamont, merely
glanced Charlotte's way. Well, she was new to the area—
some exclusivity was to be expected. It was foolish to
take offense too easily in a small town—and what purpose in taking offense anyway? Let them ignore or snub
her as they wished, so long as they did not investigate
how Charlotte Deems came to live in the little seaside
cottage where her grandpapa had gone to escape the
heat of summer months.

Lord Sebastian, however, choosing to be true to his
reputation as a force ungoverned, called out to her as
she stepped nearby. "Mrs. Deems, I saw you just now.
How dare you cheer my man's getting out?" he teased,
his mouth frowning but his eyes smiling.

Lord Lamont gave him a dark look for his trouble, and
Charlotte could have wished Lord Sebastian had been a
little more genteel, not calling to her as if she were a
common milkmaid. Still, country manners were less formal, and to be following her own advice, she had no
desire to snub the man. She turned her steps, the better
to intersect where the small group stood. "Are you captain today then, Lord Sebastian?" she called back.

"I am. And am most days, for that matter," he assured
her as she stepped up to the group. "I am rather clever
in how I place my fielders, you see. A natural leader."
He boasted so broadly, down to puffing up his chest, that
it made his claim palatable if not downright amusing. He

might be a wild, unchecked creature, but he was an engaging one as well, capable of self-mockery. Jarvis would have sooner perished than make a joke at his own expense.

"A natural leader? Surely not in how you instruct your batsmen, as the last out proves," Charlotte countered.

"Why, you horrid woman!" Lord Sebastian made a face at her, making her laugh aloud. "I detest plain speakers, I would have you know, Mrs. Deems."

"Then you will have to detest me."

"So I shall."

Miss Talbot gave a flicker of a smile—she was clearly not quite certain humor was at play and feared offending—and her father scowled. Lord Sebastian may have noticed the responses of his companions, but he grinned at Charlotte all the same. She suspected he was more than used to doing as he pleased, used to ignoring those who would censure him. By reputation, he'd been doing as he wished for years. Out of defiance of a too-stern father and a mad mama who could not watch over him, it was said.

"When do you play again?" she inquired.

"Today, you mean?"

"Not when do you bat again, but when does the team play again? Is there a schedule?"

He gave a little shrug, more with his head than his shoulders, the gesture of someone trying to be casual about something they in truth cared about. "We try to meet every third Saturday, if enough players can be had."

"Oh," she said with genuine disappointment. The time for cricket play was too short, she thought, limited by the vagaries of English weather to the late spring and summer months. She'd hoped there might be a match every week. Ah well.

"Today is just practice, though. We try to do that once or twice a week."

Charlotte gave a satisfied nod. "Excellent! When do you practice next? May I bring my son to observe?"

"Of course," he said, something unexpectedly warm in

his voice, and perhaps also in his gaze. Charlotte felt her lips part, felt faintly dazzled by the impact of it. It was a singularly . . . *intimate* moment, something shared between just the two of them. Perhaps Lord Sebastian recalled how he'd rescued her son, perhaps he realized anew the risk he'd taken by hanging half his body from the rough, unreliable edge of a cliff? Whatever his thoughts, there was no denying that a kind of bond had been formed between the two of them, a connection through Oscar, who last night had literally been a step from death and whom Lord Sebastian had dragged back into the arms of the living.

Charlotte felt a new rush of gratitude, now unhampered by last night's fear, and she allowed her thankfulness to flood into her gaze.

A startled look filtered across Lord Sebastian's face, and then he gave her the simplest of nods, an acknowledgment.

"We should be practicing again on Wednesday," he told Charlotte, but it was Miss Talbot who murmured something affirmative at his side, capturing his attention anew. For a moment he looked dazed, but then his focus centered once more on Miss Talbot.

"Will you come?" he asked her. Another warmth, more intimate yet, invaded his features. The gaze he gave Miss Talbot was eager and hopeful and *hungry*.

It warmed Charlotte's blood, and here she was ten feet away and not even the recipient of it. But there had been a moment . . . she'd felt the impact of Lord Sebastian's regard . . . and, oh, if only Jarvis had ever once centered the whole of his regard on Charlotte in such a way! What could have happened between them? What coolness could have resisted such warmth? To see how Lord Sebastian looked upon Miss Talbot was to wonder what it would be like to be so conspicuously cherished. . . .

But she must not become maudlin or foolishly romantic, Charlotte silently chided herself. This man was a rakehell, the very kind of creature who had a talent for making one feel as if one stood at the center of his universe—but it would be folly to think his attention toward her was anything other than transient. He had a way of looking at a woman, any woman—and any glances he might send Charlotte's way would not measure against the way he looked at Miss Natalie Talbot.

For Charlotte to long for hungry, love-starved gazes—well, it was the height of foolishness, was it not? Her husband was dead . . . so what point was there to indulging in romantic folderol? Who was there to be romantic with? She *could* marry again, she knew she even *should,* to protect herself, but more important to protect Oscar. But to hope for romance . . . well, she could not afford such frivolous, youthful daydreams.

Charlotte mumbled her farewells to the group, telling herself that she was grateful Lord Sebastian had shifted all of his steady gaze to Miss Talbot, for then he was too occupied to call out anything more in Charlotte's wake.

Another fellow called to her instead: Oscar cried "Mama!" as soon as she stepped into Mrs. Hyatt's garden. He had been happily digging in the dirt with a stick alongside the two youngest Hyatts, but even the fascination of other youngsters had not dulled his enthusiastic greeting for his mother. He was not so quick to want to leave, however, which suited Charlotte well enough for it meant he had enjoyed being there. She felt a pang that Oscar was very unlikely to experience siblings of his own, but there was no point in bemoaning those things that could not be changed.

After a few more minutes of dirt digging, Oscar was persuaded to drop his stick, take his mama's hand, and wave farewell to the Hyatt girls, and then Charlotte bid Mrs. Hyatt a good day. Oscar quickly tired of walking, so Charlotte put him on her hip for the rest of the quarter-mile walk. His two-year-old banter, a mix of nonsense and real words, was today largely incomprehensible to her adult ear. Charlotte said "oh" and "mm-hmm" all the same, all the while thinking how lucky she was to have her son, dirt and all, well and hale. All due to an act of bravery by a lawbreaker in gentlemen's clothing.

After mounting a small rise, Charlotte was able to spy her cottage, not far from the cliffs. She loved the sounds that carried from the river below, the movement of water, the shouts of sailors and merchants, the scent of river water and how it was occasionally overpowered by the tang of ocean that mingled at the river's mouth. She could not approach her home without having to cast an admiring eye toward the charming scenery nature had painted all around her cottage.

In her two months here, she had grown used to the patterns of the place, the lean of this tree, the size of that boulder, and today she spied at once that something was different about the cliff's edge. Intrigued, she veered her path just a little, approaching the cliff, realizing it was the very spot where Oscar had been in such dire danger last night.

She walked to where she had stood in the darkness, and now by day's light saw that she was not mistaken. Someone had taken a tool to the edge, cutting away the path that had led to the little ledge below, leaving no access to it now.

The alteration had to have been made by Lord Sebastian, for who else would think to do it? He had returned here and made sure Oscar would not have a second chance to take the dangerous and misleading path to nowhere.

Charlotte felt a second warming of her blood, not a man-to-woman affinity as she'd known earlier, but one that had everything to do with gratefulness. He had thought to do this thing, had saved Charlotte from the labor of it—that is, if she were to have ever thought of it herself—and all for no reward. It had been a . . . a *thoughtful* act.

It did not matter that such a noble word as "thoughtful" did not coincide easily with that of "smuggler." With this man, Charlotte was learning, she must simply add "unique" to the already curious combination of words she'd pinned on him: "glib" and "quick-humored" and "raw" and "ungoverned," perhaps even "dangerous."

If she had not known it before, she now knew Lord Sebastian was a man of contrasts.

There was one more word she could add to her list

to describe him: *caring*. Altering the cliff had been a considerate, even noble act. And even if it had been someone else who had altered the cliff, still Charlotte had seen the candid longing in his face as he'd gazed at Miss Talbot; she knew that people called him a cares-for-nobody, but now she also was convinced that people were wrong.

Charlotte shook her head, for she'd seen something else as well. She had not been so rattled by Lord Sebastian's intense gaze that she had missed Lord Lamont's expression: Miss Talbot's father had taken no pains to hide his dislike of Lord Sebastian.

To long for someone's love, but never to receive it—Charlotte knew very well how that felt. She could not help but fear Lord Sebastian had fixed his heart on a lady whose hand would be unobtainable.

Engaged in criminal acts or not, strange ways or no, Lord Sebastian had proven his behavior could be admirable . . . but what would his wild side do if the nobler side of his character was denied in love?

Charlotte shook her head again and hoped she was wrong. She dreaded, for his heart's sake, what she suspected lay ahead for Lord Sebastian Whitbury.

As he walked back from the cricket game toward his home on Severn's Well's highest hill, Sebastian reflected that nearly everyone he knew would consider him a callow youth. He was but two-and-twenty, so there was some basis for this conclusion—although few people could know that he had not been childlike for a very long time. At least not a child in spirit, for there had been too few people in his youth to nourish any childish fancies he might have once had.

He hitched the sack of cricket bats higher on his shoulder, and worked to push aside old thoughts of childhood. That childhood had been a dark place, lightened only by the love of his brothers. Now that their father was dead and buried, there was no point in lingering on old wishes that had never stood a hope of coming true. His father had never changed into a kinder, less judgmental being, and his mother . . . Sebastian could not remember a time when his poor, mad mother had looked at him with comprehension, let alone love.

But, to think of love . . . That was to change the subject to one Miss Natalie Talbot. He knew his feelings for the pretty black-haired woman would be called puppy love—for that matter, they probably were to one degree or another. She certainly was the first woman he'd ever fallen for. But, oh, how glorious a thing love was, even be it puppy love!

The irony was that some of the residents of this village, the home he had recently returned to, would be surprised to learn that the purportedly wild and untamed youngest Whitbury son was not so proficient at this game called love as their whispers would have it.

While Sebastian had shared a dozen beds or more despite his meager years, which of them had been couplings made from *love*? None. Love was another thing altogether. He'd never felt anything beyond simple lust. A giggle here, a tumble there. It had all been in good sport, and nothing beyond that. He'd been happy enough to play the role of dissolute younger son.

Now, however, he knew the difference: lust was mere wanting; love was ever so much more complex. He found, much to his surprise, that Miss Talbot's happiness mattered to him. Her benevolent glances toward him mattered. Touching her hand, her hair, mattered to him, and he longed to touch his mouth to hers. Winning her admiration mattered. There could be no casual parting from her side. To leave her, to never see her again—that would be a wrench so as to stop his heart—if not forever, then at least for long enough to inflict a terrible wound there.

The happy news was that Sebastian dared to think he might have, somehow, managed to capture Miss Talbot's admiration. She treated him graciously. She gave him her smiles, smiles he thought might be warmed by touches of friendship, and perhaps even attraction. He thought she lingered in his company, as he pined to linger ever in hers. She was shy, yes, and demure, with so little physical contact between them and too few words crossing her lips—but eyes could speak loudly in a language all their own, and Sebastian was convinced those lovely brown eyes of hers had whispered a secret message of affinity to him.

The only fly in the ointment was Miss Talbot's father, Lord Lamont. Sebastian could not really fault the man for looking askance at a third son offering for his daughter, even the third son of a marquess—for Sebastian knew his reputation was not good. Until now it had not mattered, his reputation, nor his lack of funds, nor his idleness—not until he'd met Miss Talbot, not until it came to impressing a potential bride's father.

For "bride" was the correct word: Sebastian wanted to marry Miss Talbot. The problem lay in convincing her papa to grant consent, for Miss Talbot had yet to reach her majority age of one-and-twenty.

As Sebastian approached his home, his muscles protesting the incline of the road leading up to it and the weight of the bats he carried, he wondered yet again what profession he could pursue.

Were it a perfect world, he would somehow be able to make a living from the game of cricket. But no matter how much he enjoyed playing the game, liked that the townspeople came to watch it, liked providing the world with a bit of entertainment—it was just a game, and there was no profession to be had from it.

Oh, perhaps he could become a schoolmaster, one who taught the game to the lads—but that would require he also be proficient at something worthy such as Latin or Mathematics. Sebastian shuddered. He did not mind totaling figures, but to have to teach the study to students . . . ? He was sure he had no skill in that regard.

He just had no idea what skill he *did* possess.

No matter. First he would complete the smuggling he had agreed to do, earn the large reward he'd been promised, and then he could decide how best to use the funds to create a future. Once Lord Lamont saw that Sebastian had money of his own, the man would be more than content to allow his daughter to marry a marquess's third son.

Besides, when it came to employment, Miss Talbot would probably want some say in any venture her husband was to undertake. Yes, most certainly he needed to discuss any such future plans with Miss Talbot. That is, if ever they could have a conversation that took place more than five feet from her father's side. Give Lord Lamont his due: he knew how to guard his daughter's person. Knew it too well, allowing her to leave his side only long enough to complete a dance. And a dance was not the easiest venue in which to conduct a serious conversation—wooing Miss Talbot was difficult enough, never mind trying to have an earnest discussion of the future with her.

Sebastian approached the front door of his childhood home, which now belonged to his brother Gideon, the present marquess of Greyleigh. The door did not open, but Sebastian did not wonder at the fact his approach appeared to be unnoted by any servants. The butler, recently hired to replace the far younger and more reliable Mr. Frick who had gone off to fight against Napoleon, was five-and-seventy years of age. At least that was the age the "new" butler admitted to. Sebastian had no doubt the fellow was creeping his painstakingly slow way to the door, belatedly alerted by a call from some more observant footman, even as Sebastian reached for the handle. Sure enough, Widell was on his feet from his chair in the hall, halfway to the front door.

"Lord Sebastian! Let me help you with that," Widell offered, still shuffling forward, meaning perhaps the door or the bag of bats, Sebastian was unsure which.

"My thanks, but I have it," Sebastian said with a nod to the butler as he passed him, heading for the stairs and his chambers.

Sebastian took no offense or outrage at the butler's limited usefulness—he had grown used to having a bevy of inadequate servants about the house. What else could one expect when his older brother made a point of hiring the old, the lame, the infirm, and any other motley being whom society had otherwise abandoned? One-eyed maids, ex-soldiers who had no fingers on one hand, and a gardener who sang bawdy songs when he'd nipped too much whiskey, all abounded around the house. They were the recipients of Gideon's philanthropic nature, and by-and-large everyone else's forbearance. In fact, despite its collection of oddball servants, the house was now a far happier home than the one the three brothers had endured as children, and the peculiar service was the price paid for such harmony.

Besides, Sebastian thought with a lopsided grin and a shake of his head, he liked learning new bawdy songs from Pepperidge, the gardener.

The stairs were mounted in a trice, and Sebastian was a little surprised to enter his chambers and not be greeted by his valet. He liked the way young Timmons was inclined to natter on, another friendly voice filling this house that had once been too silent, too cautious. He liked being surrounded by people, by the noises and murmurings of a content household. In the childhood shared with his two brothers, they'd had only each other to care for—there had been no kisses, no gentle hands brushing the hair from their foreheads, no soft laps welcoming their presence.

And so Sebastian had grown to manhood knowing he craved touching, in its many forms, as others craved music or art. He had been too long deprived of soft touches and murmured endearments. He knew he sought it out, that he turned to touch, to embraces, to physical contact, as flowers turned their faces to the sun.

It was hardly a wonder that he had made Mrs. Deems seal their bargain with a kiss, with the touch of her lips on his. He could tell himself that he made her kiss him because the act was more likely to bind her thoughts and her tongue. The truth was, however, he had thought of a kiss, not to bind her but because he had wanted to banish the fear from her blue eyes. Eyes so unlike Miss Talbot's brown ones—or even his own, for that matter. Mrs. Deems's eyes were the color of a bird's egg—not some exotic bird itself as were his, he thought wryly. No, he had asked for a kiss as an offer to make a pledge between them, that she might believe he meant her no harm.

She had cringed away from him, had feared his dark garb and his unmistakable defiance of the rule of law. And if there was one thing Sebastian could not bear, it was a woman's gaze filled with fear. He'd lived too long with a brutish man who possessed a stinging tongue, too long with the fear and confusion that man had inspired in Mama's already befuddled mind.

"So you intimidated Mrs. Deems into giving you a kiss?" he asked himself, his tone bitter as he crossed to toss the bag of bats inside his wardrobe. He caught sight of his reflection in the nearby cheval glass, saw he shook his head in self-disgust, and guiltily turned away to throw himself flat out on his bed.

But at least the kiss had had the effect he'd wanted: gradually she had lost her dread of him. If only she had known how powerless he was, how hobbled by her fear! The kiss had been all pretense, for he would have done nothing to her, not even if he'd known she was going at once to the authorities. He could not harm a woman— and certainly not her child. Not even though revealing his mission on the cliffs would destroy all his hopes, his plans. She had been the one utterly in control, if only she had known it. He'd bluffed her, matching his words and actions to his reputation, and so had been able to take a promise from her lips.

He thought about that for a long time, staring at his chamber ceiling.

It was not in Sebastian's nature to remain somber for long, however. He found he was grinning, despite disliking his own actions, despite the threat that loomed now that Mrs. Deems knew his secret. He grinned out of remembering the kiss he'd shared with her, and at their banter this afternoon, because, simply put, he liked to flirt. So as not to lie to himself, he admitted with a growing grin that the kiss had been as much about flirting as it had anything else.

He was good at flirting. He liked to find the shyest or

least pretty girl in a room, and win from her a smile and a dance. He liked to see their shoulders relax as they began to believe their evening was not completely wasted or ruined or misspent—although some mamas would argue the misspent part, since Sebastian had never done one thing to prove himself a worthy sort.

In fact, he rather suspected it was his questionable reputation that had caught Natalie Talbot's attention. He was not the sort of gentleman with which Lord Lamont tried to surround his debuting daughter.

But he could be, soon; all that was needed was for that ship, now a day later than hoped for, to arrive.

Too, for Mrs. Deems to remain silent about his presence on the cliffs.

She had sealed a bargain with her vow and her kiss . . . but was that really enough? Sebastian's smile faded and he frowned up again at his ceiling. So much rode on her silence, on secrecy being maintained. . . .

Sebastian rose from the bed, his crisp movement reflecting that a new decision had been made: he would call on Mrs. Deems tonight, and she would have to do more than merely kiss him.

Chapter 4

Yes, tonight Mrs. Deems would again be called upon by Sebastian. For now, however, there was other business to which he must attend. He must call upon Titan, who was to be found near the kitchens.

The kitchens were connected to the main house by a long corridor, so that the food never had to go outside before reaching the dining table. More important, at least as regarded Titan, the kitchens and corridor were always warm.

Sebastian found the dog, a large fellow with a huge head that had suggested his name, in the spot that had been made up in the corridor. Titan lay upon thick counterpanes, the corner of one now pulled over him as a cover, leaving only the dog's big head and thick tail exposed.

At the animal's side sat a young groom named Jacob. It was his turn to sit with the unwell animal, a job passed between four of the stable lads when Sebastian could not be there himself.

"How is he?" Sebastian asked at once.

"Still ailing, m'lord," said Jacob, looking worried.

Sebastian bent down to scratch the dog's ears. "Hey, Titan. How's my boy?" he murmured. The dog thumped his long, thick tail against the floor twice, and lolled his eyes upward toward Sebastian, but he didn't lift his head.

"Is he still taking water?"

The groom nodded. "A bit. And this morning I got 'im to take a piece of bread soaked in beef broth."

"No meat yet, eh? Well, the bread is something at least." Sebastian stood and offered a hand to the groom. "Go on then, Jacob. I will stay with Titan for now."

Jacob took his master's hand and was hoisted to his feet. "Shall I have Ned come in an hour, m'lord?"

Sebastian nodded, and Jacob turned to go, leaving Sebastian to put his back against the wall and slide down to sit next to the ailing dog. He reached to fondle the big, droopy ears, and made murmuring, comforting noises.

It was not that Titan was a beloved pet from old. The oversized mutt had only been at the house a year or so. But Sebastian and the dog had immediately formed a companionship—the large abandoned dog needing food and shelter and attention, and the man needing to share affection. Most nights Titan slept on the floor at the foot of his master's bed, a situation that suited both man and dog, each enjoying sharing the room with another living creature.

"Did you eat something you oughtn't have?" Sebastian murmured to the dog, the same question he'd pondered for two days now.

"Most likely."

Sebastian looked up, not having heard his brother approach. "Gideon," he greeted him. His brother's appearance, a peculiar combination of white-blond hair and palest gray eyes, were so familiar to Sebastian that they had no power to surprise him as it did those first meeting Gideon, but the hint of a concerned frown between his eldest brother's brows caught his attention.

"Do you want me to have the apothecary come to see him?" Gideon asked, bending down to pet the animal. Titan thumped his tail once in a listless greeting.

Sebastian shook his head. "I already talked to the apothecary. He says he knows only to keep the animal warm and dry and see he is offered water frequently. He offered to bleed him, if I wished."

"Do you?"

Sebastian shook his head again. "Perhaps later. If he takes a turn for the worse."

Gideon settled into a crouch, folding his hands before him. "Elizabeth wants to know if we should set a place for you at supper tonight," he said, his tone more somber than the words required.

"I am sorry. I know I have not been good about arriving for meals—" Sebastian began, but Gideon waved his explanation away.

"You are a man grown, Sebastian. We do not need to know of your comings and goings. Asking if you will be at supper is really just Elizabeth's way of making me come talk to you."

Sebastian went back to petting the dog, avoiding his brother's gaze.

"She worries about you," Gideon said. Out of the corner of his eye, Sebastian saw his brother shrug. "First she worried about you when you were making noises about leaving Severn's Well again—"

"She does not like me to be dissolute," Sebastian said, looking up long enough to throw Gideon a crooked grin.

"But now she's worried about the fact that you no longer talk of running off to Brighton or London."

Sebastian had not spoken of his infatuation with Miss Talbot with either Gideon or his brother's wife. What was there to say? *"I adore Miss Talbot, but her father thinks me a great gudgeon"?* He certainly could not confess that he'd made plans to earn a small fortune—that event would be much simpler to explain after it had become a fact. But neither Gideon nor Elizabeth was stupid, and they had to wonder why Sebastian's malcontent at being in Severn's Well had suddenly altered, becoming an eagerness to remain. They had to sense the restlessness that now filled Sebastian was of a wholly new variety.

"Of course, I told her she was worrying needlessly, that it is in fact a good thing that we hardly ever see you about the house anymore, that you have found things in Severn's Well to occupy your time and attention. You have places to be, people to see." Gideon hesitated, then added, "Miss Talbots to court."

Sebastian did not need to say a word—a glance between the brothers confirmed what Gideon had guessed.

Gideon gave a brief, acknowledging nod, then reached down again to pet the ailing animal. "Hey there, Titan, old boy. You must get better, you know. My brother has a soft heart, even if he seldom lets anyone know about it. So you'd better not die on us, or else I'll have a big, slobbering mess of a man crying all over my shoulder."

Sebastian did not respond, but there was no mistaking Gideon's message: beware of where you lay your heart. It would seem Gideon, too, questioned if Lord Lamont would ever think Sebastian was the man to marry Miss Talbot, Lamont's only daughter.

Only, Gideon did not know that Sebastian stood to earn a large sum of money, probably enough money to change a stubborn father's heart. If not that, it might at least be enough money to tempt Miss Talbot to defy her papa and elope with Sebastian—an act she'd refused three times to date.

But she'd refused a man with empty pockets.

"I could give you money with which to set up a household—" Gideon began, but now it was Sebastian's turn to wave away his brother's words. There was no reason Sebastian could not live off the profits from the family estate— no reason but pride. He had taken estate money before, not long ago at all, and had wasted it as thoroughly as any prodigal son could. He'd used his brother's money to go searching . . . but now that he'd found his future in Miss Talbot, the idea of taking even more rankled.

"Tell Elizabeth not to worry," he said firmly, reaching to fondle the dog's ears again. "It is not good for the baby." Elizabeth was expecting her first child in three months. "Tell her all is well."

Gideon sighed and stood up. "I will tell her. But she'll worry all the same. She says your heart is almost as soft as your head."

Sebastian took no offense, because he knew Elizabeth did not mean any; she liked him, even if he sometimes exasperated her with his aimlessness. An aimlessness he meant to put aside, now that Miss Talbot had entered his life.

"Tell her to take a glance in her own looking glass," he quipped.

Gideon grinned, as did Sebastian. They both knew Elizabeth was not the softhearted one; it was the Whitbury sons who all shared an excess of empathy.

"Just remember that soft hearts are easily bruised,"

Gideon said, his tone ending in a question, seeking assurance.

"I will remember," Sebastian agreed.

Gideon looked as if he would say more, but he shook his head instead. He pointed down at the dog. "Get better!" he ordered Titan, then turned. "We will have a place set at table for you," he called back over his shoulder, making Sebastian give another small grin. He might be a fifth wheel at his brother's table, but not because he was unwanted or unloved.

As he pet and murmured to Titan, Sebastian pondered what it would be like to bring his bride, Miss Talbot, to dine with Gideon and Elizabeth. He had no doubt she would be made welcome. From there his thoughts wandered to a vision of Miss Talbot—Natalie—residing at a table of their own, the gracious hostess. And when their guests had left, then he and she would retire to their chambers, and he would take down her dark hair, and pull her close for a kiss . . .

But his imagination stopped short there, for he had not kissed Miss Talbot, not yet. Her sentinel of a father had allowed no opportunities. When he thought of kissing Natalie—well, truth was it was Mrs. Deems's kiss that intruded. That was understandable, of course, since he'd had the opportunity of kissing one and not the other.

All the same, it was a bit of a relief to glance up and see that one of the grooms approached, ready to take over the dog-watching from him and relieve him from an excess of self-questioning.

"Time for a meal," Sebastian excused himself to the dog as he rose to his feet. "Then I am off to a night of dancing." He did not add that he needed to be seen out and about in social settings. He hoped, were he accused of waiting for a smuggler's ship, to use such an event as an alibi. His plan was to arrive, then slip away to wait on the cliffs, then slip back into the party or club or coffee-house some hours later, hopefully seeming to have been there the entire time. At least it was better than no alibi at all. Last night he'd come back to a party only to find the house dark, the party ended, he recalled with a small laugh and a shake of his head.

It was to be hoped the scheme might work to better advantage tonight—no, even more so, it was to be hoped that the ship would arrive and such subterfuges could be at an end altogether.

At any roads, he'd need better luck tonight, for he must leave a party to call upon Mrs. Deems; he must present her with his improved notion on how to fix her silence.

He reached up to scratch his chin, a slightly nervous gesture, for he was well aware she would not like it, not at all.

Charlotte offered a final curtsy to her dance partner just as Lord Sebastian Whitbury was announced. She glanced up to confirm she'd heard the butler call his name, and was unprepared for the prickle of sharpened awareness that struck her.

Although, she chided herself, she ought not truly be surprised at it. Lord Sebastian was a handsome man. Not "pretty" as some men were, nor was he ruggedly dashing—he was somewhere between, and fetchingly so. She thought it had something to do with the smooth planes of his face, which led the eye to the striking cheekbones near his peacock-blue eyes. In the general run of things, Charlotte did not particularly find blond gentlemen attractive—Jarvis had been dark-haired—but Lord Sebastian's hair was not quite what one thought of when one thought "blond." It was colored somewhere between wheat and honey, having brown undertones that might become more prominent if he ever gave up his cricket and stayed out of the sun. For now, even held in a neat queue, the color was a gloriously rich gold in the warm touch of the many candles lit for Lord and Lady Wilburham's ball.

His gaze swung her way, and Charlotte had just started to offer a nod in response when she realized he gazed beyond her. She turned, spying at once what had surely brought Lord Sebastian to this night's affair: Miss Natalie Talbot.

The other woman, resplendent in a white silk gown with an underskirt the color of palest apple green, had also looked up at the arrival of Lord Sebastian. Her heightened color told a tale, one Charlotte had no doubt Lord Sebastian would be delighted to see for himself.

She felt a soft smile touch her lips—for who could resist anything so tender as a moment of regard between two young, eligible, hopeful souls? Never mind that Charlotte feared she was beyond ever again knowing the innocent enthusiasm that betokened the spark of attraction. It was somehow reassuring to know that others could yet believe in its existence, its possibility of leading toward love.

"I sound as if I am a hundred years old," she silently chided herself, but her smile lingered on her lips all the same.

Not that tonight was about attraction, not for Charlotte. She'd made up her mind. No more evading reality: she needed to protect Oscar, and the only way she could be sure of that protection was to marry.

She had come to Severn's Well two months ago well aware that a woman without some manner of man in her life was a suspect creature. When Jarvis had died she'd been forced to move back in with her mama, but Mama's meager income had been severely strained by trying to support two, never mind three. Charlotte had had nothing to contribute to the household, because Jarvis had repeated her father's poor planning—no, he had topped it, by leaving her nothing at all, not even a small jointure.

Her papa was dead, her only uncle senile, bedridden, and unwelcoming, and her presence in her mother's home had been a financial drain her mama could not long withstand. Even if the two women had chosen to take in some manner of work, Charlotte had known she could not stay there long: her mother had grown hopeful of a second marriage, to a man who made it clear he wanted no children in his household. Should Mama marry, her life would improve dramatically—how could Charlotte stand in her way?

So Charlotte had moved away, to where there was no

one who cared what became of her and Oscar. To where
there was no male to fill the role of overseer, guardian,
protector.

Her husband Jarvis, dead of a fever, had been a clergy-
man by trade and inclination. He might as well have
taken a vow of poverty for all that he left his widow.
Charlotte had not truly understood, until it was well past
too late, that Jarvis had put most of their income back
into the little church that he had loved so well. The beautifully carved pews, the colored glass windows, the
leather-bound prayer books . . . It had not been the
generosity of the parishioners that had bought it all, but
instead Charlotte and Oscar's future.

The only place she had now to call a home was Grandpapa's summer cottage, long since willed to his only
granddaughter, a place she'd only visited once in her
youth, a place her family had not spoken of in years. She
would not have come here, would not have returned to
the scene of her family's shame, except the cottage was
paid for. She could live here without paying any rent,
only the taxes that came due. Here she was able to plant
a garden, perhaps have chickens, perhaps take in sewing
or laundry. Most important, however, she could hide
here. She could keep her secret hidden, which she highly
doubted she could have done for long in London.

Her secret . . . There was one other way to keep her
secret hidden: if she were to remarry.

It had only been five months—six in a fortnight—since
Jarvis had died, but that indecently short time was not
what really gave her pause at the idea of remarrying.
Oscar was two years old; Charlotte could outright lie and
say Jarvis had been gone over a year, if she cared to.
Who would be bothered to verify her claim? For that
matter, who in Severn's Well would care if she married
after only a half year's mourning?

No, what gave her pause was the idea of again being
bound to a man who did not love her. She was not as
hopeful as she'd once been, not as willing to believe that
things could work out. Did she believe love was impossible to find? What did it mean that she was not even

wanting to try to find love? Had she changed so much? Was she now incapable of softer emotions?

No, at least not completely. Her love for Oscar was real and strong and good. It was just that it was one thing to be thrown in prison, another to voluntarily walk into one. And marriage felt very like a prison.

It was what she was going to have to do, however. It made the best sense.

That was what tonight was for. She must put herself in the marriage mart, such as Severn's Well and nearby Bristol provided. She must be seen, for without being seen she would never attract an offer. So she had come to dance, to smile, to let it be seen that she was eligible. She'd left Oscar with Mrs. Hyatt, and she'd put on her dancing slippers and come to a party.

It did not matter that her stomach felt sour, or that she suspected her smile was something more like a grimace.

"Mrs. Deems." Charlotte was pulled back to the moment by a voice near at hand. She looked up with a quick, polite smile to see Mrs. Houghton, a woman who often shared the same pew at church with Charlotte. "May I present our local apothecary, Mr. Walbrook? Mr. Walbrook, this is Mrs. Deems, recently from London."

"Mr. Walbrook, how do you do?" Charlotte said, curtsying to his bow. *And so it begins,* she thought, trying not to clench her teeth.

"Very well. And you?" Mr. Walbrook said in a pleasant manner.

She murmured that she was well, and stifled a sigh even as she considered Mr. Walbrook's worth, for that was her duty tonight. Clearly, he was also on the marriage mart. She had been in Severn's Well long enough to learn something of who was already wed and who was considered desperately in need of a wedding. Mr. Walbrook was one of those so regarded—he had achieved the age of thirty without so much as a hint of a connection. He was not a handsome man, having a rather prominent nose and hollow cheeks, but Charlotte had no care for beauty of person over disposition. If she must seek a mate, then what she would seek above all else was kindness. Unless she learned otherwise, Mr. Walbrook must be viewed as being as worthy as any other soul here tonight.

Still, poor Mr. Walbrook, that he must endure this process of meeting and greeting and dreading and evaluating— then a flash of humor twisted Charlotte's lips, for she must do exactly the same. Did Mr. Walbrook pity her?

"Pity is not necessarily a bad thing," she silently told herself. At least it showed a capacity for compassion.

"Would you care to dance, Mrs. Deems?" Mr. Walbrook inquired in a shy demeanor, one perhaps encouraged by her smile.

"Of course," Charlotte said.

Mr. Walbrook seemed to enjoy his country dance with her, although he was not given over to frivolity. He seemed, in fact, rather sober. All the same, he remained at her side afterward, long enough for Charlotte to make inquiries into his work. His unhandsome face brightened as he discussed the various herbs and restoratives with which he worked, and Charlotte found herself wondering if he were kind, for he certainly was not fascinating. Still, he was softspoken and pleasant in a somber sort of way, and she vowed she would grant him another dance or two before deciding he would not suit as a husband.

Still, it was a bit of a relief when she moved away from his side. She wondered if he was aware of how often he blinked as he spoke, his eyelids and mouth making an odd little cadence between them. Watching the frequent blinking, in time with every other word he spoke, had been oddly exhausting.

She abandoned a passing desire for refreshments, and settled on one chair out of a dozen that filled an alcove— clearly arranged for some more private moments that guests might wish—and puffed out her cheeks once in a sigh of relief.

"Go away, Mrs. Deems," came a quiet voice behind her, causing Charlotte to twist in her seat.

"Lord Sebastian," she said in surprise, only then spying his length stretched out across several chairs. "Are you hiding?"

"From everyone but one particular lady." He made a little shooing motion at her.

Charlotte resettled in her chair, facing him, making it clear she wasn't going anywhere just yet. "May I presume this particular lady you await is not myself?" she teased. She felt oddly pleased to have encountered him—perhaps because his personality was so at odds with Mr. Walbrook's sober demeanor.

"I would hardly be telling you to go away if it were," Sebastian pointed out. He made an attempt at glaring, but it was ruined by the quirk of his eyebrow.

"Whom do you await?"

"Go away, Mrs. Deems," he repeated as though with a great expenditure of patience.

"I like it here. I think I will stay."

His glare was now more sincere, but then he shrugged, a strangely graceful gesture, given that he was lying on his side across the chairs, elbow bent and his head resting on his palm. "Stay, then."

"You do not mind an audience?"

"Not at all," he said archly.

She clucked her tongue. "You should know it is unlikely that you will make me feel so guilty that I leave."

"Nor was I trying to."

"Yes you were." Charlotte grinned.

He did not answer, but his air of indifference had faded—an answer in itself.

"I have obviously interrupted a prearranged scheme. Someone is to enter a seemingly empty alcove, and—voilà!—there you are. Do I have the right of it?"

He grunted, displeased with her.

"Are you going to propose?"

"I am going to propose *something,* if it is any of your concern," he said with obvious reluctance.

"Oh, do sit up, Lord Sebastian. Your lady is here," Charlotte announced in a whisper, not at all surprised to see Miss Talbot had appeared at the mouth of the alcove. "Do not mind me, Miss Talbot," she called out softly, not wanting that lady to retreat as she seemed poised to do.

"Sebastian?" Miss Talbot questioned, just as he sat up. He smoothed his hair with one hand, threw Charlotte a disgruntled glance, and patted the chair beside him.

"Miss Talbot, do please have a seat," he invited. His smile was warm, sincere, eager. Charlotte felt a flicker of regret for interrupting his moment—but it was quickly followed by pure curiosity to see if he would, indeed, ignore her presence.

The other woman hesitantly entered the alcove. "I do not have long," she cautioned Lord Sebastian, even as she threw Charlotte a puzzled glance.

"Do not mind Mrs. Deems," Lord Sebastian told his lady. "She is overfond of spying on others. But we have nothing to hide."

Do you not? Charlotte thought with a twist of her lips, recalling his smuggler's garb. She highly suspected the revered Miss Talbot knew nothing of that side of Lord Sebastian.

"In fact, Mrs. Deems means to guard the entrance for us, so we are not interrupted by others," Lord Sebastian said, never taking his eyes from Miss Talbot.

It would be simple to denounce his little lie, but there was no profit in doing so. Why stand in the way of an infatuation? It certainly did nothing untoward to her, one way or the other. Charlotte stood, fanning herself leisurely as she moved to the mouth of the alcove, stopping there and playing the part of guardian.

Perhaps she heard a light chuckle, but she could not be sure. She did not glance back to see if Lord Sebastian smiled. It would be an arch smile anyway, so why look since it would merely vex?

"You know why I wanted to speak with you," Lord Sebastian said to Miss Talbot, his voice low. It just carried to Charlotte's ears, but would not survive the din of the amusements just beyond the alcove. She was a little startled by his directness, going straight to his point, but perhaps time really was as short for the two young lovebirds as Miss Talbot had claimed. Very much so, to judge by the long, mildly frowning glance that Lord Lamont was casting about the ballroom.

Chapter 5

"Two minutes, Lord Sebastian, if that." Charlotte turned her head long enough to warn. She caught a glimpse of the lovers' hands clasped together, and something in her center gave a lurch—had she and Jarvis ever held hands? A few times, when they were newly married. When they were yet hopeful . . .

"Say yes," Lord Sebastian urged his lady, all playfulness gone from his voice. "Say we may elope tonight.'

"No, Sebastian, no. Elopement is too much a scandal. I do not want to marry that way," Miss Talbot said, but her tone was not utterly convincing.

"Scandals die away. We would hardly be the first pair in love ever to elope."

"You said you were improving your lot," Miss Talbot suggested, a question hanging between them.

"I am, I am."

"Then we can wait."

"Your father—" he said impatiently.

"He talks of betrothing me to someone, but it has not happened, has it? It is just talk, for now. We have time. How soon before your fortune is made?"

"Well, it is generous but hardly a fortune," Lord Sebastian corrected, and Charlotte gave him points for honesty.

"The money for our future then," Miss Talbot corrected.

"Soon. Any day. That is, the task is soon, but the reward . . . I have no control over when the reward comes. It is promised, though."

"And you believe in the promise?"

"Yes." He spoke emphatically.

"Then we wait. We wait so that Papa will want to bless our union. So we can have a proper wedding."

Lord Sebastian made a small noise, and Charlotte thought perhaps he went to speak but stopped himself. There was silence, as though he were thinking—or perhaps the two were kissing? "Lord Lamont approaches," Charlotte cautioned, only then glancing over her shoulder. They were not kissing. They were not even holding hands anymore. Lord Sebastian fought a frown, and Miss Talbot smiled encouragement.

"She is right, you know," Charlotte said quietly as she moved to where they sat. "Why seek out scandal when it can be avoided by the passage of a little time?"

Lord Sebastian scowled at her, but it was not a ferocious scowl—if anything, he looked a little hurt. Charlotte took Miss Talbot's arm, pulling the other lady to her feet. She turned her at once, and began strolling casually toward the alcove's entrance.

"I shall try that vinegar paste on my muslin to see if the stain comes out," she said loudly, just as Lord Lamont entered the alcove with a scowl already fixed in place.

"Oh . . . oh, yes, do that, Mrs. Deems." Miss Talbot tumbled at last to the ruse Charlotte provided. "It can be most effective." Her color was high as she turned to her father. "Papa! Do we leave so soon?"

"No," Lord Lamont said, his brow clearing as he made a bow to Charlotte, who curtsied in return. "Mrs. Deems, you are well?"

They chatted for a minute, and then Miss Talbot was led away on her father's arm, leaving Charlotte to turn back into the alcove. Lord Sebastian was hidden once more from sight.

"They are gone," she told the chairs, above which Lord Sebastian's head then appeared. He glanced to see that she'd told the truth, then sat up fully.

"Thank you, Mrs. Deems."

"You are welcome. I . . . I remember wanting to steal a few moments alone with Mr. Deems." Once, a thousand years ago, when she was young and confident that wanting something could make it so.

"Lucky Mr. Deems," he said.

She gave a little shake of her head, a denial, but hoped he would not take it as a dismissal of his teasing tones.

He surprised her by holding out his hand, a clear signal that she was to come to his side. She did so without demurring, although not reaching to take his hand, which then settled in his lap as she sat beside him.

"Your love should not require you to sit in the dark, stealing moments," she cautioned.

"I know," he said. He brought his hands together, letting them fall between his knees, his elbows braced on his legs, his forehead practically touching the chair before him. "Miss Talbot is shy. Even retiring. I am impatient and unreserved. What I would say aloud, she begs me to keep between us. She is a little afraid of her father, I believe."

"Many a girl is." It was pleasant, in an odd way, sitting in the semidark and conversing. Charlotte did not miss her marriage, but she did miss the companionship, even though it had been a poor, limited thing. She tilted her head a little to one side, considering Lord Sebastian. "Tell me what makes you so wicked," she said. "Have you killed a man?"

He made a motion with his shoulders, either a shrug or a quick, silent laugh. He shook his head. "No. I was in a duel once, however, over a wager the other gentleman did not want to pay. He said the terms had been unclear. I said he was a tightfisted bastard. In the end I convinced him that paying with his blunt was better than with his blood."

"Pistols?"

"Swords."

"Indeed! How brave of you. Duels are usually with pistols these days."

"I did not want to kill him. Nor, for that matter, be killed myself. Swords seemed less risky than pistols."

"Well, that *was* a little wicked of you, since duels are illegal. But have you done worse?"

He slanted her a grin. "Stole a kiss from Vicar Wembley's daughter."

"Miss 'Untouchable Honoria' Wembley? Truly? I am impressed. Although I have to say that most kisses are not really stolen. I suspect Miss Wembley was persuadable."

Lord Sebastian gave a short laugh. "I do not know whether to be insulted or not! Either I had a willing accomplice in the feat, or else I am so glib of tongue that I could persuade the usually unpersuadable. I am either a boaster or a smooth-tongued devil. Which do you think me to be, Mrs. Deems?"

"A little of both?" she suggested.

He did not laugh, but she thought she saw an amused gleam in his eye, evident despite the half-light in the alcove. If he had laughed, she knew she would have joined him, knew that a smile hovered ready on her lips.

"I have thought of something that may make you think me wicked," he said, rising to his feet. Just that quickly the mood had shifted. The humor was gone, his face serious.

If he had meant to intimidate her by standing and growing so suddenly sober, he had succeeded. He was not unusually tall, although he seemed so now when they were alone together in this dimmed space, he standing above her.

Charlotte stood as well, and refused to step away even though the impulse occurred to her.

"You are aware of my pursuit of an evening on the cliffs," he said.

She nodded, feeling a sense of caution spread through her being. Why did he mention this here, now?

"You should also be aware that my pursuit relates directly to my ability to secure a future—that is, the obtaining of my reward. The one you overheard me speak of tonight with Miss Talbot. Everything I want"—he grew very still for a long moment, very watchful of her expression—"everything rests on my being successful. And, my dear lady, the most worrisome thing that stands between me and success is you."

"But you have my word on that score, my lord," she pointed out. She glanced at the alcove's entrance, not because she feared he might attack or hurt her, but because she sensed it might be wise to leave, to flee, before he could go on, before he could say aloud the dark promise she saw in his gaze.

"But I find it is not enough. I do not know you. No one in Severn's Well knows you, not well. No one can say if your word, your kiss, is a thing of honor."

Charlotte lifted her chin. "Do you think I do not know what others speculate? That they wonder how I live, since I do not take in laundry or sewing or—?" She took a deep breath, trying to steady herself, to cut any unfortunate words from falling off her tongue. "I have funds, my lord, and that is all you or anyone need know about my personal affairs—"

"Hush, madam," he said in a soft croon, very gently laying his forefinger to her lips. She ought to push it away, but he held her with his gaze, leaving her oddly frozen in place. Her lips tingled where his finger touched.

"You have a secret, I would venture," he went on, speaking low but firmly. His gaze searched hers, and she could tell from the leap of interest there that her own eyes must have revealed too much, that she'd been unable to hide guilt from his gaze. She parted her lips to speak, to try and undo the damage, but he interrupted her. "That is not the matter at hand, Mrs. Deems. The matter is this: I do not know you, and therefore cannot trust you, no more than you can trust me. Too much is at stake."

"Because Miss Talbot will not elope with you," Charlotte stated.

He did not flinch or deny it. "I have a secret. You have a secret. And waiting for disaster, well, that is not something I plan to do. Besides, what I want from you, what you will do, is not such a terrible, wicked thing. No harm will come to you." He took his finger from her lip, allowing her the ability to speak.

"What do you want?" Charlotte asked, chagrined that the words came out in a dry-mouthed whisper.

"Merely this. That you wait with me, every night, on the cliffs. Until the ship I seek arrives."

Charlotte frowned. "But why?"

"Because it makes you my accomplice, Mrs. Deems."

"Oh," she said, stunned by the claim and its implications.

A soft smile spread slowly over his mouth. The sight of that smile acted as a goad. "An *unwilling* accomplice," she shot back at him.

"So you will say. But will you be believed? And even if you, a newcomer, are believed over the local son, what else will the good people of Severn's Well say you did on the cliffs, alone at night, with me?"

She made a sound, somewhere between a growl and a moan, and shook her head. "No. I cannot leave Oscar alone in my cottage!"

"I have considered that. I have another accomplice, my valet in fact. He will stay with your sleeping son while we await the ship's arrival."

"You could have him stay with me and Oscar both. He could guard us." That would be better than being separated from Oscar, from having to stand at this man's side while he broke the law.

"But he could not guard your tongue, Mrs. Deems. Only being implicated along with me—by my valet's testimony, if necessary—will be sufficient to assure your silence."

Anger swept through her, instead of the dread or apprehension she might have expected. "What terrible thing do you smuggle, my lord? I deserve to know what sin I am being forced to commit."

He shook his head. "I am sworn not to tell anyone."

She could not refuse him, she saw that in his gaze. So she said the most hurtful thing she could think of. "I thought we were becoming friends, Lord Sebastian."

"Thick as thieves." His tone was light, but he lifted his chin, as if he'd taken a blow.

"I do not appreciate your humor."

His mouth thinned, no sign of that humor there now. "I am sorry for that, Mrs. Deems. I am sorry for everything. But, take heart. The ship is due any day. This will all be over soon enough."

"And what will keep me quiet afterwards?"

She regretted asking as soon as the words were out, for what if the answer were something far more sinister than merely having to wait in the dark on the cliffs above the river?

"Afterwards does not matter. Scream it from the cliffs if you like, after."

Charlotte felt her shoulders relax, even as her gaze narrowed. "You do not plan to use this locality again?"

"I do not plan to smuggle again. Ever."

"You are to smuggle only one time? But what could be worth so much, for so little effort?"

His impudence returned in a flash. "A kiss perhaps? They are usually gotten after a great deal of effort—but are greatly worth it, I find." His blue eyes, made even darker blue in the half-light, danced with amusement.

He must not have expected a reply from her, for he stepped away, giving her no opportunity to try to argue with him.

He turned at the last moment before crossing out of the alcove. "Mrs. Deems, I do thank you for your service tonight, providing a pretense for Miss Talbot."

She almost said "You are welcome," out of habit, but just managed to stay the reflex. What an odd, vexing man!—to force something on her one moment, and praise her the next. "Only see how you have repaid me," she said coolly.

He lowered his chin to his chest for one long moment, an unexpectedly sheepish gesture, than looked up again.

His expression was lost to shadows, but the set of his shoulders had nothing sheepish about them now. "Some things cannot be helped. I am leaving this party now, as must you. My valet and I will arrive at your door within the hour. Please be dressed in all dark layers, with something to cover your head. It is cold on the cliffs."

"How am I to get home? My neighbors, Mr. and Mrs. Donfield, took me up in their carriage to come here tonight."

Lord Sebastian stared at her, a gesture she was starting to recognize meant he was thinking. "It is too far to walk, and dark besides," he said, frowning.

"And, besides, Oscar will not be abed so soon. So you see—"

"Your son will like my valet, Timmons. They will get on well together. Timmons can put him to bed."

"He will not go to bed for a stranger."

"Then your boy will stay up late." This was said without anger, but finality; Lord Sebastian was through debating. "Tell one of our host's servants to give Mrs. Donfield the message that you found another way home," he instructed. "Then meet my carriage around the corner, on High Street, in ten minutes' time. It is a plain coach, with no crest."

Charlotte drew herself up, not sure if she were brave enough to press on with denials—but her opportunity was lost, for Lord Sebastian strode from the alcove without glancing back.

She gave a blustery sigh, as much from aggravation as relief. She did not have to follow what he said! She could stay where she was, not leaving the party . . . and she did not think Lord Sebastian would know that Oscar was with Mrs. Hyatt. Even if he did, she found it hard to believe that he would go to threaten her son in some way. To threaten Oscar was to tip his own hand; anonymity was the smuggler's best friend.

However . . . eventually Charlotte would have to go home. Either Lord Sebastian would be waiting for her there, or else simply come the next night, or the next. Where would she go if she chose to flee the cottage, to abandon this new life she was trying to carve out here for herself and Oscar in Severn's Well? So, unless she ran, eventually she and Lord Sebastian would meet again—and if he was not angry now, he would be then.

She could go to the authorities. She knew where Mr. Wallace, the head Alderman of the village, resided; it would be simple enough to ask to see him despite it being half past nine in the evening. She could tell him what Lord Sebastian was about, could have the man caught and arrested. He probably *deserved* to be arrested for attempting to smuggle in French brandy, or sugar, or slaves, or whatever nefarious cargo he thought to profit from.

Except there was a fly in that ointment, for Charlotte did not want authorities giving her own circumstances any consideration. They might not, not necessarily . . . did they know that her cottage had once been a smuggler's den? That there was a hidden door that had once led down to the water's edge, a door now made even more hidden by a layer of stucco over all its edges? Would she be accused of conspiring with Lord Sebastian, by virtue of the home she had chosen? Could she plead ignorance? Would she be believed? Would anyone see a resemblance between Charlotte Deems and a little girl who had played at the cottage one summer, years ago? Would the authorities go to London to see that Charlotte had taken on the married name of Deems, but had once been a Charlotte Ackerley? And what other official inquiries would follow in that wake? What other pretense be exposed?

"You had better be good at this smuggling!" Charlotte said quietly but very fiercely, her gaze riveted on Lord Sebastian's retreating back. He had to be good at it, for if he were not caught, then she would not be caught either. She must guard her secret by guarding Lord Sebastian's presence on the cliffs near her home.

She would join him at night, and she would do her best to see that this smuggling was successful. She would do as he demanded, because she must.

Chapter 6

Ten minutes later, under a cloudy sky that stifled nearly all the moonlight, Charlotte walked around the corner on to High Street. She spied the carriage, a coach that looked very like a hundred other coaches; it was dark and uncrested, as he'd said, an appropriate design for a man who meant to engage in illegal activities. Its lamps were not lit. She thought the carriage was black, but it could have been some other deep color made darker yet by the night's caress.

"Don't dawdle, miss," came a quiet instruction, not unkind, followed by movement atop the carriage. It was the driver, turning from her to face the horses, rearranging the reins in his hands. This was not Lord Sebastian; it must be his valet, serving as coachman.

"Mrs.," Charlotte corrected automatically.

"Yes, ma'am," the driver said, glancing quickly back at her. He touched his fingers to the brim of his cap, then made a motion with his head. It was not impolite, but it also clearly indicated that she should climb into the coach.

Charlotte took a deep breath, not letting it out, and reached for the door handle. Moonlight slanted into the coach's interior, and she was, truth be told, relieved to see Lord Sebastian sitting inside. Various plots from Minerva Press novels had sprung into her mind, but Lord Sebastian's presence served to dispel the worst of them. *So I am not to be kidnapped and sold into white slavery,* she told herself in morbid amusement as she released the breath she'd been holding.

Or, mark that, it was only to be a limited form of

slavery. She was being compelled to be at Lord Sebastian's side, atop the cliffs, but only for a few days. She suppressed an impulse to give a nervous little giggle.

"I would not have expected you to be smiling," Lord Sebastian said, his voice reaching across the night like the hand he extended to her.

"I feel a bit ridiculous," she answered, accepting his hand. She was pulled up into the coach. The door was closed behind her before she could even seat herself, plunging the coach's interior into unpenetrable gloom. The coach began to roll forward at once. Charlotte gained a seat at last, but not before she had to put out a hand and brace herself against Lord Sebastian's shoulder—in the dark of the carriage, she was glad it was his shoulder that her hand had found, and that she had not put her thumb in his eye. Gouging him would have hardly improved his mood.

It was an idea to keep in mind, however.

"You were discreet?" he spoke out of the darkness.

"Very discreet. I am sure no one saw me leave the party."

"Good."

Silence reigned for a full minute. If it had not been for his breathing and the faintest glimmer of some metal—his watch or fob?—Charlotte could have believed herself alone in the carriage. She'd had enough time to realize that the leather flaps that served as window covers had all been lowered. No wonder the carriage's interior was especially dark. No one could identify any occupant of the coach, that was for certain.

"How long has your husband been dead?" It was a conversational question, albeit a morose one—and how like this Lord Sebastian to say "dead" instead of one of the euphemisms such as "gone" or "taken from us." Perhaps that was one of the reasons why people thought him wicked, because he did not care to wrap what he said in clean linen.

"Do you mean the local rumormongers have not spread that news yet?" She did not think she sounded bitter, even if she could easily feel that way. Truth was,

she'd avoided answering the question of how long Jarvis
had been gone.

"Not to my ears," he answered.

She'd been here two months. She knew that was hardly
any time for newcomers to a small village, but gossip
was not her friend. Gossip threatened to reveal her secret. She should have changed her surname, made something up . . . But to wander too far from the truth was to
trip oneself up. Charlotte knew she was not a good liar.

"People say you have a sadness about you yet. As if
your loss was recent," Lord Sebastian said. There was
something . . . poignant in his voice. Or was that her
imagination, brought on by darkness and regrets?

"Not sad," she said. "Just not happy."

She still had not answered his question—oddly enough,
she did not want to lie to him, even though she'd
avoided, without qualms, giving the truth to other
strangers.

He did not press the matter, thank goodness. Instead
he said, "We have to go past my home. I have to retrieve
dark clothes that I have hidden there. I do not dare leave
them in the coach, because my brother also uses it."

"Ah yes, your brother the marquess. Does he know
what you are about?"

"No one in Severn's Well knows but you. And we are
to keep it that way."

"He would not approve?" In the dark, the toe of her
slipper bumped into the toe of his boot. Most men would
have moved their foot, but Lord Sebastian did not. Charlotte decided she would not retreat either—besides, she
thought with an unwitnessed, malicious smile, if he said
aught to anger or alarm her, it would make it easier to
stomp on his foot.

"Would Gideon approve?" Lord Sebastian sounded as
though he was giving the question sincere consideration.
"I am not sure," he said at length.

He had a nice speaking voice, warm and deep. But
not like a preacher's voice—which was well enough with
Charlotte. She had heard too many sermons in her day,
and not all of them of a Sunday.

"My brother is not much of one for approving the means to justify an end," Lord Sebastian continued. "But in some ways, I think he would be happy I have chosen to do *something*."

"He has called you idle?"

"He has called me many things. Which brings us to what you are going to call me, since we are to spend one or more nights together."

"Call you? Why, Lord Sebastian, of course," Charlotte said. It was, after all, the style afforded the younger son of a marquess.

"Sebastian without the 'lord' will do."

"I should think not!"

"Do as you will then, but I intend to call you 'Charlotte.' 'Mrs. Deems' makes you sound old beyond your years."

"I am complimented, I am sure," she said tartly.

He laughed, a sound even richer and warmer than his speaking voice. "Admit it."

She pursed her lips, but such an admission cost her nothing. "I admit that 'Mrs. Deems' always makes me think of Jarvis's mother, even though she passed away shortly after we married."

"Jarvis? Mr. Deems's Christian name was Jarvis?" His tone was ripe with mock horror. "It makes me think of 'larvae.'"

To her surprise, Charlotte had to swallow a laugh. "There is nothing wrong with the name 'Jarvis,'" she said, falsely prim. Better prim than frivolous—it was too easy to lose one's sense of propriety in the dark, or so Jarvis had always said.

"Then why did you not name your child 'Jarvis the Younger'?"

Now she could not help a small laugh. "Sir, you are correct. I admit I could not be so unkind to my child."

"Forfeit! Your admission means you lose, I win, and I am merely 'Sebastian' to you, and you merely 'Charlotte' to me."

She wondered what his intent could be—or did wicked rakehells ever bother to form an intent? Did they care to pursue anything beyond a moment's enjoyment? Or was it fair to label a young man as a rakehell, especially one who could look at Miss Natalie Talbot with such devotion shining forth in his gaze?

"Why is such informality between us necessary?" she asked. "Do you think to somehow magically mend fences and make a friendship grow between us?"

"Yes."

She laughed again; he was so frank in his manner. "But why?"

"I am sure I do not know. You are a sharp-tongued baggage, Charlotte, and I am equally sure I would be better off leaving any such friendship behind."

"Miss Talbot would approve that stratagem, I should think."

He was silent for a long moment, and Charlotte began to wonder if she had offended him although she'd had no such intention.

"I believe Miss Talbot would not deny me a friend or two," he said at length. It was evident from his voice that he had truly given the matter his consideration. "Not even of the female variety. After all, I mean for *her* to be my friend, the friend of my heart."

"Lord Sebastian—!"

"Just Sebastian."

"Sebastian then," Charlotte said, astounded to feel a flicker of real emotion at his words. He had taken her little quip too much to heart. But how curious that she could be concerned at hurting his feelings in some way! She was, though, and she sought to make it up to him. "I think you have just flattered me, calling me 'friend,' when you obviously hold your friends dear."

"Madam, I do."

He sounded so genuine, any words she might have uttered caught in her throat. She wished she could see his face, see if he was sincere, or if he teased at some deep, even cruel level.

Still, she did not need to see his expression. She could give in, a little. Even if he were entirely insincere. For her own sake, not for his, she could do that.

"Very well," she said, sounding a bit wistful. "I should like to hear someone call me 'Charlotte.' It has been . . . a long while." She felt an urge to give in just a little more, to relent and tell him how long she'd been widowed—but she tamped the notion down. She liked this man, despite everything, but she would be a fool to trust him.

The carriage slowed. "We are arrived," announced Lord Sebastian. . . . She supposed she could think of him as just 'Sebastian' now, since that was what he insisted upon.

Charlotte lifted a leather flap to glance out one carriage window and then the opposite, seeing only more darkness. "Where is the house?"

"There is a rise to your left. The house is beyond that. It is too difficult getting things in and out of the house unnoticed, at least for me. Easier for Timmons, however. He brings the necessary items here, to this clearing, out of sight of the house, and leaves them in oilcloth inside a hollow tree. Then I can take what I need as I need it, or leave them for him to clean, or whatever needs doing."

The carriage rocked for a moment, the result of Timmons climbing down from the box. He did not open the door, and Charlotte concluded he was probably securing the team to a tree or bush, in order that he might retrieve his master's black clothing from its hiding place.

"What if someone finds your belongings? Or Timmons turns traitor?" She felt as if she should whisper, just knowing his brother's house was not too far away. She was, indeed, beginning to feel like an accomplice.

"Life is not without risk. For instance, my choosing not to remain at your side four-and-twenty hours a day in order to utterly assure your silence."

"I am glad to hear that." She tried to make it sound like a declaration, but her voice betrayed her with a squeak at the end. The very idea!

A slow rumble of a laugh filled the carriage's dark interior.

"If you give me reason to think I should give you all

my time and attention, I will," he said. "I would be a silent, secret guest in your home, ever spying on you. I find I rather fancy the idea."

"Miss Talbot would not," she shot back.

He drew in his breath. "You know how to sting a man, Charlotte. But that is not why I will not stay at your home. There must be some level of trust between us two."

She was not persuaded for a moment by his talk of trust. "And besides, your brother would note your absence from his home."

"That too." She could not tell if he laughed, or maybe that was the sound of a mouth held tight with annoyance?

The carriage door opened then, allowing in what little moonlight escaped from behind the night clouds. Timmons, who pushed down a dark muffler from his face, held a lantern. It had three solid metal sides, with light coming only from the fourth side. It had a panel that could be slid up or down, allowing more or less of the light to shine forth—a smuggler's lantern. She recognized its purpose at once, for there was one very like it gathering dust in the small stable behind her cottage.

By the lantern's limited light, Charlotte could see that Timmons seemed younger than she had expected. His face had a smooth quality that made her wonder if the valet had yet reached twenty. He handed in a bundle tied with string, which Sebastian accepted.

"Thank you, Timmons."

The young man touched a hand to the brim of the hat pulled low over his eyes, accepting his master's thanks. "To the usual place now, my lord?" he asked, raising the muffler once more to obscure his features. Their driver dressed so as not to be recognizable, Charlotte thought to herself, but that was no wonder given the task he and his master had undertaken.

"No," Sebastian said. He turned to Charlotte, the outline of one side of his face caught by the sheltered lantern light. "Where is your son? Or is someone with him at your cottage?"

Charlotte caught her breath on a long hesitation, not wanting Oscar to be any part of this lunacy—but she could hardly leave Oscar at Mrs. Hyatt's all night. What manner of gossip would *that* create? A widowed mother not retrieving her child before dawn?

She looked to the valet. "Do you know where Mr. and Mrs. Hyatt live?"

Timmons nodded. "Yes, ma'am."

"We go there," Sebastian ordered at once. "Quietly. We will keep the coach back, away from any lights coming from the house. And then on to Mrs. Deems's cottage."

Timmons nodded again, indicating he knew where Charlotte's cottage resided. That thought made her give a quick frown. Not that it was any secret that she'd taken the old cottage on the cliffs, but she had to suppose these two conspirators had used her home as a mark of some kind in the past. Did they know it had once provided secret access to the Severn River below its cliffs? Had they used it for smuggling purposes before she had returned to claim it? But no, the hidden door was hidden yet, unusable because of the stucco that had covered it for some fifteen years.

The carriage door closed again, plunging them once again into deepest gloom. At once Sebastian began to make shuffling noises, the whispery sounds of fabric moving. His movements stirred the air, teasing Charlotte's nose with the occasional subtle scent of forest that had come in with the bundle Timmons had handed in.

"Hold this, please," Sebastian said, and fabric was pressed near her face.

"I have it," she said. She lowered the fabric to her lap and ran her hands over it, quickly realizing it was a coat. Ah then, he was changing into his dark clothing. What color had his breeches been? She thought back to earlier tonight, and blushed when she realized his breeches had been buff—he would be changing them for black ones, right here, right now, with her in the carriage with him. It felt quite scandalous, even though there was no way she could see anything untoward.

Indeed he did change, to judge from the sound of shoes being dropped to the carriage floor, and from the stockinged foot that bumped repeatedly into hers and the grunts and one small oath he uttered.

She could feel the heat in her cheeks, and was glad of the blackness that hid her growing sense of fluster. Part of her wished he'd been polite enough to ask her permission first, but that was a foolish thought—regardless of her "permission" he must change his clothing. If anything, she ought to be grateful it was dark.

Still, the mere sound of fabric moving, the occasional brush of a hand or a foot against hers, was enough to paint a mental picture for her. She was a widow. She'd borne a child. She knew how men were made, what intriguing differences were hidden by their clothing. In her mind's eye she could envision what she could not actually see: his fingers spreading open the collar of his shirt, the fabric being pulled over his head, the exposing of his chest. . . .

"When—" She had to stop and clear her throat. "When you are on the cliffs, you should wear your hair back and tuck it under your coat," she suggested, just to interrupt the intimate sounds so close at hand.

"That is what I do," he acceded through the dark.

She remembered him letting his hair down around his shoulders when first they had met, how it had acted like another cape for his coat, except that its color had clearly been light. Anyone seeing his hair thusly would remember it well—it could identify him easily. Why she should say anything that might assist him in breaking the law, she did not know. Actually, she did, because now she might also be implicated along with him. Even if she was found innocent, she could ill afford the notice, the attention, it would bring her way. Protecting him was protecting herself.

He heaved a sigh, one that said he was done twisting and pulling, that his smuggler's costume must now be in place. His hands touched hers, making her give a startled hiccough. "I can take that coat back now."

She pushed the coat into his hands, and listened as he

gathered things, presumably bundling them together for Timmons to take care of later.

"If I were clever," he said as he worked, "I would cut my hair short, to make myself harder to distinguish."

"Then why do you not? In London, everyone has short hair now, even many of the ladies. It is the fashion."

"I suppose that is why—so as not to follow fashion. But, no, I lie. Truth is, I did not have a valet for a while. My brother's household was . . . disturbed for a while. There was money, but chaos reigned. It seemed imprudent to bring anyone into the house then, not even a new servant. So I let my hair grow. For a while I liked it thus. It suits my reputation, I am told."

"But you do not like it long anymore?"

He made a noise, a verbal shrug. "I just never chose to change it."

"You have a valet now."

"Timmons is young, only sixteen."

"Sixteen! And he is our driver? Are we safe?" she said with a thread of alarm in her voice.

"Very safe." There was a smile in Sebastian's voice. "Timmons is young in age and in some kinds of experience, but he knows horses."

Indeed, the carriage had rolled along nicely, with no suspect lurches despite having no lamps lit against the darkness. The valet had the lantern, she supposed, which might provide a little light by which to be sure of the road ahead. "But he is not experienced in cutting hair?"

"I fear not. Frankly, I am terrified to let him come near me with scissors."

"For fear of your life?"

Now Sebastian did laugh, a quiet, soft laugh. "Hardly. He likes me, and being my valet. He likes driving a team secretly in the night. He gets to use skills that might otherwise be wasted. He's a clever little rogue."

"Whyever did you hire such a young person?"

"I did not. Gideon, my brother, did. Then asked me if I knew what to do with the little thief. That was what Timmons was until Gideon took him in, a thief."

Charlotte was again glad for the darkness, for it hid

that her mouth had rounded in surprise. "But are you
not afraid he will steal from you?"

"I pay him an extra twenty quid a year not to steal
from me. It's a bargain we made. Besides, he was only
a thief in order to eat. His father beat him, so he ran
away, and then he stole. Now that his belly is full and
his thieving little hands put to constructive work such as
polishing the harnesses or driving horses, he's less
tempted to be light-fingered."

"You are very forgiving."

"Not me so much, but Gideon is. However, it is not
my brother who would sport a head of butchered hair
were I to allow Timmons to have his way at me with
scissors—and so my hair grows longer by the day."

"You could have the lad trained."

"That is my intention. I will take him with me when
I establish my own house." It was not spoken, but Charlotte sensed the unsaid pronouncement: "And when I
can pay for that training myself."

So, the rakehell *did* have some intent other than enjoyment on his mind. Miss Talbot's hand, for one, and a
former thief's training in the art of being a manservant,
for another.

"I am not so sure I would want a former thief in my
household, were I to be your bride," Charlotte said.

She thought he did not mean to answer, but at length
he said, "You have a point. Then I will simply have to
withhold that little tale about Timmons from Miss
Talbot."

Charlotte parted her lips to warn him that hiding
things—even little things such as this—was no way to
start a marriage, but then she clamped her mouth closed.
Who was she to hand out marital advice?

The carriage rolled to another stop, but unlike the last
one, this was near a house. Timmons opened the carriage
door, letting in only moonlight and a tiny glow from the
lantern he carried, for he had stopped the team of horses
well back of any light shed forth through the house's
windows. It was enough to see, however, that Sebastian
was indeed now dressed all in black, even down to the

kerchief tied about his neck, ready to be hoisted to obscure his features.

Charlotte hesitated before rising from her seat. "Are you not going to caution me to pretend to the Hyatts that I am with the Donfields?" she asked finally.

"I could, but I cannot control what you say when you are inside, away from my side, so it would be a waste of my breath. Are you telling me I should come to the door of the house with you?" He started to rise from his seat.

"No," Charlotte said at once, putting her hand on his arm. There was just enough light that she was able to see him glance down at her hand, which she quickly removed. No, he must not come to the door with her. What would the Hyatts make of seeing Lord Sebastian Whitbury at her side? Exactly what she herself would think in their shoes: that a liaison was about to occur. A stupid liaison, if Sebastian and Charlotte were so foolish as to appear together before the Hyatts—but people liked to watch others behaving foolishly, liked having something to gossip about, no matter how unlikely its basis in reality was. "No," she repeated. "I will go alone. I will avoid saying anything to indicate you are here."

Sebastian did not appear either triumphant or mocking—he just gave her a steady look, one that made her think again of his comment about trusting one another.

"I have a thought," she heard Sebastian whisper to Timmons as she stepped away from the coach toward the Hyatts' front door.

It was simple, so easy. Oscar was fetched, the Hyatts secured a promise that Charlotte would mind their daughters while they attended a midday musical assembly in nearby Bristol two days hence, and Mrs. Hyatt's eldest girl saw Charlotte to the door. If the six-year-old noted the coach well down the path or was curious about the occupants, she gave no sign of it.

With Oscar on her hip, Charlotte was back in the coach in short order, surprised to find that Timmons and his master had traded places.

"Good evening, Master Oscar," Timmons greeted Charlotte's son from his seat inside the coach, and she understood in a moment that the two men had switched so that Timmons and Oscar might begin to grow familiar with one another. Somehow that made it more real that Charlotte really was going to be forced to wait and watch on the cliffs with Lord Sebastian, and some of her resentment bloomed anew. But there was no point in letting Oscar sense this, for he must endure the company of Timmons, and vice versa. Better that they should not have her angry disapproval stirring the pot as well.

As it happened, Oscar fell asleep in Timmons's arms, where he had been playing with the valet's coat buttons.

Once at her home, Oscar settled without incident into his cot beside Charlotte's bed. Everyone was quiet, breathing a communal sigh of relief when her son snuggled down into his blankets without waking.

Charlotte turned, meeting Sebastian's gaze with her own. "I must change clothing," she mouthed to him. He nodded, and the two men backed away from her bedchamber, and Charlotte gave another sigh of relief, this one just for having the men out of her private space.

"I saw a stable at the back," she heard Timmons say quietly, but she was unable to hear Sebastian's reply, which was no doubt to unhitch the horses and take them there until the time came for the two men to leave later.

She did not linger, for she feared disturbing Oscar. Since Jarvis had died, there had been no money to afford the services of a maid, so all of the dresses Charlotte now owned could be donned unaided. She'd never been more grateful for that fact.

She heaved another relieved sigh when her clothes were changed and Oscar had not been wakened. She prayed he would remain asleep at least until her return, for he would most certainly be unsettled to find Timmons in his mother's place, but there was naught she could do about the possibility.

"How long do we wait out there?" she said quietly as she came from the bedchamber, dressed in a mourning gown of black wool. She left the door open, because the heat from the grate in the main room was enough to warm all of her little cottage now, since the bitter cold of winter was behind them.

"Only until one o'clock," Sebastian answered just as quietly as he pulled on black gloves that he had produced from a coat pocket.

Why one o'clock, she wanted to ask him, but he made a motion with his head, indicating they should leave, so she swallowed the question. She pulled on her cloak, also wool, dark blue, and raised the hood against the late-night cold that would sweep up the cliffs from the river below.

Timmons handed his master the lantern, now severely shuttered. Charlotte knew the light could be hidden entirely, by lowering the sliding panel all the way down, not leaving a tiny rectangle of light as it had now. Lord Sebastian motioned Charlotte out the door, moving right behind her. She swallowed, and sent up a quick prayer that Timmons had an aptitude with children in case Oscar awoke, and stepped out into the night. She watched with an agitated feeling as her own door was closed against her, and as the smuggler at her side reached to take up her hand.

Chapter 7

They stood a moment, allowing their eyes to readjust to a lack of light. The numb feeling Charlotte had felt for a moment began to fade, starting with her hand, which she was now acutely aware was clasped in his own.

"Why one in the morning?" she asked, to fill the awkward silence between them.

"A ship not at anchor late into the night is a ship with nefarious purposes. Or at least that is how the local members of the Customs guards see it. After one, it is too dangerous for an intelligent smuggler to even attempt to ply his trade."

"But I thought ships moved at all times of the day and night, to make the most of the Severn's tides." She had been in the vicinity of the river long enough to know the Severn, flowing as it did into the Bristol Channel and eventually the Atlantic Ocean, had not only a tide, but one capable of viciously dragging unwary ships down in troubled areas. Where river met ocean water, whirlpools formed—it was a difficult port. And because it was difficult, it attracted smugglers, men who were willing to risk sailing when and where those with legal trade dared not.

"If you are using the Bristol port, yes, with its quays and its crews to keep disaster at bay, it is used at all hours," Sebastian answered her as he pulled on dark leather gloves. As he moved she saw that he had indeed stuck his hair under the collar of his coat, hiding its length. "But more to the point," Sebastian went on, glancing down at her, "the patrols are doubled at one in the morning, because it is known that most smuggling occurs after then. Besides, as I told those who hired me,

I must have some time in which to sleep. I have to go on with my daytime life, for appearances' sake. Even the wicked must rest, so we agreed there would be no signaling after one."

He took up her hand at once, and began to walk forward with long strides, forcing her to scurry in order to keep up with him.

"You need not hold my hand. I will follow you," she said, but she could not be sure he heard her over the night sounds of wind and leaves, as well as their clothes rustling and the small crunch of their shoes against the earth. He certainly did not release her hand. He did not hurt her, did not squeeze her fingers, but his hold was firm.

A rock skittered from under her foot, and she almost turned her ankle—she might well have if not for his steadying grip on her hand. Perhaps . . . could it be he did not so much mean to hold her hostage as to give her a support against the vagaries of moving quickly through the dark?

He gave her little time to ponder if he was being forceful or considerate, however, sweeping her along. He was in a hurry. She suspected he worried that he had already missed the signal he awaited. What would it be? A rocket, such as military men used to light a battlefield at night? No, that would not serve, not if the smugglers meant their business to be kept secret. A "hello?" shouted across the water—but, no, that would leave too much to the chance direction of the wind and proximity. The lantern then. The ship would have a shuttered lantern not unlike the one Sebastian carried, and they would have a prearranged signal, a certain number or length of times for which the shutter was opened and the light within exposed, the direction prearranged. Of course. Charlotte should have known that at once—her grandpapa had told her such tales.

Sebastian did not stop until they had reached a large evergreen at the very edge of the cliff. The tree's top half, a blackness against a charcoal sky, was bent permanently inland, pushed constantly by the winds that swept up from the river's edge far below. Half its roots were exposed, the soil eroded away, leaving the roots to stretch out like entreating fingers over the precipice on which the old tree struggled to cling. A treacherous and eerie drop-off, just discernible, was only a few feet from where Charlotte stood at Sebastian's side.

"Of course," she said, her voice very soft. The smuggler beside her would not appreciate loud tones.

"Of course what?" Sebastian did not look at her; he looked out upon the water, searching the river and the channel out beyond its mouth. His voice was equally as hushed.

"Of course you would need some kind of marker, so the ship knows which direction to shine its signal."

"Hence the tree," Sebastian agreed.

"You do not keep your secrets well, Lord Sebastian." She stumbled over his name a little, belatedly recalling she was to leave off the "lord."

He did not correct her, and despite herself she liked him all the better for it. He was not overly proud or carping—she would have expected either quality from a man willing to stoop to importing illicit goods.

"I feel compelled to point out that one tree looks much like another, especially in the dark. Especially from the distant deck of a ship."

"But if you combine such a tree with other landmarks, a seasoned sailor will find his way along the coast easily enough."

She conceded the point with a shrug, but he probably missed the gesture since he continued to peer toward the water.

"Let us move," he suggested at length. It was an excellent idea if they were to stave off the chill of the evening. Spring might have arrived, but the cliff side was seldom warm, ever cooled by breezes fresh off the river, and tonight was no different.

They could not walk far, just in a semicircle near the tree, perhaps fifty feet in an arc, but it was better than standing still. Sebastian alternated his glances between the ground at their feet, the water, and her face, speaking softly of the weather and the crops sprouting in local fields.

She could have laughed at the parody they made. They might as well have been at a party, promenading among other guests, making small talk. Really, for a smuggler his manners were very refined—but he *was* a marquess's son. He'd been trained since birth to be refined. *Preferable to the alternative,* she thought to herself, and almost shuddered at the very idea of being out here, on the cliffs in the dark, with a rougher sort of man. An odd kernel of something like gratitude filled her, for things could have been so much the worse this night.

They stopped for a moment, his attention keenly focused outward, but then his shoulders relaxed. He must have thought he saw something, but had not. "Let us speak of your secret, Charlotte."

She had not been expecting his gaze and his attention to shift so suddenly back to her, nor that his words would pierce her sharply. Did he perhaps know something? Had he just been playing coy until now? As a member of the family of prominence in the area, he was positioned to hear of anything untoward that affected the village. Had word spread from London? Did he know her secret, that she lived off the income generated from selling jewels that were not yet rightfully hers?

"If I have a secret, what is it then?" she challenged. It was the wrong tone, one that spoke more of guilt than denial, but her surprise had turned her voice brittle.

He gave her a long considering look. "I do not know. But I know you have one."

She almost breathed out a sigh of relief—he did not know. "*Me?* I am not the one awaiting a ship full of untaxed goods," she pointed out.

"There is something you do not want others to know about you," he insisted. "What is that?"

"If I did not wish people to know something, it would hardly behoove me to tell *you.*"

"I will not tell."

Now she laughed, a cynical sound.

"Who would I tell?" He sounded so sincere, so reasonable.

"There is nothing *to* tell," she lied baldly, meeting his gaze. Even in this small amount of light it was possible to see he was disappointed in her answer.

He accepted her lie, or chose not to challenge it. Either way, he looked out to sea once more. "Tell me about Oscar."

She scowled. Why did he want to know anything about her son? "What is there to tell?" She wondered if her shrug was as nonchalant as she tried to make it. "He's a fine boy, but he is only two."

"Humor me, for I have quite run out of 'weather' comments."

Oh. Perhaps he really was just attempting to change the subject. She was too easily spooked tonight—but what sane woman would not be in like circumstances?

"He looks like his father, at least through the eyes," she said, giving in to the need for conversation, for normality in a bizarre situation. "He does not speak much yet, but the words he has are fairly clear. My mother was worried when he was nearly eighteen months old and still had not tried to say anything—but he was quick to walk, only ten months old."

Sebastian nodded, and by wordless consent they began to stroll once more, her hand still caught in his.

"They say children tend to be walkers or talkers," she elaborated. "Truth to tell, I was surprised that he was not more like his father, talking, always talking—" She cut herself off abruptly, ashamed at the disloyalty that had started to trip off her tongue. It served no purpose to dishonor Jarvis's memory—even if she only spoke the truth.

"Charlotte?" Sebastian asked, concern in his tone.

"I . . . I stubbed my toe."

"Do you need to be seated or—?"

"I am fine, just fine."

"Are you sure?"

"Quite." She stepped forward, propelling them both into walking once more since their hands were yet linked.

"So your husband was a great talker, was he?" Sebastian mused aloud. It was difficult to tell if he was only making conversation or finding humor at her expense, but she was saved from having to answer by his going on. "In my family, I was the talker. Gideon can be taciturn, and Benjamin tends to keep his own counsel, so it was left to me to be the magpie."

"Well, someone has to do the talking in a family, surely," Charlotte offered—it was a kind of apology to her dead husband. Plus it served to keep Sebastian speaking, filling up the night, making the time pass.

"My father did not think so. He had no use for my tongue. Which only encouraged me to make even more use of it, naturally. I chattered because I knew it vexed him so. It was my form of defiance." He glanced down at her. "I hope you encourage young Oscar in more useful pursuits?"

"I hope I do, too. Did you and the old marquess often have quarrels?" She was just making conversation—albeit intriguing conversation that gave her an insight into what could lead a man toward a willingness to break the law.

"Quarrels!" His voice was soft, but rueful. " 'Quarrels' is too kind a word."

"So you were unruly?"

"Indeed." He gazed outward, but Charlotte would have guessed a different view filled his vision, memories of unhappy times. "But I was only unruly because he was so harsh."

"Cruel?" she ventured, struck by the sadness in his voice, his posture.

"Not in the usual way. Oh, he struck us, his sons, but it was his words, his deeds, that were cruelest."

She shook her head. "I am sorry to hear it."

"Well, we had each other. We boys."

Charlotte spied a large rock, and moved to sit on it, tired of strolling. Sebastian finally surrendered her hand to glance out to the water again.

"You have two brothers, I believe you said?"

Sebastian nodded. "Gideon, the marquess, as you

know. And Benjamin, the middle brother. He is married now, and owns his own stud for racing horses which, thanks to his wife's keen eye for horseflesh, is thriving." He sat down beside her, forcing her to share the limited space. He set the lantern near their feet. "Have you any siblings?"

"None," she said, pushing an errant strand of hair from her eyes. "I was born late to my parents, who never had another child." She hoped he could not feel the tension that filled her at the personal slant their conversation had taken.

"Where are your people? Your parents?"

"Dead," she lied. Only her papa was gone—but Mama might as well be, so caught up was she in forming a new marriage, a new life for herself. Perhaps once Mama was married to her new suitor and the two legally bound . . . but Mama's suitor had made it plain enough that grandchildren were for visiting, not for living in one's house. There might be the seasonal family reunion awaiting there, but not a home.

"What about your husband's people?"

"Jarvis was estranged from his family. He chose the church when his father had wanted him to go to the army. There was a bitter quarrel. They never reconciled."

"You have no one?" Sebastian questioned, sounding shocked.

"Oscar," Charlotte pointed out.

"But no one else," he stated, and shook his head in commiseration. "I am sorry to bring up your losses. I am certain you cannot appreciate the reminders."

"All I want is to live quietly in my little cottage," she said, and saw his face fill with color even through the gloom.

"Then God speed the ship to this shore," he said, his voice strangely gruff. He rose to his feet, walking away from her, only to turn and walk back.

He stooped before her, drawing his watch from his vest pocket. Even though he stooped, she became suddenly aware of his size, of the shoulders and hips and height of a man. Of the foreign nature that was male. She was glad for the cold night, for the way the breeze carried away a sudden warmth in her face. It was too easy to remember how man was made to fit his mate, how the marriage bed had not been the duty her mother had described—at least, not when Charlotte had yet hoped to love her husband. It was too easy to long for the intimacies a man and woman might share but which she never really had.

Sebastian lifted the lantern, lighting the watch face, then made a sound rather like a growl. "Two more hours."

She made a sound in her throat, a discontented sound that suited her mood on several levels.

He looked up at her, a scowl formed between his eyes. "That is too long a time to be at odds. No more talk of personal matters, as they only stir unfortunate memories. You were in London not so long ago—"

"Two months."

"Still, the tattle is fresh enough to be of interest. Speak of that."

And so they passed the time, with Charlotte telling every anecdote she could think of that would not tell him more of her life in London than she wished revealed. She spoke to pass the time, and to forget the sudden flush of ardor that had struck her.

When he looked at his watch and declared the evening at an end, she was surprised that the two hours had passed so quickly.

This time, he did not take up her hand, but offered her his arm to escort her back to her cottage. Timmons was asleep in her only chair, not counting the two spindly wooden ones pushed up to her small dining table. His head lolled against the chair back until the door closing startled him awake.

"The lad slept through," he muttered to Charlotte as he blinked the sleep from his eyes.

She tiptoed into her bedchamber, seeing for herself that Oscar was contentedly asleep, and lingered a moment to watch him breathe and dream. She took off her cloak and hung it on its peg, then went back to the front room.

The two men were already halfway out her door, but at her appearance Sebastian stopped. He gave her a long look, then nodded. "Tomorrow night, Charlotte," he promised. His voice, pitched low so as not to disturb Oscar, sent a shiver up her spine.

She did not need to answer, for he moved at once to close the door behind him. She stood still, listening until the sound of hoofbeats and carriage wheels faded, lost beneath the usual sounds of the wind outside and the fire on the grate within.

How . . . peculiar. She felt rather as she had the first time or two that Jarvis had singled her out, had sought her company. Not flattered—she did not feel giggly or silly or tingly, but . . . aware. But of course, she told herself, how could she *not* be aware of Lord Sebastian? He was handsome, he had a vibrant manner, he was up to no good, and he had forced his company upon her.

Still, when she turned to enter her bedchamber, she felt impolite? Slow-witted? Disappointed? That she had found nothing to say in return to him. What should she have done? *Thanked* him for usurping her time, for making her into an accomplice of sorts? Of course not.

She changed into a night rail, threw more wood on the fire in the front room, then fell into bed, half afraid she was too provoked to find any sleep. But slumber claimed her almost at once.

If she dreamed, she did not remember them come the morning when Oscar awoke her with a repeated cheerful chorus of, "Mama? Mama?" The dreams must have been pleasant ones, though, for she was left with a sense of tranquility she would not have expected after last night's escapade, and it was easy to return her son's good morning smile.

Chapter 8

After lunch the next day, the groom and Sebastian shared a grin over the large head of Titan. The dog was sitting between them, the top of his head as high as the bottom of Sebastian's waistcoat.

"Only one day later and look at 'im, m'lord! 'E's better, ain't 'e?" Jacob asked with all the enthusiasm of someone who already knew the answer.

"He is decidedly better," Sebastian agreed, reaching to brusquely rub the dog's ears. Titan thumped his tail against the floor.

"It's getting hard to keep 'im 'ere," Jacob said. " 'E keeps straining at 'is tie."

"Take him for a longer walk, then, and then move him into my room for the rest of the day. That will be easier on everyone."

"Especcially the kitchen staff," Cook said from the table just inside the kitchens. She sent a speaking glance from where she stood peeling carrots. "Dogs in the kitchen!"

"Be fair!" Sebastian cried in mock outrage. "There was only one dog, and he was in the corridor."

"One huge dog," Cook said on a sniff, but beneath her censure hid a smile.

Sebastian grinned back before he turned to the groom. "If Titan still seems well tomorrow, he can have the run of the place again."

"Yes, sir," Jacob agreed with a satisfied nod before he untied the dog and led him away.

Sebastian flipped back his coat and put his hands in his pockets, contentedly watching as the oversized mutt walked away, clearly in better health. However, now that his visit to see about Titan was settled, Sebastian found himself at odds, with nothing to do. It took him only a moment to decide to stroll down the hill and into the village—where there was always the possibility of spying Miss Natalie Talbot.

The wind picked up his loose hair as he walked, sending its length dancing about his head. Should he cut it as Mrs. Deems had suggested he ought? Would Miss Talbot like it shorter? She very well might, for it would be more fashionable. There was a barber in Bristol that Sebastian knew of—he must send the man a missive and have him come to cut his hair. He had enough of his quarterly funds left to afford the cost of having the man come from the bigger city.

He could always ask Gideon for more money, for that matter. Gideon would give it to him. But after his one foray into debauchery in Brighton—financed by estate money that Gideon had given him—Sebastian found it increasingly difficult to take money without ever giving anything back.

It would be good to have his own funds, once the ship had arrived and he had discharged his task.

That thought had him thinking again of Charlotte Deems—she clearly held no sympathy for smugglers. Why? Most people who lived along the river secretly approved of a spot or two of smuggling. It was a way to have desired goods without paying the exorbitant taxes on them. Would she feel any different if she knew he smuggled not goods, but a single person? That this duty had been handed to Sebastian upon the orders of the Prince Regent?

He would never know, because he could not tell her that the Prince of Wales had, through an emissary, agreed to award Sebastian ten thousand pounds if he could manage to get a certain Frenchman off one ship and onto another, all in secret.

He did not try to fool himself by thinking he was doing something noble—it might be an entirely ignoble thing, so far as Sebastian knew—but he knew he had agreed to do it because his country's prince had wanted it done. And, he thought with a wry grin, he'd agreed for the money. The Regent needed a favor, and Sebastian needed blunt. For this he would tempt the fates and hope his one try at smuggling was a successful one.

He thought, then, of how he had changed his clothing in the carriage, with Charlotte not even a foot away. He'd known at once from her sharp intake of breath that she'd quickly discerned he was undressing. He was glad she had not turned missish on him—after all, what harm had come of it? He grinned a little, remembering both her verbal discomfort and her unspoken acceptance of the situation; she had not carped at him nor even bid him cease. He doubted the unmarried Miss Talbot would have been so temperate in the same circumstances—but that was the advantage of having his unwitting ally be a widow. Married women seemed better able to accept that men had things to do that sometimes had very little to do with being gentlemanly. Married women understood that there were times when a man might be half-naked in the dark. . . .

Sebastian grinned, and turned his unruly thoughts to another topic: it was a fair day, the afternoon sunshine making him wish he was playing cricket. There was neither a game nor practice today, however. That left him free to wander between the scattered shops of Severn's Well, which suited him well enough, especially since each door he entered held the possibility of revealing Miss Talbot within.

The luck was not with him today, however. Miss Talbot was not abroad. Still, he got a book from the lending library, bought a hot crossed bun from old Dick Fairley's cart, and spent a half hour instructing some of the local lads in how to properly wield a cricket bat, using a stick as a substitute.

His only surprise came upon stepping into the apothecary's shop. Miss Talbot was not here either—but Mrs. Deems was, along with her little boy. Neither of them looked particularly pleased. For that matter, neither did the apothecary, Mr. Walbrook.

"I do not need anything to make Oscar sleep, Mr. Walbrook," Mrs. Deems was saying through narrowed lips. "He sleeps quite well enough on his own."

"But most of the local mothers do like to have it on hand, for those nights when the little man is restless."

"I am sure a simple case of restlessness does not call for laudanum!" Mrs. Deems replied crisply. She turned to leave, Oscar's hand in hers, and startled visibly when she saw Sebastian had entered the shop. "Oh! Lord Sebastian."

"May I assist you in some way, Lord Sebastian?" Mr. Walbrook said almost over Mrs. Deems's words.

"No, thank you," Sebastian answered. He would have tipped his hat to Charlotte, but he'd already removed it upon entering the building, so instead he offered her a short bow. "I was looking for Mrs. Deems here, and as you see I have found her. Mrs. Deems?" He offered her his arm. She hesitated only a moment, then took it.

He pulled her from the shop, settling his hat once more on his head, faintly amused by her pursed mouth.

"Insufferable man!" she said once the door had closed behind them. "He thought I should be giving Oscar laudanum to put him to sleep each night!"

" 'Only a drop or two,' " Sebastian quoted. He laughed when Charlotte's mouth rounded into an O of surprise. "I know, because it is exactly what he says to every mother for three miles around. He is a bit famous for this little bit of advice. The happy news is that most people agree with you, Charlotte, and prefer to save laudanum for more dire conditions."

"Why do they tolerate such a charlatan?"

"Walbrook is not so bad in most things. He just believes in the 'silence is golden' rule for children, I am afraid. Besides, the nearest surgeon is in Bristol, and who wishes to travel to Bristol just to obtain megrim powders?"

"I suppose," Charlotte gave in with little grace.

They all stopped then, in order to allow Oscar to stoop down and examine an insect crawling in the dirt. The lad had a natural curiosity, his intent expression now reminding Sebastian of the boy's mother.

"Tell me, is Oscar ill?" he asked. "Is that why you went in to Mr. Walbrook's?" Sebastian inquired politely.

"No." Charlotte blushed, intriguing him.

"Tell," he commanded her with a grin.

She shook her head.

"You know I will just make you tell me tonight."

Charlotte slanted her gaze his way and grimaced.

"Tell me now or tell me later, after I have hounded you for hours."

She must have believed he would indeed hound her, for she sighed and gave in. "I just . . . he seemed a pleasant sort the other night. I wondered if Oscar would . . . would like him."

"Oh." Sebastian felt a small disconcerted ripple fill him as comprehension dawned. She was husband-hunting! That was hardly any surprise; looking for husbands was what unmarried females did, even widows. Or rather, especially widows who had children to feed.

"Oscar may like the man, but Oscar's mother does not," he observed. He meant to make her smile, or at least relax her shoulders, and he was glad when he saw she did both.

"No, she does not," she agreed. "I hope escorting me out of Mr. Walbrook's did not interrupt your business?"

He shook his head. "I am practicing being idle. I have been so busy of late, I have almost forgotten how to waste time. I am finding I have nearly lost the knack."

She might suspect he was following her, minding where she went, watching whom she talked to. If she did, she did not let on.

"Where to next?" he asked as Oscar at last lost interest in the insect and stood up.

"Home."

"That is a fair walk for you. Can Oscar walk so far?"

"I carry him most of the way," she admitted.

"Not today. I will carry him for you."

"It is not necessary—"

"No, it is not, but I will do it all the same. I have

grown bored with being completely idle today. It is too
exhausting, all this tarrying. I insist you let me be of
some use."

She seemed yet reluctant, but in the end she nodded.
"As you wish. Thank you," she said, then turned to lift
Oscar. She passed him into Sebastian's arms, and they
both watched as the little boy looked up at him with a
questioning expression. Then the pin that held Sebastian's cravat in place caught the lad's eye, and he reached
eagerly to try and pluck it off.

"He likes most women, but some men alarm him,"
Charlotte said softly, obviously not wanting her tone to
upset the boy. "Clearly you are not one of them."

"Children like me," Sebastian informed her. "And
dogs. And cats. And horses. And women. All women
adore me, did you know that?"

She laughed at that, shook her head, and led the way
out of the village toward her cottage.

He would not say anything, of course, but he could
not help but realize Charlotte had no carriage, not even
a gig. He already knew she quickly grew thin-skinned on
the matter of her income, and would not appreciate having this shortage pointed out, but he could not help but
feel sorry for the lack. She would have to walk every-
where, and carry all purchases the long distance to her
house. Neither did she have a maid—clearly money was
a problem for her. It was evident that her husband had
not left her much in the way of a widow's portion.

His sympathy, however, was tempered by the suspicion
that the Widow Deems was keeping some kind of secret.
She had admitted to nothing—but he'd seen the alarm
in her eyes when he'd accused her of having a secret.
She was open on the subject of some things. Sebastian
did not doubt that her husband had been named Jarvis,
or that her son was legitimate—there was only pride in
her gaze when she spoke of her child, no shadows
there . . . but money. Any subject to do with income
caused her to take a defensive retreat.

Was she a wellborn lady, now ashamed of her slide
into near-poverty? Was she a husband-hunter who knew

that having a child lessened her desirability, especially combined with a lack of a dowry? Did she really have no family, or had she been banished for some sin or crime she'd committed? Had she taken what money she could from some relative or guardian and fled? Perhaps to escape drudgery? Or to protect Oscar?

What if the widow supplemented her income by turning smugglers in to the authorities? But, no, there had been no arrests of late. Living in Gideon's home as he did, Sebastian would have heard of arrests, for Gideon was the largest landowner in the area. What affected Severn's Well affected him, so the Aldermen of the village were quick to keep Gideon informed.

Still, to know Charlotte's secret could be the final tie that Sebastian could use to bind her into silence as regards his own intended crime. He may have been asked by the Prince's friend to do this favor for His Royal Highness, but Sebastian was under no illusion that both Prinny and his interceder would deny all if Sebastian were caught. The key to it all was secrecy—and that was the key to Charlotte as well. If he knew her secret, Sebastian had little doubt he could control her.

She had run from London, that was evident. London would be the place to go to investigate Charlotte's perfidy, whatever it may be.

Except, Sebastian considered with a wry interior shake of his head, even if he were free to leave the cliffs and go to London, he did not want to.

It was foolish to let Charlotte keep her secret from him—but unless some dire reason arose to change his mind, he did not want to know it.

Besides, the threat of implication was enough to buy her silence for now. She would not go to the authorities, Sebastian believed, because she did not want the authorities to pay any particular attention to her.

Gideon is right, Sebastian thought, *I do have a soft heart, more the fool me.* He shrugged, turning the motion into a bouncing ride for Oscar in his arms. The little boy laughed and cried out, " 'Gain! Do 'gain."

"Oh no!" Charlotte said with a smile. "You may regret starting that. He'll never tire of it."

"Madam, I do regret my little game," Sebastian said twenty minutes later as they stepped up to her home. Charlotte watched as he set Oscar down, making sure her son was steady on his feet before he himself stood up slowly, shaking his arms as if to restore feeling in them. "Do you feed him bricks?" he demanded. "He must weight five stone!"

"Hardly," Charlotte corrected with a grin. "Thank you for carrying him. He does get terribly heavy after a bit."

"Next time, you carry him, and I will carry an anvil and think myself the luckier."

Now she had to laugh, which helped to cover the sudden fluster she felt at the idea of there being any "next time." Would they have any contact after he'd met his ship? It would probably be best if they did not, nothing beyond the most casual of meetings such as occur in a village. Surely he was only making a jest.

"Well then," she said, the fluster increasing instead of fading away. "I guess I will see you tonight."

Sebastian nodded, and might have spoken, but Oscar interrupted.

"Mama!" he said, leaning his weight against the front door, clearly wanting to be let in.

"Good-bye," Charlotte said, turning at once to scoop Oscar up. She pulled the handle down, lifting the simple mechanism out of the latch on the doorjamb, allowing her to push the door open. She stepped in and spun at once, closing the door between her and Sebastian.

She heard the sound of his boot heels as he strolled away, not moving from where she still held the door handle until Oscar protested with a babbled exclamation and a wiggle. She lowered him from her hip, and wondered why her heart was racing so. Sebastian had not threatened her . . . or even flirted with her. But of a sudden she'd felt awkward in his company.

It was curious that she had spent hours with him last night alone in the dark, and never felt awkward. Scared at first, annoyed sometimes, even amused—but not awkward.

A shiver coursed through her, giving her the unflattering notion that she trembled with all the grace of a dog casting off water, as she ruthlessly decided the impression was not worth exploring. She *ought* to feel awkward in a smuggler's company.

She moved toward the kitchen, filling her mind quite deliberately with thoughts as to a dinner for her and Oscar, only to stop short when she saw through her kitchen window that something was altered. She moved closer to the window. There, covering the floor of the small two-horse stable, was fresh straw. And in the back part, sheltered by the roof, sat a new pile of hay.

While she had been gone someone had brought straw and hay. She had no doubt it had been Sebastian's valet, Timmons. Now there was hay for Sebastian's horses to eat while they waited for their master each night.

How would Charlotte ever explain new straw and hay to anyone who might come by? Would they believe her if she said she was thinking of obtaining a horse? What about after Sebastian's horses had stood there for several hours tonight—how could she explain away the droppings?

Had Sebastian done this in order to further incriminate her? One more step taken to "persuade" her not to reveal his smuggling?

Charlotte frowned. Or could Sebastian have done this in order to keep his cattle comfortable, not to mention quiet?

It would be more intelligent to suspect the former—but the latter seemed more in keeping with the little she knew of the man.

For that matter, whoever came by her cottage? A tinker had come by once in his wagon. The surgeon, if she sent for him because Oscar was ill. Mrs. Hyatt had stopped in twice, once to greet the newcomers, and once to share a bounty of eggs. Charlotte's cottage was out of the way, isolated. Callers were not very likely, really.

All the same, Charlotte found herself sending up a little prayer that tonight would be the night that Sebastian's ship gave its signal.

Chapter 9

Sebastian knocked softly on her door shortly after Charlotte's small mantel clock had chimed ten that night. Oscar was already asleep in his cot. She opened the door, letting Sebastian and Timmons in. Sebastian doffed his large, floppy dark hat, nodded at Charlotte, and set down a tied bundle next to her door. She guessed it must be clothes inside the oilcloth.

Sebastian spotted her eyeing the bundle. "I am supposedly at a card party. I will return there after our task." He spoke low, in deference to her sleeping child.

So, the bundle *was* clothes. He thought to give himself an alibi, albeit a flimsy one, since there would be a three-hour gap between times he could be confirmed as being seen there. But she supposed it was better than no alibi at all.

She retrieved her dark blue cloak, nodded to Timmons, who belatedly thought to doff his hat, and reached for a bundle of her own. She slipped it under her arm and then moved out into the night with Sebastian at her side.

"I noticed last night that you wore no gloves," he commented. "Do you not have any dark ones? I do not mind if you wish to wear light-colored ones, as you can always hide your hands within your cloak—" His voice rose at the end, turning the comment into a question.

She hesitated a moment, and then decided she was being prideful by not wanting to tell him the truth, to no purpose. "I only have one pair of gloves, my lord. And, yes, they are white. I try to save them for Sunday wear."

He looked stunned at this revelation that she was so

lacking in this area of basic apparel. She'd had two other pairs when she'd first moved here, but the lace pair had been ruined when she tried to launder them, and one of the pretty kid leather pair had gone missing. She supposed she would find it one day in her garden, buried for some unfathomable reason by her son, but it certainly was nowhere in the cottage.

"I beg your pardon," he stuttered.

Charlotte offered him the briefest of smiles, and started walking briskly, glad for the plentiful moonlight that guided her steps. She did not give Sebastian a chance to take up her hand as he had yesterday—but she doubted he would even try now that she had flustered him.

"How large a card party is it you are presently missing from?" she asked back over her shoulder.

He fell into step beside her, settling his hat once more atop his head. "Kingswell's," he answered.

Charlotte nodded with understanding. Mr. Kingswell of Bristol only threw card parties, and often, and large ones at that. It was rumored he survived off the advantage that always went to a gaming house, although he'd be horrified to have his "parties" called a club. He teetered on the very bounds of gentility by hosting his "friends" in his own home and not making them pay a membership fee. He had many rooms filled with a variety of card and dice games, food, wine, cigars—someone would be hard-pressed to prove Sebastian had been missing from the company there.

They came in silence to the cliff's edge by the slanted evergreen. Sebastian put down his lantern, checked to see it was properly sheltered, then stood again in silence, staring out at the water. "Three days late," he said on a sigh.

"Do you fear the ship is sunk?" Charlotte asked as she stooped to untie her bundle, a blanket wrapped around a small casket and a length of linen cloth.

"No," he said, glancing at what she did. They kept their voices low, so as not to carry. "It is too soon for that. I knew I might have to wait as much as a week. The ocean has no respect for man's timetable."

She shook out the blanket, a dark color, spreading it for them to sit on. Sebastian moved to straighten the two corners nearest him.

"This will be better than sitting on cold, bare ground," he said with a nod of approval.

"If it was as windy as last night, I would have brought another, to wrap around me," Charlotte said. However, there was little wind, for once, tonight. The clouds were few and thin, allowing the moon to shine its light down on them. It provided poor cover for a smuggler, but Charlotte enjoyed being able to make out the features around her, including Sebastian's expressions.

She sat on the blanket, tucking her feet up under her skirts and cloak for added warmth, and Sebastian threw himself down beside her on his elbows just like the day on the common.

"How goes your courtship of Miss Talbot?" Charlotte asked, to make conversation.

He growled. "She was at Kingswell's, glued so tightly to her father's side that we were only able to exchange nods."

"Lord Lamont *is* zealous in his vigilance over the company Miss Talbot keeps."

Sebastian shrugged, but he was not so nonchalant as he tried to appear—his growl and the pout on his mouth proved that.

"One can hardly fault the man," Sebastian said, "since he is only trying to assure the best alliance for his daughter. Besides, he keeps other suitors at a distance as well. He is doing me a service, if you look at it that way."

"And you think he will warm to you once you have a pocket of money to call your own?"

"I do."

"But surely your pockets are not really so empty as you like to claim. The Greyleigh estate prospers, does it not? Your brother is not likely to let you starve or sleep without a roof over your head, is he? Lord Lamont need not fear that his daughter would be a penniless pauper, should she marry you."

He cast her a dark look, but she saw the misgiving in his gaze. "Lord Lamont is not just worried about a roof over his daughter's head, but any son-in-law's *purpose* in life. He would think a man must have goals. I daresay it is my idleness to which he objects, more than anything else. Unfortunately, it is difficult to be anything *but* idle when you have no real income from which to build an occupation of one's time."

That was probably true, to one extent or another. No father would want his daughter to marry a man with no ambition. "An idle person is the devil's playfellow," as Jarvis had been fond of preaching. But what father would pass up the chance for his daughter to be assured at least a comfortable home and food on the table, albeit at a brother-in-law's tolerance? Charlotte had only been in Severn's Well for two months, and even she had heard of the unusual magnanimity and compassion of Gideon Whitbury, Marquess of Greyleigh. That, and one had only to mention the marquess to see Sebastian's affection for him glow forth. Only a simpleton would think the youngest brother would ever be allowed to fall into a state of destitution.

If Sebastian never formed an ambition in his entire life, any wife of his would still at "worst" be dining at a marquess's table. She would be afforded the social triumph of rising to the level of Lady Sebastian Whitbury. Lord Lamont was but a baron—what could possibly make him want to deny his daughter an ascendancy all the way up to the wife of a marquess's son?

Charlotte glanced at Sebastian, and felt a qualm for his sake. He did not know, he refused to realize . . . Lord Lamont did not like *him*. Perhaps it was a combination of many factors: his mad mother; his leisured days playing at cricket; his third son status. His reputation bordered on that of a libertine. Or perhaps it was Lord Sebastian's wit—a father might find it vexing, even though Charlotte found Sebastian's wit more charming than not, despite herself and the circumstances of their acquaintance.

Whatever had caused it, she would wager every last penny she had that Lord Lamont had no use for Sebas-

tian Whitbury. Lamont would never agree that his
daughter should marry the man, no matter the prece-
dence it would bring her. Unless it was to be a fantastical
sum, Charlotte could not imagine that Sebastian's soon-
to-be reward could be enough to tempt Lord Lamont
where other advantages had not already.

She parted her lips to tell Sebastian as much—but how
could she? What proof did she have but simple logic?
How could she say such hurtful words? It was possible
she was mistaken—even though every fiber of her being
told her she was not. Besides, perhaps he would manage
to convince Miss Talbot to elope with him.

"What have you there?" Sebastian asked her now, unaware of the turmoil of her thoughts. He nodded toward
the small casket she had brought.

She reached for the casket and opened it, showing him
the contents.

"A sewing box?"

She lifted out a pair of scissors and a comb. "I never
thanked you properly for saving Oscar. I thought you
might want me to cut your hair, as your reward, since
you are leery of letting Timmons do so."

"I do not need a reward. I am only glad Oscar is safe
and well." He eyed the scissors with doubt. "Do you
have any notion of how to cut hair?"

"I cut Oscar's."

He grunted, a faintly approving sound.

"I used to cut Jarvis's. And he had to look presentable
for his sermons every Sunday. I know how to cut the
style à la Brutus."

"Indeed?" At least he did not reject the idea outright.

"Or do you wish to keep your mane? It is rather fetching, despite fashion. It suits a smuggler to look rather
like a pirate."

He lifted an eyebrow. "You are certain you know what
you are doing?"

Charlotte nodded, smiling encouragement at him.

"I would not be able to go back to the party."

"Oh! I suppose not, not with suddenly trimmed hair."
Charlotte made a little face, feeling faintly disappointed

she could not do him this favor, and started to put the comb and scissors away.

He cleared his throat, the sound causing her to pause. "Could you do it justice here, in mere moonlight?"

"It is light enough tonight." She glanced up at the moon, and then back at him. "But we could wait until we return to my cottage," she suggested.

He considered for several long moments. "No," he said at length. "I do not want to disturb your son, nor do I wish to be out later than necessary. Let us do it now," he decided all at once. He drew off his large, floppy hat, pulled his hair free of his coat collar, and pulled out the ribbon holding it back.

Charlotte stood, glancing around. "Why do you not sit on that rock from last night, to act as a chair." She gathered up the length of linen, and preceded him to the stone.

He sat so that he could gaze out to the water. He looked puzzled for a moment while she draped the linen around his shoulders, then he realized her intent and reached to hold the two ends together in front. "To keep the cut hair off my clothing," he noted the linen's purpose aloud.

"Most of it, anyway." She clicked the scissors, eyed the shape of his head and his handsome face, then stepped back to meet his gaze. "You are sure?" she asked. "Part of me hates to cut it."

"Cut away," he said blithely. "For if you think to play Delilah to my Sampson, I assure you that my strength is not in my hair."

No, not at all, she thought to herself as she began to comb the golden-hued length. Sebastian's strength lay in his humor and his devotion—things Lord Lamont seemed unlikely to prize.

She gathered his hair in one hand and took a large snip at the back, severing the length. "Well, it is started," she said, feeling a bit wistful. She would trade her own ordinary brown for his gold tresses in a moment, were such a thing possible.

"Excuse me a moment." She moved to the cliff's edge, and bent down carefully, intending to drop the hank of

hair over the edge for the wind to scatter. She remembered how she had saved the wisps of hair from Oscar's
first haircut—but there was nothing maternal in the feel
of Sebastian's hair in her hand. If anything, it possessed
a bit of sinfulness to it, this act of cutting something so
eye-pleasing, just to suit fashion. Would she remember
it as sinful decades from now, when Charlotte recalled
this night? She did not know, but she did abruptly decide
she wanted a memento, something to remind her of her
strange, oddly intriguing time at a smuggler's side.

At the last moment she plucked out a lock of hair,
hoping Sebastian did not notice, and then let the rest of
the golden strands go; they fell to the cliffs, the light
breeze doing its best to tumble this evidence of human
proceedings above. Charlotte moved back to the small
casket, pretending to be looking for something there, but
instead stashed the lock of hair inside. She prayed it was
only a little adventure, that they would not be caught
out—but, either way, she would have her memento.

"The rest of the hair I cut will blow away or be less
noticeable, being shorter," she explained as she returned
to his side.

"Thank you for not leaving such identifying evidence
about," he said, more serious than usual.

"You would have scattered it about if I did not."

Any seriousness retreated as he grinned up at her.
"True."

"Hold still," she said, and began cutting in earnest.

Sebastian gazed out to the river and the channel on
the horizon, but he had to frequently remind himself he
was here to watch for a lighted signal. He wanted to give
himself up to the simple pleasure of having his hair
played with, but his vigilance was required outwardly.

Still, Charlotte's fingers moving through his hair, across
his scalp, touching, soothing, made him want to relax and
simply give himself over to the pleasure of the moment.
He wished he could close his eyes, or perhaps start to
purr—he did, just to hear her laugh. Perhaps, when his
hair was done being trimmed, he would lean into her

touch and beg her to continue her gentle handling some more, he thought with a wry interior sigh.

He knew the caresses she delivered were the very thing he most craved in life. He knew he valued women for the softness of their touch, for the gentleness in their gazes and in their approach to living. He knew he marveled at their small hands, strong enough to knead bread one moment, then gentle enough to give the lightest, sweetest touch to one's cheek in the next.

He knew he had longed for years to see the humanity in his mama—Gideon remembered their mama having lucid moments, but Sebastian did not. For him she had never been tender, only frighteningly peculiar and detached. So some people might think he longed only for a mother's caress. Some might find his inability to forego touching as a sign he sought another woman to grant him the mothering he'd never had—but it was more than that. What he craved from a touch was the thing both his parents had denied him: love. The simple physical manifestation of love.

He did not want Miss Talbot to mother him. He wanted her to love him, to reach for him out of a kinship of hearts, one that only deepened any desire between them. He wanted, in the truest sense of the word, a helpmeet. A mate. A match to his essence, perhaps as different as one piece of a dissected map puzzle from another, though made to fit together to form a whole.

And yet . . . and yet, it was difficult to stifle an elemental pleasure at Charlotte's touch. She was not Natalie Talbot, and she worked with precision and purpose, not with the lingering touch of a lover—but there was something too fundamentally intimate in this act they shared. She was impossible to ignore or take for granted.

A woman had never cut his hair before. Sebastian had expected it to be much the same as when a man cut it . . . but a man had a different touch than did a woman. He was aware of the roundness of her breasts under her black dress, no longer obscured by the cloak she'd flung back over her shoulders to get it out of the way of her arms. He was aware of her scent—soap and rosemary, the rosemary no doubt a holdover from the chicken dinner he'd smelled upon entering her cottage tonight. He noted the tip of her tongue at the corner of her mouth as she worked, and smiled secretly to himself at the temptation that little bit of pink tongue had even for him, a man in love with another woman.

If Charlotte really wished to marry, he thought to himself, she ought to advertise that she cut men's hair. She would have several offers inside a week, he was willing to wager, once they saw that pink tongue and once they had experienced Charlotte Deems standing between their legs as she worked to even out the fringe on their foreheads.

He began to wish he'd taken off his coat, for he found he grew too warm under the coat and linen fabric that protected it from the work of her hands.

At length Charlotte stepped back, and Sebastian experienced a moment of relief to have a few feet between them.

"Done!" she pronounced, shifting her head from side to side, evaluating her work in the light of the moon. After several long moments, she nodded in satisfaction. "Yes, done."

She stepped toward him again, this time to carefully pull the linen away from his neck. He stood, brushing at his shoulders, feeling the inevitable prickle of clippings that clung to his neck. He ran a hand through what was left of his hair. "It certainly feels short," he acknowledged.

"I put a hand mirror in my sewing box. If you stand with the moon behind you, you should be able to make out your reflection," she offered as she moved to the cliff's edge again, to shake out the linen.

"Be careful," he cautioned before he bent to retrieve the mirror. He gazed, a little shocked by his altered appearance, and ran his hand through his hair again. He nodded. "It looks fine."

"What faint praise!" she pretend-scolded, folding the linen and bringing it back to set it to one side of the blanket.

"No, truly. You did well." He continued to examine

his reflection in the mirror, angling his head this way and that. "I doubt I could have done better with a barber from Bristol. I'd forgotten my hair has a bit of curl to it when it is not dragged down by length."

She nodded. "You have the perfect hair to achieve the Brutus effect, all tousled half-curls." She gave a theatrical sigh. "Oh, to sprout such a glorious color and crop of curls atop my own head."

He wondered if it was possible for her to see the blood that rushed into his cheeks despite the grayness of moonlight. She might not have meant to flatter, but he flushed with color as if she had. He ran a hand through his hair again. "But your hair is very pretty, a nice rich brown color," he assured her.

" 'Rich' is being generous. I will let you tell me my eyes are a pretty bird's-egg blue, but I am well aware my hair is very ordinary," she said on a laugh, not self-effacing, just honest.

"Your eyes are a pretty bird's-egg blue," he chimed dutifully.

She laughed, pleasing him because he'd only hoped to make her smile, as she sat once more on the blanket. She continued to smile slightly as she stared out to the river, evidently joining him in searching for a light. A ship was passing down below, a light on its deck, but he'd already told her last night to watch for an interrupted light, not a steady one.

"I know you cannot say much, Sebastian," she said, her tone having grown sober despite the lingering curve of her mouth. She glanced at him as he took a seat next to her. "But I do have a question about your ship that I would like answered." The humor had faded away. "Honestly, please."

"If I can speak, I will be honest," he said. The breeze, just a flutter compared to usual, moved through his shortened locks, reminding him of Charlotte's fingers in his hair.

"I want to know if the cargo being smuggled into England is slaves. Besides being illegal, it is a cruel institution, and I pray I do not in any way contribute to it."

She looked so earnest, so concerned for people she

did not know—but it was easy to put her mind at rest. "No slaves, I vow."

She let out a breath, clearly relieved. "I believe you," she said.

He felt a new warmth fill him, unlike the uncomfortable warmth he'd experienced while she stood between his legs, trimming his hair. This was a gracious glow, the result of a compliment. She believed him. Despite their awkward association, she had chosen to take him at his word.

They sat in silence for several minutes, until Sebastian pulled up one leg and hugged his arms around it. His first impulse had been to take up her hand, but he restrained himself. "I just thought," he said, "how will I explain this to Gideon and Elizabeth?" He unlinked his hands long enough to point at his shorn hair.

"Tell them Timmons did it," she suggested.

"Ah!" he conceded. "That will do." He rocked a little in place, as one does while waiting for the time to pass, or for impulses to abate.

"Come now, we are too soon silent. Surely there is much more to be discussed between two people," Charlotte prompted.

Sebastian nodded, even though he personally thought their silences had been comfortable enough, if one discounted the time during which she'd cut his hair. Never mind his impulse to touch her hand with his own—that impelling force, that craving of touch, was an old itch he knew how to ignore when he must.

"Tell me why you play cricket," she suggested.

"Why?" he said on a laugh. "Because it is fun."

"What makes it fun?" she asked. Now it was her turn to recline on her elbows, a rather unladylike posture that made his grin widen. She certainly had lost any dread of him she'd had.

He went on to explain. He'd learned to love the game despite never having attended school outside his home. His tutor, thank goodness, had heartily approved of exercise, cricket especially, and had without doubt used the game to draw off some of his three pupils' energies. Since three was hardly the number for a good game of cricket, it had been Sebastian who had organized matches involving all the local lads.

"And you are still organizing matches like that," she pointed out.

"That is what I would really like to do, you realize."

"Organize cricket matches?" she questioned, grinning.

"You laugh, but, yes. Most schools have a team. The game is growing yearly in popularity. There are some competitions that occur, but I would like to see a regular circuit of matches. A town to town sort of thing, where people would know that two teams are coming, and everyone would turn out and make a day of it. Not something that's advertised by flyers and only happens a time or two a year, but regularly, on a schedule."

"Oh, I should like that," Charlotte said, her eyes gleaming.

"Yes!" Sebastian cried, immediately making a face for having spoken too loud. It was just that he'd been pleased by her accord. He had been thinking for a long while now that the game was in need of organization and structure, that most towns and cities would welcome a rotation of this sporting event among them, and it was pleasant to have someone agree with his notion.

"And we could charge each town a small fee," he went on, having lowered his voice again, "enough to cover the expenses of travel. And there ought to be uniforms, do you not think? Nothing so stiff as a soldier would wear, but perhaps matching waistcoats? Or hats, to make it clear at a distance who played for which team. We'd confirm the rules, so that the entire kingdom plays the same game, probably to the standards drawn up by the Marylebone Cricket Club in London. And—and why are you laughing at me?"

"I am not laughing at you, but at your enthusiasm," Charlotte explained. "Why, I think your devotion to the game would make you a perfect speaker to be called before Parliament! Your brother could go to the House of Lords, and put forth a recommendation for the Cricket Act."

He tried to keep a frown from crossing his features, and to ignore the sting he felt that she did not take him seriously. "You tease me."

"Indeed, I do not," she said, looking shocked. "I was quite serious. I happen to agree with what you say, and personally I believe that Parliament should provide funds for the establishment of a National Cricket Standard. Or perhaps a Council of Cricket."

He gazed into her eyes and saw sincerity. The sting he'd expected never came, but was displaced by gratification. "It is just a game," he said, feeling a little stupid for having spoken his thoughts aloud and for taking umbrage unduly.

"But it is the grandest game, do you not think?" Charlotte said on a breathy sigh as she reclined further, half turning onto her side, her head cradled on one arm. Sebastian caught his breath, stirred both by her words and the casual pose—oddly intimate—she had placed herself in. He'd never seen a woman lie down in such a way, except in a bed. He knew Charlotte was earnest, and her gesture provocative without intention, but the accidental nature of its design could not keep the moment from striking Sebastian as ripe with sensuality.

He quickly turned his gaze from hers, not trusting his voice to be steady enough for a response, and hoped she noted his nod.

A half-minute of staring out to the river did nothing to calm the inappropriate stirring of his blood, so Sebastian leaped to his feet and walked away from Charlotte. Thank God, she did not follow him. He moved within an arm's length of the cliff's edge, struggling to master this errant attraction that moonlight and a woman's words and motions had stirred in him. He loved Miss Talbot, adored her in fact. This was only a random, regrettable moment, the disadvantage of being the male of the species. Man was made to seek—and sometimes could not help but be stirred by sudden urges.

He could, however, master his urges. He could choose. And he chose Miss Talbot. Clearly. Without doubt. It did not matter that Charlotte's tongue at the corner of her mouth had affected him, nor that her increasing trust in his company flattered him, nor that her admiration of his favorite sport filled him with gratification. Or, rather, it did matter—but only so far as in a friendship.

Would it be possible for them to be friends when the smuggling was behind them? He hoped so, he truly did. Natalie and he would have Charlotte and Oscar over for meals, and they would be good neighbors and friends. Sebastian felt better for having made that decision—he need not dispose of Charlotte's company; he needed only to know his feelings for her were those of friendship and mutual interests.

Still, he did not return to her side for over half an hour, looking away from her out to the water.

When he moved back to where she waited, he found she had slipped into slumber. Carefully, he crossed the edges of the blanket over her, a shield against the light breeze. She stirred and blinked up at him.

"I was just covering you, Charlotte. It is still two hours to go," he informed her quietly. She nodded once, blinked, and went back to sleep.

He woke her shortly after one o'clock, and gathered the casket and the linen while she rubbed the sleep from her eyes. When she rose, he threw the blanket over one arm, and offered his other to her, which she took.

Once inside her cottage, he put down her belongings and gathered up his own bundle. Without speaking, he gestured toward the kitchen, where he went and changed into clothes more suited for the card party he could not now return to, not now that his hair had changed entirely. But even in just returning home, it would hardly do to be seen in his smuggler's garb. It would be difficult enough to explain his change in hair, should Sebastian run into Gideon before making good on an escape into his private rooms.

He came back into the sitting room, his bundle retied, and was faintly disturbed to discover Timmons was gone, no doubt already hitching the horses to the coach. Charlotte sat in her one comfortable chair, just fighting off the return of sleep.

"Timmons said he moved the horse droppings into the copse nearby," she said sleepily. She yawned, hiding it behind her hand and looking a little embarrassed. "So it may look odd that I have straw and hay, but at least there's no evidence that horses stood here. Thank you," she said, giving him a nod of appreciation.

"That was Timmons' doing, not mine," Sebastian said, giving credit where it was due. "I am glad he thought of it. Well then. Good night," he said to her, then gave a small, lopsided smile. "Or rather, good morning."

"Good morning," she said back, then rose to open the cottage door for him.

He slipped out the door, and saw the coach standing ready, Timmons already on the box, the coach door open and waiting for him. Charlotte closed the door at Sebastian's back, cutting him off from the warmth and light of her cottage, and from the possibility that he might linger there awhile longer tonight.

Sebastian gave a quick frown, then moved to the coach and climbed in, settling against the squabs. He sighed, feeling oddly unfulfilled. That was not to be wondered at, of course, for yet again there had been no signal signifying the expected ship's arrival. It would be there tomorrow, he thought rather fiercely, as if his determination could make it so. There ought to be only one more night waiting on the cliffs, with Charlotte at his side.

Sebastian sighed again, and wished he might go back to the card party, for the company. He ought to sleep, but he suspected sleep might be elusive tonight—wine, women, and song seemed to suit his mood. Well, not "women"—Miss Talbot had won his esteem and he would not betray her for a mere moment's touch—but a bit of company would do. Only, it would be too difficult to explain away his hair. He could tell a lie about going to see a barber in Bristol, but it was a silly lie and easy to prove false. Better to just go home, and in the morning tell one and all that he'd finally allowed Timmons a turn with the scissors.

He ran a hand through his hair just to feel its shortness once more, and thought of Charlotte, and sighed again.

Chapter 10

Charlotte moved toward the small stable—free of any sign of horses if one discounted the fresh straw and hay—in order to put away the hoe she'd just been using on her garden. The garden would provide some nice fresh produce over the summer, and perhaps a little for putting by into the winter, but she would have to be sure to buy extra produce from local farmers. Certainly she'd need potatoes and apples and herbs, to supplement the bread, meat, macaroni, and rice that could be had from the village market all year round. Milk, butter, and cheese could be had from the Dairyman who drove his cart from village to village, and Mrs. Hyatt was always more than happy to sell extra eggs.

The Hyatt girls had come and gone already, their parents clearly pleased to have enjoyed their musical midday without children underfoot, perhaps as much as Oscar had enjoyed having visitors. Were there any other chores in order this late into the afternoon? Charlotte had already restacked some of her firewood to better shelter it from rain. Mr. Hyatt had been so kind as to chop into smaller pieces the rounds of wood Charlotte had bought upon first coming to Severn's Well. She found she liked the popping and hissing of wood burning, ever so much more than the coal she'd used in London.

There were quite a few things to like about living in the country, even about living unwed.

If she remarried she would still have a garden, but she would most likely have servants to work it for her. Even the apothecary would not want his wife out in the sun, scraping at the earth like a tenant farmer—except perhaps to harvest herbs for his salves and potions. Not that Charlotte had any intention of marrying the laudanum-giving Mr. Walbrook. No, her search for a father for Oscar must begin again. Tonight. But not today. Today she had a treat in mind.

"Our work is done for the day, Oscar," she said to him, stooping down next to where he worked so diligently at dislodging an imbedded stone from the garden bed with a stick.

He looked up at her, listening, the brown hair so like hers shining in the sunlight. It was still cool enough that Charlotte had put knitted breeches under his long smock, both garments now edged in dirt.

"Do you want to go watch the men play cricket?"

"Yes!" Oscar said at once, dropping the stick and standing, taking the hand she reached down to him.

They moved into the house, washed their hands and faces, and Charlotte hung the apron she'd been wearing on its peg. They donned their outer garments, and began to walk toward the village and its common. Charlotte cast an uncertain glance up at the clouds that had gathered since last night. Well, if it rained, she and Oscar would get wet. The pleasure of watching cricket outweighed the risk of a little dampness.

The possibility of rain had not discouraged the cricketers either. The practice consisted of a line of bowlers delivering pitches to batters, with balls scattering in a dozen directions and shouts of "Mind the ball there!" to one another. Over Oscar's occasional bursts of chatter, Charlotte could hear that there was some manner of instruction on leg position which Sebastian led. And a half-dozen men practiced making runs, with one of the scoring lads counting off the time loudly so they could tell if they were improving.

Oscar was content to watch the men for a while, but eventually that was too inactive for a lad of two. Charlotte walked with him as he retrieved balls that rolled near, keeping an eye open so that none should come down and strike them as they entertained themselves. They piled the retrieved balls together for the players to fetch, except for one they then kept to play a catching game of their own. Oscar threw the ball, Charlotte went to get it, and then she rolled it back so that it stopped at his feet, ready to be taken up and thrown again. Oscar laughed every time the ball went nowhere near his mother's outstretched hands and she made a pretend pouty face.

"The wind is picking up," came a familiar voice.

Charlotte turned, not surprised to verify it was Sebastian who had spoken. Oscar spied him, too, and ran over to where his mother stood, alternately hiding his face in her skirts and peeking out to shyly smile at Sebastian.

She had not seen Sebastian's shorn hair in daylight, of course, and was struck by how flattering it was. He had nicely shaped ears, close to his head, and the cut only served to draw that much more attention to his uniquely colored eyes. He saw the direction of her gaze, and ran a hand through the gentle curls, tousling them even more than was fashionable.

"You did well by me," he said.

"I did," she conceded with a smile. "You look very dashing. What did your teammates think of this new look?"

"They hated it."

Charlotte stared in surprise.

"They said now I will win the hearts of *all* the girls in the village, not just half of them as before."

She laughed. "I daresay they are right."

"But that would include *your* heart, Mrs. Deems."

She knew teasing when she heard it. "Ah, but am I a villager yet? I have only lived here two months. I believe I have to live here two decades to be called a local. So my heart is unavailable to you, you see."

Sebastian grinned down at Oscar, who was trying to draw his attention by alternating hiding his face in his mother's skirts and then revealing it for a long moment. Oscar hid his face again even as he chortled, a purely delighted sound that Charlotte had realized adults could not imitate, and Sebastian shifted his grin up to Charlotte, clearly amused by her son's antics.

"Alas, I cannot argue against your logic, Charlotte," Sebastian said. "At least you are not one of those foolish city folk who think they can belong by mere dint of living here."

"There is truth in that," she said, unable to keep a wisp of regret out of her voice.

"Charlotte, I was only funning." Concern erased the amusement from his face. "Severn's Well is more accepting than they pretend to be. Only see how they welcomed back their prodigal son, me."

"It must be good to have a place that has always been home," she said wistfully. She glanced up at the worrisome gray sky overhead, then down at the ball in her hand, and offered it to him. "Time to head home, I suppose," she admitted as he accepted the ball.

Oscar let go of her skirt for a long, smiling stare up at Sebastian. Of a sudden he cried out, "How you?"— his version of "How do you do?"—and to her surprise, ran to fetch a ball. He picked it up with a show of effort, and at once turned to run back and offer it to Sebastian.

Sebastian stooped down to accept the ball. "Thank you," he said, then stood and scooped Oscar up into his arms.

Oscar did not protest or suddenly go shy again, surprising his mother once more. "I ball?" he asked.

Sebastian glanced at Charlotte.

"He is wondering if you would play ball with him," she translated. "You do not have to, of course. We did not mean to interrupt your practice."

Sebastian waved her concern away. "It is but practice. I am the team captain, so I can play ball in any way I wish, even be it with this good little fellow," Sebastian said, setting Oscar back on his feet.

He took over where Charlotte had left off, retrieving Oscar's wildly thrown balls, complete with a pouty face that made Oscar laugh. Charlotte leaned against a tree to watch.

She was amazed. Not so much at Sebastian for taking the time to play with a little boy—Sebastian was indulgent with people that way, she was coming to find. He had an ability to seem gruff on the outside, but it went no deeper than that. She wondered if his reputation as a miscreant wounded his sensibilities at all? She imagined it did, even if he would never let it show. But it was Oscar who really amazed her at the moment: he had not only greeted Sebastian—an honor never bestowed on anyone other than his mama or grandmama, but he had also invited Sebastian to play with him. Not another child, but an adult.

Of course, Oscar had been too young to initiate much of anything while Jarvis was still alive, so there was no fair comparison to be made there—but it warmed her mother's heart to see her son reaching out to a man as he did now. If she'd doubted before the wisdom of remarrying to obtain a father for Oscar's sake, she could hardly doubt it anymore. Thank goodness Sebastian had responded so easily and readily to the request. He was laying a groundwork for another man to follow, allowing Oscar to grow in confidence in his dealings with new faces. It was kind of him to take the time to indulge her son.

Charlotte gazed at Sebastian, and thought that he was, in his own fashion, a good man. Better than just a good man, really. Miss Talbot was fortunate to have this man in love with her. Did she realize that?

Of course, what did Charlotte know of love? Only that she'd never had it, not with her husband. Or had she expected too much of him, of marriage? She did not know, but she knew she was grateful to Sebastian for playing a game of ball with her son.

After a bit, the sky threatened even more than it had, for although the clouds had not increased, the wind had. Charlotte announced it was time to go, and Oscar must have been tired and longing for a lie down, for he did not protest.

Sebastian picked Oscar up, carrying him to Charlotte. As he passed the boy into her arms, Sebastian stepped close, his mouth not far from Charlotte's ear, no doubt to be heard over the rising wind. "Tonight," he said, his breath stirring a wisp of hair and making a shudder run through her in reaction.

"Do you think the weather will cooperate?"

He gazed at the sky and gave an uncertain nod. "Perhaps. Perhaps not. I must watch, all the same."

"I understand."

Neither said that she must watch with him, but it was there between them.

"Do you want me to carry Oscar—" he began to offer.

"No," she said quickly, then smiled to soften the rejection, a quick movement of the lips. "You should stay and practice."

"Are you saying I need it?" he demanded, pretending to be insulted.

"As I recall, the Gentlemen lost the last match," she stated as she settled Oscar on her hip.

Sebastian narrowed his gaze at her, but there was no real anger there. "You are cruel, Charlotte Deems," he said.

"Well, you, sir, are not. Thank you for playing with Oscar. It was very kind of you." She turned away, but not before seeing surprise cross his face. She wondered if he had grown used to being thought a profligate—so used to it that he'd forgotten what it was to be admired. He had certainly forgotten to hide his better side from her.

As they moved away, Oscar waved for a considerable length of time over her shoulder at Sebastian, who must have been waving back to engage Oscar's attention for so long. Charlotte did not wish to be seen glancing back, however, so instead she concentrated on the weather. She concluded the wind may have pushed away the rain, but she would rather not be caught in a downpour if a little haste could make the difference. Besides, haste carried her outside the reach of anything Sebastian might call out after her, which suited her perfectly. She'd had enough of Sebastian's company for one day. Their conversations always left her feeling . . . rattled.

There was enough in her life to be rattled about as it was. Money, raising her son alone, keeping her secret—

even keeping Sebastian's secret. She had wished before that all this business on the cliffs might be over soon, and now she wished it doubly. Lord Sebastian Whitbury was a difficulty in her life, albeit a charming one. She'd be well rid of him, once he had no reason to come and fetch her from her cottage each night.

Yes, once he was done interfering, she could go back to having the plain, normal, quiet existence she'd come to Severn's Well to find. It would be a little boring compared to the past few days, no doubt about that, but she did not need "excitement" in her life.

"I most certainly do not," she said aloud.

" 'Bastian," Oscar said, responding to his mama's conversation as he saw fit. He looked back the way they had just come. " 'Bastian," he repeated, looking up at his mother.

She sighed. "Taught you his name, did he?" she asked. "I missed that interchange. I was not listening as you played, obviously."

" 'Bastian," Oscar said happily.

After they had arrived home and Charlotte had sliced a pear for Oscar to eat as he sat on a round of wood that served him as a little stool, she moved to her room. She made certain the window curtain was closed, only then kneeling to pull up the two loose floorboards that she knew were there, just under the edge of her bed. She reached into the hole this revealed, and took out a tin box.

She removed the lid, and did a mental assessment of the jewels lying inside the box. They were all there, what was left of them. She'd sold perhaps as much as a third of her jewels so far, in order to afford the move to Severn's Well and to set up her household. She'd needed a few things she had not been able to bring with her, such as her bed, not to mention stocking the kitchen.

These jewels were all she had left, once Jarvis had died. Everything else but her clothes and the few belongings she and Oscar had brought with them, had belonged to Jarvis's beloved church, St. David-in-the-Fields.

Not that the jewels really belong to me, she thought

with a flash of anger, *not yet*. Her jewels, brought into her marriage, had upon that marriage no longer been hers to dispose of. As did everything that was hers, clothing, books, even the children she might bear, the jewels had become the property of her husband.

Jarvis's will had been specific that she was not to have control of the jewels until Oscar achieved the age of five-and-twenty. It had not been stated, but the implication had been that once Oscar was old enough, he would then decide if he wished the jewels for his own purposes, for his own wife, presumably—or whether he was going to allow his mother to retain them.

Part of her understood that Jarvis had been trying to preserve the "family" jewels for their children—but by so "preserving" them he had kept Charlotte from being able to use them. She did not doubt he had never foreseen she would be in such straitened circumstances . . . if he had foreseen it, he would not have put so much of their personal monies into the church he'd been beautifying. He had planned, she knew, on having years in which to reap the rewards of being the rector at a handsome little church, one that he'd hoped would become a fashionable wedding and baptismal favorite.

She sighed, recalling the cost of the baptismal font alone. It had been lovely, all Italian marble and gilded filigree—but its cost could have housed and fed Charlotte and Oscar in London for a year. Instead, upon his death Jarvis had left his family the grand total of forty-five pounds, two shillings, and sixpence. That was it. That had been all of the earthly worth left to Charlotte.

So, when Jarvis's solicitor had asked for the family jewels, Charlotte had given him one-tenth of what they were in reality. He had questioned with a small frown if the handful he held were the extent of the jewels mentioned in the will, and Charlotte had bald-faced lied to him, saying "Yes." There had been a long, silent stare exchanged between them, but Charlotte had been so benumbed by Jarvis's sudden death and the realization of her destitution, she knew she had shown neither fear nor remorse.

"They are my jewels!" she said fiercely now, as she had a dozen times before. Only, legally, they were not her jewels at all, not yet. Not for three-and-twenty more long years.

For three months, while the estate settled and St. David's awaited their new rector, she had lived in dread that someone would recall the rope of pearls she'd worn before and had not turned over to Mr. Ulrich, the solicitor. Or the opal earbobs she'd often worn to outings about town. Or any of the other jewels she'd never had any reason *not* to wear.

So she had left London, had come to her grandpapa's long-abandoned summer cottage. For two months she had awaited a knock on her door, the solicitor come with a magistrate at hand, to arrest her for theft. Theft of her own jewels! It was so unfair—but, no, they were Oscar's jewels under the law.

If she could, she would have saved them for him. But they had to eat! They had to live. Jarvis had left his family as good as nothing—so if it took this kind of thievery to keep body and soul together, Charlotte had long since made up her mind to do it.

Two months of freedom from London, of thinking about her precarious situation had opened her eyes, though. What would become of Oscar if she were thrown in prison for theft? Would Mama pay the difference, so that Charlotte's debt was erased and she was able to go free? Mama, who herself strove to marry in order to better her own widowed state? She had no money with which to assist her daughter.

It was all so ironic. Charlotte was stealing from no one but herself and Oscar. Still, under the law she was wrong.

The only alternative, of course, was to marry. To no longer live off the proceeds of selling the jewels. Her husband would be responsible for any debt she accrued, so even if the law came for her, it would not keep her long, not once her husband was made to pay or else face imprisonment for debt himself. She and Oscar would be fine, if she married.

As to how she could marry a man, any man, without

warning him of the possible debt he assumed, without
revealing herself as a thief—how could Charlotte do
that? What sort of marriage could be built on such a
rocky foundation as that? Just because Jarvis had done
nothing to protect her or Oscar, how could she pull such
a dirty trick on someone else?

How could she not?

Charlotte sighed and picked out a piece of jewelry—
an emerald ring her father had given her the year before
he died. She reached up from her kneeling position to
put it on top of the dresser drawers. Tomorrow she
would have to take the Mail coach into Bristol, to pawn
the ring. Her funds were running low again.

She replaced the tin box and the boards, then stood.
She moved the ring into the topmost left drawer, then
had to stand still a moment, blinking away tears. It would
never do to let Oscar see her crying. When her vision
cleared, the only other item in the drawer caught her
eye: the lock of Lord Sebastian's hair.

It was silly to have kept it. If someone else ever
opened this drawer, what would they think to find this
tendril of blond hair tied with a ribbon? Oscar had the
same brown hair as his mother, so no one would mistake
it for his. But why would anyone ever look here, and
even if they did, did it matter?

"Perhaps I will gather a lock from every man I meet
until I marry again," Charlotte argued aloud, then shook
her head and smiled ever so slightly at the absurd
thought of requesting a snippet of hair from the apothecary. She closed the drawer with a sigh, and wished she
might as easily close a drawer on other facets of her life,
such as heartache and worry.

Ever since the solicitor had told her how little Jarvis
had left her, Charlotte had learned what it was to feel
hurt and disappointed. She had thought her marriage had
taught her all there was to know about that—but death
had brought the final insult.

So what was one more small ache compared to the
overall pain that she'd known since Jarvis had succumbed
to his fever? It did not matter that it broke her heart to

pawn the ring—she could not let it matter. She did not have the time or energy to spend on the luxury of regret.

Sebastian leaned a little more to his right, fully aware his arm butted against Miss Talbot's. No, not "Miss Talbot"—if he could call Mrs. Deems "Charlotte" he could certainly call his beloved by her Christian name of Natalie. It was so good to touch her, however obliquely, so good to be in her company.

They sat side by side at a musical evening, Lord Lamont for once missing from his daughter's side. That gentleman was, happily, being detained from taking a seat by Mrs. Noggetty, over some matter to do with a fence that was falling into ruin between their properties.

"Lord Sebastian!" Miss Talbot said, practically giggling. "If you lean any more into me, I shall tumble from my chair."

"Do not do that. Tumble into my arms instead."

He felt inebriated, just from the giggle she gave again, from the pretty flush his nearness had put into her cheeks. She had already told him she admired his hair cut short, and he could tell from the enthusiasm under her compliment that she liked it more than just a little.

Gideon and Elizabeth had both given the new hair styling their accolades also, at breakfast—even if Elizabeth forbade Gideon to cut his own long, shockingly pale blond queue in imitation.

"It lends to your aspect of mystery," she'd assured her husband. "Whereas Sebastian's unkempt mop had only made him look the part of pirate."

Sebastian had just laughed, knowing his longer hair had not been unkempt, and knowing that Elizabeth was closer to correct in labeling him a "pirate" than she would care to know. For that matter, the woman who did know of his smuggling had also said he looked the part of pirate.

Pirate looks and familial approval aside, Sebastian would have to thank Charlotte again for making his new and clearly well-received appearance possible.

"Has there been any advancement?" Natalie asked at

his side very quietly, not needing to mention she meant in the area of his monetary hopes.

"Soon," he assured her, even though he was growing weary of the word that kept them yet apart.

She did not know anything of what he was doing—he had allowed her to think he had invested in a ship's cargo and that he awaited news of the cargo's sale and his share of the profit thereof. He could hardly tell her he was smuggling a Frenchman from one ship to another, even if it was a favor for the Prince Regent. He had not even told his coconspirator, Charlotte—the only person he'd be tempted to tell if he had not promised utter secrecy.

"Is that what is distracting you tonight?" Natalie asked him. "Thoughts of the cargo arriving?"

"Distracting me?"

"You have not even asked me once tonight to elope with you. I would call that distracted." She gave him a playful little pout.

He sat up in attention. "Will you, then? Elope with me tonight?"

"You know my answer must always be no," she said, her mouth turning up at the corners in a shy smile. She did not seem to think he was serious. Perhaps he should have gone for insistent instead of hopeful? "We will have a proper wedding when your fortunes are made," she said, as she'd said a half-dozen times before.

"Any day now," he assured her, daring to move his hand over her gloved one. She allowed him to fold his fingers over hers.

"If you will not elope with me, will you promenade with me instead?" he suggested. He stood up, her hand still in his, silently urging her to relent.

They both glanced toward her father, and Sebastian was pleased to see the man's back was turned as Lamont engaged in a mildly heated discussion with Mrs. Noggetty. Natalie swallowed nervously and stood up as well. "Let us slip away," she whispered, a flicker of her eyes indicating the back of the hall where other couples bored with or indifferent to the music strolled.

Sebastian led the way, not stopping until they were as far from Lord Lamont as he could make them. There was no privacy, but at least they could talk. He would like to have kissed her—as always, it was not possible, not here—but at least they could look into each other's eyes and touch hands.

"I am glad we can talk a bit. I have something to tell you," Natalie said, a tiny frown forming between her brows.

"Nothing untoward, I pray," Sebastian said. He took up her hand and kissed it, actually touching his mouth to her glove. He gave her a long, lingering glance, pleased by the deepening of her blush, and only then settled her hand on his arm.

"No, not untoward," she said. She cast a diffident glance up at him. "But I felt you should know. Papa is telling me that a suitor has asked for my hand."

Sebastian came to an abrupt halt. "What?" he asked, so stunned he scowled at her.

"Oh, do not give me such a thunderous look, I pray, Lord Sebastian!"

"Sebastian. You may call me just Sebastian," he murmured, his thoughts whirling. Would her papa accept this suitor?

"Not in public!" she said. "Although I would be flattered to call you thus in private."

We never have a private moment, he thought, but then he corrected himself, remembering how Charlotte Deems had bought them two minutes alone together in an alcove recently.

"It is old Lord Heversham," Natalie went on. She shuddered. "I do not want to marry him, of course. I want to marry *you*."

"Heversham! He must be eighty if he's a day! Your father cannot seriously be considering him." He wanted to add, "Not if your father wants grandchildren!" but he could not say such a thing to Natalie. She was blushing quite enough as things stood.

"Two-and-eighty," Natalie agreed, her mouth now turned down with worry or repulsion, or both.

"There is no problem." Sebastian rallied his thoughts. "Your father cannot force you to marry. There are laws about that sort of thing," he stated.

"Of course I will not marry him. But I must pretend that I am considering Lord Heversham's offer."

"Why?" He searched her brown eyes, not sure exactly what he searched for.

"Do not scowl so, Lord Sebastian. It is all a ruse. It buys us time, you see, so we can await your change in fortunes."

He forced his brow to clear, even though a sense of doubt lingered. "That makes sense," he said slowly. "But how long can you 'think' about the offer? Surely you must give an answer soon?"

"I know how to delay," Natalie assured him.

She did. Heaven knew she had put Sebastian off enough times over the question of an elopement.

"Good," he said, feeling a bit relieved at her stated intentions. He put his hand over hers, where it rested on his arm. "I am glad you told me, in case I hear any rumors. Now I will know not to be concerned at all."

"Not at all?" she asked. The arch tone to her voice was all pretense, however, for she smiled at him.

"You coquette!" He could not even pretend to scold her, for her prettiness struck him anew, much as it had the first time he'd seen her at her debut ball in Severn's Well. Just home from a school for young women, she had looked as fresh and new as snow, but her smile had been nowhere near as cold.

"Will I see you tomorrow?" he asked as they began to stroll again.

"We go to Lord Heversham's tomorrow for supper," she said, giving him an apologetic glance. "I think he hopes to impress me by showing us his home. I hear it is quite grand."

"What about your afternoon? Could you drive or walk in the park with me? We could meet—"

She shook her head. "I am so sorry, but after we receive our morning callers, I am promised to visit my cousins."

"Could I be invited there as well?"

She laughed, a refined tinkle rather unlike Charlotte's throaty laugh. Curious, he'd never noticed there could be a difference in women's laughter before, despite the riotous couple of months he'd spent in Brighton. Of course, he'd never been in love before either.

"Natalie!" a voice called in rebuke.

Sebastian and his would-be fiancée turned at the call of her name, both sighing aloud to see that Lord Lamont approached rapidly. His expression was not thunderous, but neither was it happy.

"Whitbury," he greeted Sebastian, giving him a nod of the head, just this side of the bow a marquess's son might have expected. "I want you to come meet someone," he told Natalie, taking her hand from Sebastian's arm.

She was whisked away, leaving Sebastian to pretend, for her sake, that he saw nothing amiss in Lamont's comportment nor in having to surrender Miss Talbot's company so abruptly.

Chapter 11

Later that night Sebastian started to open the coach door in preparation of stepping down, only to be shocked by the sensation of the carriage backing up.

"What—?" he said aloud, opening the door anyway. He braced his hands on either side of the door opening, not overly concerned for his safety since the coach was moving very slowly, and stuck his head and torso out.

Timmons was already looking down at him, a finger to his lips in a hushing motion. "There's people at her house," he said in a whisper that just managed to carry over the wind to Sebastian's ears.

He looked through the stand of trees beside the road they drove, seeing the lights of Charlotte's home through the dancing leaves. Yes, there it was, just barely touched by the glow from the cottage windows: a coach. It was not directly in front of her home, so Sebastian guessed it stood, for some reason, on the road that ran on the noncliff side of her property, instead of having pulled up before the house. That was a bit peculiar.

Timmons had the horses, their heads tossing, push their own coach even further backward until they were well under the cover of trees. They were on a rough road that adjoined with the main one that ran into the village. Its traffic was so light that it was flattering to call it a road, so Sebastian did not worry much that the other carriage might meet up with theirs if it resumed its journey.

"Well done, Timmons," he told the valet. "Now we wait."

Sebastian retreated into the coach, and pulled aside

one of the window covers. Through the trees, he could just make out one edge of the other coach from here. He knew his own coach would be invisible, having no light behind or on it, and hopefully the wind would cover any noises the horses might make.

He waited, feeling a little disgruntled although he would have been hard-pressed to say exactly why. He must still be stinging from having had Natalie snatched from his side, from Lord Lamont's near-snub of him. But there was no point in dwelling on it. Lamont would be his father-in-law someday, and it would be best not to harbor any feelings of ill will against the man—even if that was easier said than done.

A quarter hour slipped past, Sebastian guessed, even though waiting in almost complete darkness and a steadily whistling wind made it seem far longer.

He took off his hat—he would not want it flapping in the wind—and reached for the door again. "I will investigate," he told Timmons as he stepped down, having to raise his voice more than he wished to. "I will see what I can see. Circle the horses, and return here in a quarter hour."

"Yes, m'lord." Timmons touched his coachman's whip to the brim of his hat, then clucked at the horses.

Sebastian waited until the sounds of hooves and harness had been swallowed by the night, then approached Charlotte's cottage with stealthy steps. He crouched low, and moved with caution to below the window nearest to her dining table.

Sebastian heard voices, but he could not make out their words. He crept to the other window, with the same result. At least he had ascertained for a certainty that Charlotte was not alone. There were at least two voices, and possibly a third.

He looked to the coach, which had indeed stopped on the road, and saw at once why Charlotte had callers: the right rear coach wheel had splintered. The wheel was only still in an O shape because of the metal banding around it. If one pit in the road was hit, the entire wheel would crumble, and without doubt the axle would be snapped.

The two horses pulling it had been disconnected, trailing their harness behind them where they had been tied to a fence. Had Charlotte talked the coach driver out of putting the horses in her stable, or were they thinking a repair might be quickly had, so there was no need to stable the animals?

A voice carried on the wind, startling Sebastian because it came from *outside* the house. Someone was approaching, no, two persons. Sebastian scrambled from the side of the cottage in a crouch-step until free of the windows, then he stood and moved swiftly around the back, seeking the hiding shelter of the stable.

A knothole, inconveniently low for comfort was just right for spying, gave him a line of sight to where several men approached the coach, one rolling a carriage wheel as he walked, another holding a lit torch aloft. Ah, one must be the coachman, and the other was certainly Mr. Pingley, the local wheelwright. There were three more— all Pingley's sons, no doubt brought along to lift the carriage while the broken wheel was replaced with the new one. It was to be a quick repair then.

There was the sound of a door opening and then there were more voices, and in a moment Charlotte, another woman, and a man moved to examine the broken wheel and greet those who had come to repair it. Sebastian shifted his position, but the knothole gave him only limited vision, and he could not at first make out who the callers were.

Once the other woman turned, her face briefly lit by torchlight, he saw that it was Miss Diana Hubbard. Then he was able to determine from the voice that the man with her was Mr. James Hubbard, her brother.

Sebastian reared back in shock. Hubbard was the local Collector of the Customs—the very man who organized and conducted the civilian Excisemen, those men who acted as guards to the nation's coastlines and gatherers of import and export taxes due the government. Locally, they raided and rooted out smugglers all along the Severn River and the channel beyond.

The authorities? Here? Had Charlotte betrayed him?

Sebastian slowly bent back down to spy through the knothole.

Hubbard and his sister were clothed in fancy dress—the man's coat and breeches were light in color, and he wore a spill of lace at his throat and cuffs. His clothes were not something he would be likely to wear for his work as a Revenue Collector, which was often outdoors and unsuited to fancy dress. He and his sister lived along the river's edge, farther south than Charlotte's cottage. Either the man played at some deep game, or else it was exactly what it looked like: he and his sister had been returning home from a night's outing when their coach's wheel had broken.

Sebastian's gaze moved back to the splintered wheel . . . that was real enough. Hubbard was known locally as a man a little too dogged at his work, but even he would not stoop to endangering or involving his sister in some scheme.

Well then, it was just damnable luck that this particular man's coach had broken down near Charlotte's home.

Sebastian cursed silently, and would have glanced at his pocketwatch to see how much time was slipping away, but the stable was too dark for that. Was he missing the ship's signal? Surely they would signal more than once? Had Timmons returned? Would he and the coach be spotted?

There was no way for Sebastian to slip away unnoted; he had to wait where he was despite the impatience gnawing at him.

Thankfully, Pingley was efficient: with much grunting as the axle was hoisted by the three lads, the wheel was changed and the lynchpin pounded in place in under five minutes.

"Much obliged, my good man! Taking you out of your warm house at night and all," James Hubbard's words carried to Sebastian. The Collector pulled his purse from his coat pocket, agreeing upon a fee that he paid to Pingley.

Miss Hubbard turned to Charlotte. "Thank goodness for the kindness of neighbors!" she exclaimed. "It would have been a cold wait in the coach if not for your being home in our moment of need. To say nothing of being potentially dangerous."

"Indeed, we are most grateful," Mr. Hubbard chimed in as Pingley and sons headed back toward the village. If they saw Sebastian's coach, would they find it odd that it was just sitting and waiting? Would they raise an alarm? Sebastian shifted from foot to foot, then forced himself to remain still.

"I am happy to have been of service," Charlotte assured the Hubbards. "I am only glad no one was hurt."

"At least we did not awaken your son."

Charlotte nodded. "He played hard today. He was tired. Well, good night then. I hope the remainder of your journey home is less eventful."

Mr. Hubbard gave her a deep bow, deeper than required by gratitude, Sebastian thought with a frown. Then he frowned again as Hubbard stepped near to Charlotte, taking up her hand, much as any friend might take up another friend's hand. How well did they know each other?

"Do say you will let us repay your kindness by calling upon us soon?" Hubbard insisted. "We would enjoy returning your hospitality."

Charlotte did not hesitate long before agreeing. "That would be lovely."

"Would Friday afternoon suit? At two?"

"Thank you, yes." She took her hand back.

The brother and sister expressed their thanks again, only then finally climbing up into their coach.

Charlotte watched until their carriage was free of her property, then crossed her arms before her, her hands on her arms, making Sebastian wonder if she was feeling chilled from the wind. She slowly turned, gazing out into the night, her gaze searching.

"Charlotte," Sebastian said softly as he stepped from the stable, but his call still startled her.

"You are here," she said, visibly having to gather her composure. "There was a broken wheel—"

"I know," he interrupted, to save her the bother of the whole story. "I saw."

"How long have you been out here?"

He consulted his pocketwatch, using the light from the windows to see by. "A half hour."

"Where is Timmons?"

"Nearby. I will go find him and tell him all is quiet now." He started to move away, then stopped, a twinge of guilt striking him. "What would you have said if they had wanted to use your stable?"

"What we planned. That I am buying a horse. Or were you in it the whole time? I do not know how I would have explained you."

He shook his head. "I took refuge there when the wheelwright got here." He shook his head again, but this time at himself. Even though the lie she would have had to tell was plausible, it did not sit well with him. He not only forced her to stand beside him as an accomplice awaiting the ship, but he had nearly forced her to lie. How she must resent him, his interference in her life.

"Speaking of your horseless stable, how do you mean to arrive at the Hubbards' home on Friday?" he asked. "It is three miles or more from here. You cannot carry Oscar for three miles and back."

"No," she agreed, looking uncertain. "I will ask Mrs. Hyatt if she can keep him for me."

"Still, it is a long walk."

She gave a little shake of her head, not a denial but an amused gesture. "Fetch Timmons," she said. "We can talk while we watch from the cliffs."

Timmons was exactly where he'd been before, and in short order he had the horses unharnessed and stabled, and was ready to stay with Oscar. Sebastian retrieved from the coach his hat, now that it did not matter if it swayed in the wind, and the lantern Timmons had readied for him. When he returned to her door, Charlotte was cloaked and ready, a basket hanging from her arm by its handle and the dark blanket once again under her arm.

Once they had reached the cliffs, Sebastian watched Charlotte set down her basket and begin to unfold the blanket. He moved to take it out of her hands, and shook it open. Instead of spreading it on the ground, he reached around her, draping the blanket over her shoulders.

"I meant it to sit on," she told him, peering up into his face, her own only a few inches away as he transferred the ends of the blanket from his hands into hers. He stepped back, because he did not really want to and he knew that not wanting to was wrong. It was wrong to feel a tingle of attraction for this woman, to let her blue-eyed gaze make him want to draw her nearer, to want to brush back the wisps of hair that had fallen from her topknot and were now forced to dance around her face by the wind.

This was attraction—perhaps different from the simple attraction that stirred every young man's blood, perhaps more complex than anything he'd known from doxies and past affairs—but it could not be anything like the passion he'd formed for Natalie Talbot. Of course it could not.

So though he could not keep himself from being attracted, he *could* keep himself from showing any sign of it, or in any way acting on it.

He realized they'd been staring into each other's eyes for too long a pause, and belatedly thought to respond to her comment. "It is chilled tonight. The wind is up. You need an extra layer."

She gave a slow blink, as if she were getting sleepy, then she shook her head in a motion meant to clear away cobwebs. "What about you?"

"I am fine. What is in your basket tonight?" he ruthlessly changed the subject, striving for a light tone. "Surely you do not plan to cut my hair even shorter?"

"I plan to feed you."

"What?" Her claim took him by surprise.

"I get hungry sitting out here for three hours," she said, and he thought she looked just a touch sheepish.

"Oh. Well." The spell, whatever had caused it, was broken; they were back to the old footing they had established. "If you are waiting for me to chide you, you will have a long wait. I think this is an excellent idea! Besides, if we should be discovered here, we can always claim we're having a moonlit picnic by the river." He gestured at the basket.

"And be dubbed the village idiots."

"As if that would change anything in my life," he quipped.

She lifted an eyebrow—a gesture of restraint—and it occurred to him that Charlotte knew another notch against his reputation was hardly likely to endear him to Lord Lamont. However if she had the same thought, she chose not to point it out.

She bent down, one hand holding the blanket about her shoulders, and began to draw the food items out of the basket, settling the bits on a napkin she spread open. She laid out bread, cheese, and beef, already sliced, and a half-full bottle of wine. "Oh," she said in disappointment, glancing back toward her cottage, "I forgot glasses for the wine."

"We'll drink from the bottle."

"How gauche," Charlotte said, smiling all the same.

Sebastian threw himself down beside the offerings. The ground was not wet, but it radiated a deep chill that made him shudder in reaction all the same. He was glad Charlotte had the blanket to act as a shield between her and the ground as she settled on the other side of the basket.

They ate for a while, in silence, passing the bottle between them, but he only took small sips. He wanted to be entirely sober and aware while watching for the ship.

When he passed the bottle back to her, she laughed lightly and shook her head at some private joke, presumably the inelegance of their serving method. She spilled a little wine down her front as her reward. She tried to brush it off with a napkin, unsuccessfully. "I will have to

launder this before I wear it to church, that is for certain," she said. She did not seem particularly vexed. That
was one of the things a man—or anyone—could enjoy
about Charlotte's company, that she was not one to stew
or fuss over matters.

He found himself wondering if Mr. Hubbard would
like this attribute in Charlotte as well. *Of course the man
would,* he thought with a frown. No man liked a woman
who carped or fretted, but the opposite. Like Charlotte.

As to Hubbard . . . Sebastian supposed the man would
be the sort a woman would view as a possible marriage
partner. He was honorably employed, he had some con-
sequence in the community, and he was not old, perhaps
thirty at the most. Sebastian assumed a woman would
find the man attractive, if not exactly handsome.

Charlotte had agreed to call upon Mr. Hubbard and
his sister . . . after an ever-so-slight hesitation. Had she
been making the same evaluations of Hubbard? Why
would she not? She no doubt wished to see the man in
his own home, where a person might learn something of
the tranquility, or lack of it, of his household. She would
be thinking of Oscar and what would be best for him,
her lively little boy.

"You are frowning. Is something amiss?" Charlotte
asked.

"Thinking." He gave her a short, vague answer.

"About the past?"

"Mmmm." The wind caught his hat, threatening for a
long moment to pull it from his head, forcing him to
reach up and hold the brim until the gust passed.

"I have been wondering . . ." Charlotte began, but she
shook her head. "No, I should not ask."

"Been wondering what?" he said, letting go of his hat
to reach for another slice of cheese.

"It is a rude question—"

"Oh, and I have not been rude to you? Making you
sit out every night with me? Making you miss your
night's rest, and you with a child who surely rises early?"
The sharp tone of his voice surprised even him—it was
growing difficult to ignore the guilt he felt at interrupting

her life, putting her at risk. She'd only been a mother searching for her wandering son that night, and in her distress had only earned more trouble. All for Sebastian's sake. Not hers, his. It did not matter that he could not trust her before, that he had not known anything of her to give her that trust . . . he still felt he'd acted as a bully.

"Ask me anything," he said, wishing it had come out sounding more genteel and less sullen.

She gave him a puzzled look. "Very well. I was wondering who raised you, since your mama was . . . not in her proper mind. Your brothers?"

This was an old hurt, oddly fitting his mood. "I had a nanny for my first five years. Nanny Brackett. Gideon and Benjamin did not spend much time in the nursery. They had their tutor, mostly."

"You had her only for five years? What happened then? Did you join your brothers with the tutor?"

Sebastian nodded, remembering. "Mama accused Papa of bedding Nanny Brackett. I have no idea if it was true." He shrugged. "Could have been. It didn't matter, though. The accusation was sufficient. Nanny left, and I began my schooling."

"You loved her," Charlotte said softly, her voice barely carrying to his ears. "Your nanny."

"Of course I did. My mother spent all her days either sneaking bits of food to hide in her room, or lying on her bed, sobbing for hours. She was peculiar. Difficult. I did not like her. I cannot remember a single time when she seemed . . . right. Nanny was the closest thing I came to having a mother." He no longer wanted the cheese bit in his hand, so he tossed it out into the night. "After that, there was only the tutor and papa. And my brothers, of course, who were good to me."

"I am sorry, Sebastian," she said.

It was not her words so much but the fact that she said them, that caused him to shudder, as if she had tickled the nape of his neck. She did not need to elaborate; he did not need to tell of a hundred other cruelties life had thrown his way. Charlotte Deems knew what it was to have suffered; it was evident in her sorrow-filled voice, in the soft, caring way she offered commiseration.

He nodded, accepting her compassion. "What about you?" he asked. He reached for her hand where it lay in her lap, covering it with his own. There he went again, touching, as was ever his wont. "Who disappointed you?"

She did not try to deny she'd been disappointed. A small, fleeting smile touched her lips. "I thought I hid it better than that."

"You do. Usually."

"We grow maudlin, sitting out here in the dark, whispering our secrets to one another," she said, perhaps more to herself than to him. She tossed her head, as if to shake off reluctance, and gazed squarely into his eyes. "It was Jarvis, my husband."

"His crime?"

She looked away then, out to the water, her gaze turned inward in memory. "He did not love me."

"Impossible," Sebastian said softly, perhaps too softly for her to hear over the wind. What man could not love Charlotte? Especially a man married to her, by her side frequently, a man who had this woman's gaze fix on him as she looked up in invitation from their bed. . . . He cleared his throat. "Did you love him?"

"I tried," she said without self-pity, without blame, even if her voice was little more than a sigh. "I tried."

Her quiet resignation made something in his center start to ache, and he felt his lips grow thin in exasperation at Jarvis Deems, a man he'd never met.

"Tell me more. Not about your marriage," he corrected that impression at once. "Tell me about someone else from your past. Perhaps a happy story?" He also looked out to the water, to give her an illusion of privacy, to let her decide for herself if she would go on, or not.

"I will tell you a secret," she said.

Chapter 12

He half twisted toward her, his heart thumping hard against his ribs, the organ seemingly as astonished as he was by her wish to share a secret. "No," he said. "You do not have to."

She smiled then, the kind of smile shared by friends. "Of course I do not have to. But this secret would eventually come out. You pose no additional threat to me by knowing it." There must have been some measure of concern on his face, for she gave a small laugh, one meant to comfort. "I have misled you. You think I am going to tell you a grand secret, but it is only a little one. You will be disappointed there is not more mystery or intrigue about my little confession."

He relaxed his posture, turning back toward the river. Strangely, he was not disappointed at all that she clearly did not intend to divulge her great secret. For a moment he had worried that the wine had set her tongue too free, and she would regret what she said come the morrow. The twinkle in her gaze told him she knew what she was about, and he was glad for it. He did not want to know her secret, not if it wasn't freely and soberly given. "Go on."

"You know my cottage?" she posed the words as a question.

He nodded.

"It belonged to my grandpapa, Wilfred Ackerley."

"I know that name," he said, frowning as he tried to recall why he knew it. He snapped his fingers and looked up at her, astonished by the memory he had summoned. "He was a smuggler! Years ago."

She nodded. "My maiden name was Ackerley. Deems
is my married name, of course. But since I took no pains
to alter my name—Oscar has the right to grow up knowing and using his real name—I know eventually someone
will learn that 'Deems' had been 'Ackerley,' and then
someone will remember a little girl named Charlotte who
played here in Severn's Well one summer."

"But I do not understand—! I mean to say, I understand not wanting your grandpapa's name bandied
about—"

"Nor his disgrace, when he was caught."

"Of course." This was history, past, done with. It was
a little embarrassing, perhaps, to have a convicted smuggler in one's lineage, but here in Severn's Well who did
not have a smuggler somewhere in their family history?
Still, she must feel the sting of the label, for she only
now revealed her past connection to Severn's Well. "Is
that why you dislike smugglers in general? Because of
your grandpapa's being caught at it?"

"Of course. But what I most dislike about smuggling
is that anyone might think to use my home as a point of
transfer, Lord Sebastian."

She had added "Lord" once more to his name, plainly
a sign of anger at him. "You think *I* have used your
home as a point of transfer?" he said, stunned by understanding her resentment. "I suppose I have, indirectly.
Not your home, but your property."

"I suppose you have. But that was not what I meant."

"What then?"

She fixed her gaze on him for a long, long stare. At
length she nodded, seemingly satisfied by something
she'd seen in his own gaze. "You do not know, do you?"

"Know what?"

"About the tunnel."

"Tunnel?" What was she talking about?

"It leads from the bank of the Severn, up to my cottage," she said, her voice dry like a schoolgirl's recitation
of facts that were old and stale for her. "At riverside,
there is a crevice in the rock wall that looks like nothing
more than a crack weathered and washed out of the cliff.

It is very narrow, going back ten feet, perhaps twelve. Nothing so large around as a barrel can pass through it—but a man, turned sideways, can. And once the ten feet have been gotten through, the crevice opens into a tunnel. It is not wide nor high—only five feet, so a tall man must stoop, but he can fit. There are rough stairs carved into the rock, that climb up and up, seemingly forever—"

She stopped to take a deep breath, perhaps a sigh. "But eventually one comes to a door at the top of the tunnel, a door designed to open outward. Only it is now stuccoed over, from the inside of my cottage. When was it sealed, you might ask." She closed her eyes for a moment, like someone looking at an old memory. "The day after my grandpapa was caught smuggling French lace. My father covered it over, to hide that piece of evidence from the Excisemen, for all the good it did."

Sebastian knew he had been staring at her for a long time, longer than he ought. He ought to be watching the river—but there was more to her story, he knew, and he could not keep himself from staring into her calm, if pained, expression.

"I never knew," he told her. "About the tunnel. Does it still exist?"

She nodded, blinking back a shimmer of tears. "I went into the crevice myself, when we first moved here to Severn's Well. It is full of moss below, and cobwebs higher up, and some of the stairs have crumbled in places, but it is still useable."

"What happened to your grandpapa? I do not recall."

"He was tried in London. Two weeks later they hanged him at Newgate," Charlotte said. She blinked again and a tear slid down her cheek.

Her recitation of the facts had been rote, but that tear proved the old memories still held their power to wound. It also proved to Sebastian that, whatever fault there had been in her marriage the majority of the blame must surely fall to Mr. Deems, for Mrs. Deems certainly did not possess a cold heart. If he had not known that before, if he had not seen her pride and joy in her son, had not heard in her laughter the ability to hope and to forgive, Sebastian knew it now. He wanted to reach out, to brush away that single tear, except that she might think he minded that she'd shed it.

"We never visited Severn's Well again," she explained. "We lived in High Wycombe at the time, but we went to London to claim Grandpapa's body when . . . when all was done, and we stayed. The Ackerley name was . . . less notorious in London."

She sighed again, but this time it was as if she acknowledged an old trouble that was in the past, unforgotten but also inconsequential to her life now.

"My grandpapa left me the cottage. Until Jarvis died I never thought I would step a foot in it again," she said. She looked down at her feet in their half boots, knocking them together, an unexpectedly playful gesture. It was as if she meant to signal that the time for somber discussions had passed.

"I like it now," she said, looking up from her feet to him. "My cottage. At first I was ashamed of it, of all it reminded me of. But it is an agreeable little place, all told."

Sebastian thought of his brother's mansion on the hill above the village and grimaced internally at all he took for granted. "Do you fear the villagers will rebuff you if they learn the granddaughter of Wilfred Ackerley has returned?"

"No, not really. Not now that I have lived here awhile. I have learned I am rare in my complete dislike of those things connected with smuggling. Others see it as a necessary evil, or even a boon. Anyway," she said, pulling the blanket tighter in an effort to ward off the hungry, searching fingers of the wind, "it seems we have both had misfortunes in our pasts." She smiled gently. "I suppose that makes us just like everyone else."

He smiled back, a lopsided affair. "I suppose it does."

"I am glad you are going to marry Miss Talbot. I am glad you will have the love you never had from your parents."

"Yes," he said, strangely unsure what to say next.

"Yes indeed." But then a flash caught the corner of his vision, and he sat up straight, memories dashed by more immediate needs. "A flashing light!"

Charlotte sat up at attention, too. "Yes, I see it!"

Sebastian leaped to his feet, offering his hands to her, helping her also to rise. They walked a little closer to the cliff edge, one of his hands still holding hers, both of them peering anxiously out over the river.

"Damn this wind!" he said. "I cannot tell . . . One long, two long." He had counted out the "longs" at three seconds each, but had that just now been a "short"? There should follow three short flashes, then one last long one. He shook his head. "I do not know—"

He stared, watching the ship move farther up the river for several long, wordless minutes, but then he shook his head. "No. No, it was not the signal. It was a play of the wind and sails, I guess. Not a signal at all." Too, he'd finally thought to attempt to identify the ship's design: this was a bark, not a brig. He was looking for a brig.

An unexpected twinge filled his chest—he felt both disappointed and relieved. Disappointment was simple to understand, since all his plans for the future hinged on finally meeting his live "cargo" and helping the Frenchman move on in secret to a new port in America—but relief? That he was not yet to be tested? That his plans for secrecy and stealth were not yet to be tried? He felt nervous at what he planned to do, but he had not thought he was afraid. So why did he feel relieved that his time on the cliffs was not yet at an end?

He had but to turn and look at Charlotte to know what was at the heart of his relief: he did not wish to surrender his time with her. It seemed too soon. It felt as if they had been telling each other an entertaining tale, and it was but half-finished.

Had they, by some miracle of circumstance, become friends? The thought made sense of everything, of his relief, his flash of regard toward her, his growing feelings of guilt that he had invaded her domain.

If she *had* befriended him, did it have to end? He would surrender his life of crime, if such it could be

called, after this one task. They were to live in the same
village. They would attend many of the same balls and
entertainments. Why did any budding friendship have
to end?

It did not. Not, that is, unless for some reason Natalie
disliked associating with Charlotte—or disliked having
him associate with her. He knew a flicker of pleasure at
the idea of Natalie feeling jealous. Too much would be a
bad thing, of course, but a little spike now and again . . .

But he was shaping nonsense from notions. There was
no reason to think Natalie would not receive Charlotte
Deems—what possible objection could she have? Even
if she knew Charlotte's grandfather had been hanged for
smuggling, would that give Natalie anything but the
briefest of pauses? Her father might frown, but Sebastian
did not think Natalie would be such a stickler. After all,
Charlotte had had no part in her grandfather's misdeeds,
having been but a child at the time. To cut those with
smuggling connections in their past was to cut at least
half the society to be found locally.

Sebastian had misdeeds of his own—ones that he had
himself engaged in, not some forebear of his. He had
drunk to excess, and lain with loose women, and reck-
lessly spent his brother's money on games of chance.
Even if these things were typical of a young man un-
folding his personality, leaning headfirst and headstrong
into the beginning of his adult life—still, they had been
of his own volition, unlike Charlotte's "stain." If Natalie
could overlook his stains—not least of which was the
blood of a madwoman running through his veins—she
would surely overlook what Charlotte had had no part
in doing. He felt sure Natalie would accept Charlotte,
for his sake, if he asked it of her.

"Do you think a ship could send a man to shore in
this weather?" Charlotte asked at his side, bringing Sebastian back to the moment. She peered down at the
dark river. "Do I see whitecaps?"

"I think so," he said with a frown.

"I would be loath to put my cargo into a small dinghy
and try to row it ashore in these conditions," she said,

glancing up at the clouds being hastily driven across the moon's face.

"This is exactly the kind of condition that favors the smuggler," Sebastian told her, still frowning. "The Excisemen tend to be less vigilant on a stormy night. They wait in their huts along the shore, hoping not to see anything that forces them to come out. It is human nature to want to be inside, out of the wind and cold."

"You sound as if you know a lot about the Customs men."

"As opposed to only the smugglers' side of things?" He grinned at her, and made a nonchalant movement of his hand. "For a while my brother Benjamin was in the navy. He had to serve alongside the Excisemen, often enough. They combine their forces at times." He grinned wider. "He does not have much use for your average Customs officer."

"Well, they are civilians, after all."

"Exactly his point, as I recall. 'They have no military discipline' was his foremost complaint. I got my information as to their habits from him."

"Would he approve of what you seek to do here?"

"Good gad, no," Sebastian said, but then he considered a moment. "He would say there had to be a better way to achieve my ends."

Charlotte shook her head, a gentle rebuke, but otherwise she did not add her censure to that of the absent Benjamin. Instead she glanced at the sky again. "At least it is not raining."

He clucked his tongue in remonstrance. "You have cursed us by tempting the gods with such a statement," he warned.

But the rain did not come, even though the wind increased. Charlotte passed the time by tidying up their picnic, and Sebastian studied the river, but neither rain nor ship arrived. He stood where he was, removed from Charlotte's side, several long strides needed to cross the distance between them. The distance allowed him a little clarity of mind, as if it was too much to watch for a ship, be mindful of Charlotte, *and* think. And he'd hardly drunk a drop.

Thinking brought him to only one conclusion, however, and that was a determination to have Timmons bring a carriage around on Sunday, to take Charlotte up. She would not have to walk the three miles to the Hubbards nor the three miles back.

He hunched his shoulders, feeling the cold creeping under his skin despite his heavy wool coat. He bent beside the sheltered lantern, and cracked the panel open just enough to light his watch's face for a moment. "Half past midnight," he announced. He stood and looked to the river one last time. "It is too rough. They will not come if they have not come before now."

"We are done for the night?" she asked, sounding eager.

Sebastian felt another flash of guilt, for keeping her out and awake, night after night—and tomorrow would be yet another night.

"Done," he said shortly, moving at once to scoop up the lantern, and also her basket so that she need not carry its weight. He started to walk away briskly, only to half-stumble over a root or a rock he had not seen. The uncertain moonlight made for treacherous footing. He recovered and turned back to Charlotte, finding she had made haste to keep up with him and now reached out a hand toward him, as if to somehow keep him from stumbling again.

He could have spoken, could have explained he'd tripped, that they needed to proceed more cautiously, but it seemed unnecessary. Instead, he opened the lantern fully, and crossed to hand her basket back to her. With his lantern arm outstretched, providing lighting by which they could make their way, he took the hand she offered him. She only made a small surprised sound when he pulled her firmly to his side. "For warmth and safety," he told her.

Without words, they fell into step, side by side.

Sebastian did not know what to think—no, more correctly, he did not think at all. He just walked, making sure the path was lit and Charlotte would not be tripped, all the while reveling in the feel of her ungloved hand tucked trustingly into his. He was tired, and cold, and his eyes and brain ached with the effort of watching for a ship's black shape against the blacker river, but all the same he embraced the shimmer of contentment that coursed through his blood. He did not have the energy— or was that the will?—to explore that simple pleasure; he just allowed it to exist.

Sebastian released her hand in order to open her cottage door for her, and she told herself she hated to let his hand go because it had warmed her own. Truth was, she had grown rather too warm when she had been all but tucked against his side as they walked—it had felt too intimate, somehow. They had just been walking, their hands entwined for safety's sake, but . . .

She had grown flushed, no longer welcoming the blanket he had so kindly draped over her shoulders—but if she felt too warm, he must be feeling at least a little chilled. "I could mull some wine to warm you before you go on your way," she suggested. "It would take hardly any time. Or I could make tea."

As Timmons rose sleepily to his feet, Sebastian declined her offer with a shake of his head. "I have to make an appearance at my club in Bristol," he said in a low voice, so as not to disturb Oscar. "I fear wine and a coach ride would make me witless."

This was the second time she had found him being cautious in his drinking. The other time had been while he watched for the ship. He would ruin his reputation as a dissolute man-upon-the-town if he was not careful, she thought with an interior twist of the lips. "Tsk, my lord! People have assured me you are very steeped in immoral ways, yet *I* never get to see you being wicked," she took him to task with a crooked little smile.

His eyes widened, and then a slow smile pulled at his lips. "Immoral? I could demand that you give me another kiss. Would that do to make me seem more immoral?"

Charlotte glanced at Timmons, who had abruptly ceased to rub his eyes, the valet glancing back and forth between the two of them with a suddenly alert expression.

"A kiss is not immoral," she murmured.

His peacock blue eyes danced. "It is if you do it properly."

She had no answer for that, so she could not imagine why her lips parted as though she meant to speak. He stared at her lips, no doubt awaiting a reply, but when none was forthcoming, his gaze at her mouth did not shift but only intensified.

"Timmons," Sebastian said, having gone suddenly quite still. "Go harness the horses."

"Yes, m'lord." The valet gave them each one more glance, then hurried out the door to do his master's bidding as Charlotte turned away, hanging her cloak on its peg with suddenly nerveless fingers.

"Charlotte?" Sebastian said.

She closed her eyes, because her back was to him and he would not see the gesture, would not see that she had to gather her composure. His nearness was making the blood trip through her veins, made her want to breathe more rapidly than she ought. It did not take much soul-searching to realize the attraction she'd experienced earlier tonight had been no accident, that it was happening again.

He waited until she was able to turn back to face him. "Yes?" she said, sounding far more poised than she felt.

"I know I have disrupted your life," he said. He lowered his gaze, now looking down to his hands holding the hat he'd removed upon entering her home. "I would like to make up for it in some small way, if you will let me."

She gave a nod, uncertain but giving him permission to go on.

"Our stables have a dozen horses and a half-dozen carriages. It would be no hardship on our household, and it would be my pleasure to send one of them to drive you to the Hubbards' home on Sunday. Please, I would like to do that, to save you the long walk there and back."

She was not particularly surprised he knew of her planned visit; he would have overheard Mr. Hubbard's request. Her first impulse was to refuse—there was already too much between them, too many peculiar moments. But he did not ask for much in this, only to lend her a carriage for a few hours. Let him assuage any guilt he felt. It cost her nothing to allow this small kindness on his part.

"That would be lovely," she assured him.

His mouth quirked, as if he could not decide whether to be somber or to smile. "Thank you."

"Thank you, Sebastian. It will be pleasant not to have to walk so far."

"Particularly if it is raining," he pointed out.

"Yes." She gave him a smile and a nod.

He nodded back, but sobriety had won out, for his nod was a trifle stiff. Tonight . . . Tonight *something* had happened, she knew. Call it attraction, or regard, or any other name—but it was hardly any wonder if he had realized that it would not suit. He was going to marry Miss Talbot. Any . . . *affinity* that might have surfaced between Charlotte and him was, at best, ill-advised.

She knew that, she thought to herself as he slipped out the door and she closed it behind him. She understood that. Sebastian was going to marry the woman he loved. As he should. Miss Talbot would be very good for him. She was fresh and graceful, and most important, Sebastian loved her. Their marriage would go forth as it ought to.

Except that Charlotte would not attend it, she decided abruptly. She would not be able to bear it, she knew that as surely as she knew her own name. Tonight she had touched on something wonderful. It had been more than the breathlessness of attraction, more than the tingle of desire. It had been happiness. Real, honest, make-your-heart-swell and your-spirit-soar happiness. Something more than mere contentment, even something more than bliss—it had felt very much like . . .

"Like coming home," she told herself in the smallest of whispers.

She'd had a glimpse of the bond that ought to have been in her own marriage, but never had formed there. To watch Sebastian and Miss Talbot unite their hearts, to know she had touched upon such joy for only the briefest of moments—Charlotte knew she could not bear it.

Tonight she had shared a secret with him. It had been nothing much, nothing that would not eventually be common coin in the community, but she was glad they'd had that moment of sharing. For now she had a new secret, a secret of the heart that she must never tell, could never share with Lord Sebastian Whitbury.

Chapter 13

Lord Lamont's drawing room was so thickly occupied by callers that Sebastian had no chair on which to sit. To be anywhere near Natalie, he'd had to take up a position standing behind the sofa on which she sat with three other ladies. Four other gentlemen jostled elbows with him.

One thing is certain, Sebastian thought a bit sourly, *when Natalie and I marry, we will have to take a honeymoon journey out of the country to have any hope of time alone together.* Not that he minded Natalie being sought out—only look at how content she seemed, even having to sit between her aunts, gorgons all. Besides, Sebastian could not really complain, for Lamont's crowded "at home" days, limited to Tuesday and Friday mornings, meant he had been able to slip in with the rest of the crush today. The butler could hardly tell him that "Miss Talbot is not at home" when he marched in as if he were part of the Mallett party.

Besides having gained entry and so overcome all obstacles to seeing Natalie today, Sebastian was pleased to note the aged Lord Heversham was not present. Undoubtedly this crush of people would have proved too rigorous an outing for Lord Lamont's preferred suitor for his daughter's hand. Besides, Heversham would need to save up what little vim he had for the dinner he was to host for the Talbots tonight.

Sebastian was not anywhere near as feeble as Heversham, however. Despite what other callers might have planned, Sebastian had no thoughts at all of leaving in a timely fashion. He did not care if that would make Natalie late to call upon her cousins this afternoon, as she'd promised to do. With any luck, he'd outwait everyone and eventually have Natalie to himself, at least for a brief while. Well, and Natalie's father, no doubt of that.

Presuming Lord Lamont did not cast him out on his ear—which was indeed a bit of a presumption.

For now, however, he must content himself with the occasional smile Natalie threw over her shoulder at him, and, by dint of the occasional half-shout over the babble of the place, the exchange of a comment or two with her.

Some of the crowd stayed the prescribed fifteen minutes of a morning call, but even with them gone too many others lingered as tea and cakes arrived.

After an hour, three cups of tea, and two slices of cake with almond paste icing, Sebastian began to think his scheme might not have been so clever as he thought. A good twenty callers still remained—he increasingly found their manner of lingering quite annoying regardless that he'd every intention of outstaying the heartiest of them— and he had run out of inconsequential things to say from the back of the sofa toward Natalie. There was no way to carry on any real sort of conversation with her.

Eventually he turned to the window behind him, just to watch a different set of faces as they passed by. There was old Mrs. Avery, walking as briskly as a young woman, no doubt on her way to make the midday supper for the vicar. Here came Mr. Marpin the butcher, a long stick hung with a dozen plucked chickens balanced across his shoulders. Sebastian lifted his brows in mild surprise to see his brother's crested coach roll by, but a quick glance verified it was the one with the broken window, and it was more than likely on its way to a coachbuilder in Bristol for repair.

Sebastian ran a hand through his hair—he was still getting used to it being short—and yawned. The trip to his club last night had seemed exceedingly long, and only worse coming back. It had been a lot of trouble for a rather fragile alibi. He felt grainy-eyed and under-rested, and he did not have a young boy to follow around all day as Charlotte did.

Ah, Charlotte.

He'd never thought the name particularly pretty before, but he'd grown used to it. It had a certain elegance to it—but that did not keep it from also being a name that could be pleasant to whisper in the night—

He shook his head, pushing his thoughts in a different direction. He could not think about last night, could not remember how her lips had parted and how he'd wanted to cross to her side and explore that mouth with his own.

It had been a rush of lust, he knew, his old habit of taking every advantage that might lead to a touch—but, curse it! It had been something more, too. There had been the white hot flash of physical desire, but that he'd been able to ruthlessly thrust aside. What was harder to ignore, harder to forget, was the *wanting*. Not sexual longing, but longing for something whole, something unique, something unfathomably *right*. For one very long moment, there had been something tender, and sweet, and *irresistible* between them.

If she'd turned back to face him a moment sooner, he would not have stopped his arms from reaching for her, would not have able to resist the need to be . . . to be *important* to her, as she unalterably had become to him.

It had not been friendship that had whipped between them—but friendship was the whole extent of what must exist.

Sebastian frowned, and shook his head, and told himself that one wildly profound moment did not a future make. He'd be a fool to let his thoughts linger on that moment, or even any that had presaged it: like when he'd placed the blanket on her shoulders and had known the first flash of wanting. He must push any such recollections from his thoughts. Even if he had not promised himself to Natalie, how could he and Charlotte build anything real or true from the coercion he'd forced her into? It did not bear thinking through, anyway, because Natalie had expectations from him, expectations they'd built together. He *wanted* Natalie . . . yes, but perhaps in a different way. He was not quite sure what made it

different, but perhaps the distinction lay in the simple
fact that Natalie *was* going to be his bride, and Charlotte
was not.

Sebastian looked back out the window, and could have
laughed. He could not help but think that fate must enjoy
irony: he had glanced up just in time to see Charlotte,
the woman he was trying to banish from his thoughts,
being handed down by the driver of the Mail coach.

The ironic laugh faded as quick as it was born, however, as it struck him that it was very odd that Charlotte
would be willing to pay the fee for anywhere the Mail
coach went. That was a significant expenditure for this
woman who only owned one pair of gloves.

He watched as Oscar was lifted down after her, the
boy's presence revealing that wherever she had gone it
had not been somewhere she did not want her child to
know about. Was the boy ill? Had she taken him into
Bristol to see a physician?

"Excuse me," Sebastian said to no one in particular
as he started to edge his way around several gentlemen.
He would go out and speak with Charlotte, to be sure
Oscar was well—only he stopped short before another
window, now seeing that another man approached her:
Mr. Hubbard.

The two exchanged greetings and smiles, causing Sebastian to take a small step back from the windows even
as he felt a flicker of relief. Charlotte would not smile
like that had Oscar been seriously ill or hurt. She and
Mr. Hubbard exchanged comments and small gestures,
and then Charlotte nodded and put her hand on Hubbard's offered arm.

Sebastian shifted back to his former window, from
which he was able to see that Charlotte and Oscar were
assisted up into Hubbard's cabriolet, a smart two-
wheeled vehicle that would be a bit crowded except that
Oscar sat on his mother's lap. Hubbard set the horse in
motion in the direction of Charlotte's cottage, quickly
rolling out of sight.

Sebastian scowled. He supposed Mr. Hubbard was a
decent enough man, was the sort of man that a woman

might admire and look toward with thoughts of marriage—but was he right for Charlotte? It was just that Charlotte was so . . . so full of life, and laughter, and so *not* like Hubbard, whose work had made him rather dour, if indeed he had not been born that way. Sebastian would like to see Charlotte's lot in life improve. He'd like her to feel as if she had found a home here in Severn's Well. He'd like her to find a husband, fine, but this time one who adored her. Would Hubbard be able to give her all that?

But then Sebastian was getting ahead of things here: there was no reason to suppose from one invitation and one carriage ride that Charlotte and Mr. Hubbard would move on to anything more than being mere acquaintances.

Anyway, it was not Sebastian's place to be troubled by any marital or romantic choice Charlotte might eventually make. Oscar was clearly well enough, Charlotte did not have to walk home, and that was all that mattered today.

He reached down to his coat pocket, assuring himself that his gift was still there, a gift for Charlotte. He'd made the purchase prior to coming to Natalie's home. . . .

How odd. He'd not thought to buy anything for Natalie. Not that she needed anything—that was the difference. Her father provided for all her needs and wants. Still, he could have bought her a posie. Sebastian glanced around the room, belatedly realizing the bounty of flowers included several posies—other suitors had thought to bring such tokens to Natalie.

Sebastian frowned, and vowed he would have the gardeners at his brother's estate put together the largest bouquet possible from the spring flowers now showing and anything that would suit from the forcing garden. He would order it brought around to Natalie's home today.

"What out there is so fascinating?" a soft voice said at his side.

Sebastian turned at once in surprise, not having expected the most recent occupant of his thoughts to be there. "Miss Talbot!" She had left her gorgon guardians to seek him out; Sebastian hoped the glow of pleasure he felt did not show too openly.

She smiled at him, a question still lingering in her eyes.

"I was just watching Mr. Hubbard," Sebastian explained at once. "He appears to have a new cabriolet, very smart."

"Where?" she asked, leaning around him to peer out the window. Her black hair was a riot of ringlets, falling artfully from the crown of her head from where a pink ribbon held them. He'd played with one of her ringlets once . . . but that had been weeks ago. Her father's vigilance since had not permitted any more opportunities for even so modest a caress.

"The cabriolet is gone already, I am afraid. Mr. Hubbard offered a ride home to Mrs. Deems."

Natalie stood up straight and wrinkled her nose. "Mrs. Deems? I cannot like her much."

Sebastian stared at her, struck dumb for several moments. How could anyone not care for Charlotte? "You mean you do not know her well," he corrected Natalie.

She looked startled, but then she gave a little laugh. "True enough. I find it peculiar that no one knows much about her. Do you find that odd? She has not been very sociable." She wrinkled her nose again. "To judge from the black she wears, I suppose she is yet in mourning, though. Do you know, how long *has* her husband been dead? Everyone is wondering, and she seems reluctant to say. Do you think her husband was real? Or has she made him up, to cover up that her son is baseborn?"

Sebastian felt his hands curl into fists and his face flush scarlet. How dare people speculate so outrageously? It was one thing to talk about *him*, he'd earned any rumors that flew around about him, but a blameless widow and her young son—!

"I assure you," he said to Natalie, aware his words were clipped because he had to work to unclench his teeth, "that Mrs. Deems was indeed married. To one Jarvis Deems, who was a rector of a small London church. She is quite respectable, and her son is entirely legitimate."

"I was only repeating what I've heard others asking," Natalie said, clearly dismayed by the reproach in his tone.

"That is called gossiping, Natalie, and it behooves you not to do it," he said, trying to soften his timbre but not succeeding very well. Several people glanced their way, perhaps not hearing their words but catching the heated accents between them.

"Spoken like someone who resents having his own exploits turned into gossip," she countered.

Sebastian opened his mouth, only to shut it again. He'd never heard her speak so curtly to him—but he deserved any sharp-tongued thing she had to say in repayment of his own cutting tones. He could not blame her. If anything, it showed she had some of the fire he'd been hoping to bring out in her, the will to defy her father, the mettle that would have allowed her to throw caution to the wind and elope with him.

He opened his mouth anew, but this time to apologize. "I am sorry, Natalie. Truly, I am. You are right, I do not care for gossip. My family has felt its sting, you know."

"Because of your poor mother!" Natalie acknowledged, the coolness retreating from her gaze and being replaced by sympathy. He thought that had they been alone she might have cupped his face with her hands, or run them through his short curls—but she was not free to do so in her father's populous drawing room. In fact, Lord Lamont had become aware that they stood together and was glaring at Sebastian from across the room.

"And," Sebastian said, speaking quickly for he knew it was only a matter of moments before Lamont extricated himself from the conversation he was in, to cross over and separate the two of them, "I wish you to know that Mrs. Deems is a friend of mine."

"You knew her in Brighton?" Natalie asked, her expression uncertain.

"No. She is a new friend, one I have made since coming back to Severn's Well."

"Oh." Her brow cleared.

He gathered up both her hands in his. "I will not have

ill spoken of her. Just as I would not have it spoken of you, my dear."

"Oh," she repeated. "Then you have my apologies, Lord Sebastian. I did not mean to find fault with your friend."

"Thank you." He lifted both her hands to his mouth, kissing the back of each in turn, not caring that Lord Lamont would almost certainly banish him for the presumption.

He and Natalie had had their first fight. They'd recovered from it. All was well. He'd even managed to include Charlotte Deems as a part of the circle his marriage to Natalie would encompass—as a friend to them both, of course.

Now all he had to do was convince Charlotte that they could be friends.

That, and ignore any further vibrations of deeper attachment he might feel toward Charlotte.

He had a man's appetites. He could not help it if he was not blind to Charlotte's charms, both in her person and in her manner. A man would have to be made of stone not to find something about Charlotte Deems that moved him. But, damn it, he also had a man's brain. He would use it to ignore that which was unsuitable. Or if he could not ignore it, at least not respond to it. Their friendship might have to change, having a few less intimacies in their conversation, a few less touches, but that was probably for the best anyway.

"You are in the same situation as my sister," Mr. Hubbard said to Charlotte as they drove toward her home.

It had been kind of him to offer to take her and Oscar up, to spare them the walk home from where the Mail coach had left them at the north end of Severn's Well.

"What is that?" Charlotte asked.

"Living outside of the village, in an isolated place. Our home is very comfortable, but sometimes I worry that she is alone there with just a few servants while I am busy with my Revenue work. Like your cottage, our home has no immediate neighbors."

"Is your home near the river?"

"Yes, but not on cliffs as yours is. We are almost on a level with the river."

"I look forward to seeing it tomorrow."

"I think your lad will like to feed the geese that have recently returned there," Mr. Hubbard suggested. Oscar turned his head to look at the man who had said his name, but when Mr. Hubbard did not meet Oscar's gaze, he went back to looking at the passing scenery and pointing at things that caught his fancy.

Charlotte could wish that Mr. Hubbard would actually talk *to* Oscar, but she knew that some men were not entirely comfortable with children. Bachelor gentlemen were perhaps even more of that persuasion. It was nothing that time and familiarity could not change.

"It is my work to keep smugglers from being successful," Mr. Hubbard went on, "and to see they come to justice. But even more than that, I like to keep the residents along the river comfortable. It is the backbone of our life, this river, and the threat posed by any kind of ruffian is a major concern."

Charlotte swallowed the impulse to grin, for she doubted Mr. Hubbard would appreciate that she found his recitation just a trifle pompous. She supposed he was trying to impress her—which was rather flattering, that he should even want to try.

"So I pray you will tell me if you see or hear anything untoward near your home, especially at night. I am prepared to allot a patrol specifically to your part of the river, if it seems warranted."

"You are very kind," Charlotte said, hoping she sounded grateful and calm, when in fact alarm raced through her. She'd known all along that Sebastian risked being caught out, but hearing the possibility from Mr. Hubbard's lips made it seem more real, more dangerously possible. "I will let you know if there are any difficulties at all," she said, striving to sound confident and undisturbed.

At her cottage, Mr. Hubbard leaped down to offer her a hand down, and he lifted Oscar from the cabriolet with a pat to her son's head. He offered her a graceful leg in farewell.

"My sister and I look forward to tomorrow," he assured her before he climbed back up into his carriage and rolled away.

"Firsty, Mama," Oscar said with sudden insistence. Charlotte took him by the hand and led him into the house to fetch him a glass of water.

As her son slurped and spilled down his shirtfront, Charlotte gave an internal sigh and considered the absurdity of her situation.

She had made up her mind to find a husband, and Mr. Hubbard was about as likely a prospect as she could hope to find in the district. But he was also the man most likely to arrest Sebastian. That was the last thing she wanted to have happen—even if she could not like that he acted the part of smuggler. "The trade," as the locals called it, had taken her grandpapa from her and had humiliated her family. She hated the idea of how getting caught would affect all of Sebastian's schemes. Did he know how much he risked? Did he know that the greatest pain from smuggling came not at being caught; the greatest pain came from dealing with its aftermath. Those who dared to love a smuggler, also dared living with the threat of a terrible loss.

Love. She had thought the word, but not as she was remembering her grandpapa. It had been Sebastian's face that had risen before her mind's eye.

She shook her head, hoping to shake any tears from her eyes, for tears served no good purpose. They changed nothing. So then, what might serve? She could talk to Sebastian, beg him to cease—but she knew it was too late for that. He had made a commitment, even be it to seafaring knaves, and he would see it through.

So what option was left? Only to do everything she could to keep Mr. Hubbard's attention centered away from the cliffs near her house. By words, actions, or misdirection, she vowed she would do her best to protect Sebastian.

Chapter 14

Just after ten that night, Sebastian's coach stopped, once more at a short distance, situated off the main road near Charlotte's home. While he changed into his dark smuggling clothes inside the coach, Timmons crept up to Charlotte's cottage to be sure there was no one calling on her tonight.

By the narrow beam of light he allowed from the lantern Timmons had left with him, Sebastian made a point of moving his gift from his regular coat pocket to the long, dark wool coat he wore while waiting on the cliffs. That was when it struck him that he'd forgotten to order a bouquet of flowers be delivered tonight to Miss Talbot.

Oh well, nothing he could do about it now. Besides, she would enjoy receiving them more tomorrow—*after* she'd had to suffer through her undoubtedly tedious supper with Lord Heversham.

Feeling disgruntled, Sebastian bundled his routine clothes into the protective oilcloth and secured the bundle with its length of rope.

"All's clear," Timmons said five minutes later as he opened the coach door. Sebastian nodded, picked up the lantern and the bundle, and sprang forth from the carriage.

"I would like ten minutes alone with Mrs. Deems," he told his valet. "Wait here, and do not unharness the horses."

Timmons, wise beyond his sixteen years, nodded without questioning these statements. He settled onto the coaching box, while Sebastian turned and walked the dividing distance to Charlotte's front door. He set down the lantern and the bundle, and knocked.

Charlotte answered at once, already dressed in her cloak.

"Is Oscar asleep?" Sebastian asked her, not crossing her threshold.

She nodded.

"Then join me outside for a moment."

She gave him a puzzled glance, and complied by slipping out the door and closing it behind her. "Is something amiss?" she asked at once.

"Not in the way you mean."

"The Revenue officers—?"

He shook his head. "There has been no sign of interest from that quarter, or at least none that I have been able to scent. Their cutters have been patrolling farther out, in the channel, and their riding officers have been more interested in the flat shore at the river's mouth."

"Then what—?" she asked.

He took up both her hands in his, making a point of also capturing her gaze. "Charlotte, I have been wrong to make you come out to the cliffs and watch with me."

She started to speak, but he overrode her.

"What if we had been seen, or even arrested? I would have done my best to take all blame onto myself—but what if you'd had to stand before a Bristol magistrate? What if he were harsh, or stupid, or unbending? You could have been separated from Oscar."

Charlotte caught her breath.

"I cannot allow that risk to stand any longer. I release you from any requirements. In fact, I forbid you to be out on the cliffs until this is all over. I will send you a note.

"Do not worry," he went on. "No one has seen us together, out there." He gestured toward the cliffs with his head, his hands still clasping hers. "Should I be taken by the Revenue men, I will deny vehemently any suggestion that someone had ever been watching with me."

Her eyes were wide with surprise, but there was somehow a quiet gravity in them as well. "But if I am not there to be seen as your accomplice, what is to keep me silent?" she asked with calm reasoning.

"Nothing," he said truthfully. He squeezed her hands. "I hope you will not go to the authorities, but I will do nothing to compel your obedience."

"But why? Why now?" She spoke so softly he had to lean down to be able to hear the words. "Why take this chance when your ship must arrive any day?"

"Because—" He had to pause, to take a deep breath and gather his wits, which felt frayed. "Because I feel you have become a friend to me, Charlotte. I cannot compel a friend to do anything, especially something dangerous to her and her child's well-being. Or, by calling you my friend do I presume far too much?"

"You do," she said, but then she smiled, the smile chasing some of the gravity from her gaze. "But that is part of your charm, my lord."

He felt a responding smile flit over his face. "Then I will presume again, and ask are we indeed friends?"

She had to swallow before she could answer. "We are."

A weight he'd been unaware of until this moment lifted from his chest, and he smiled even as he expelled a relieved sigh.

"I am glad." He squeezed her hands again, to keep from pulling her into his arms and hugging her close.

"Then please accept these as a gift, from one friend to another," he said, letting go of her hands to reach into his coat pocket. He pulled out a smallish packet wrapped in paper and tied with twine. He pressed the thin packet into her hands.

She looked up at him, a question in her eyes.

"Open it later," he instructed. Later, because then he would not be here to see her smile in acceptance or frown in rejection. He knew that either response was more than he was capable of enduring right now.

He nodded at her, and stepped back, out of arm's reach. "Good night," he said, then bent to retrieve his bundle and the lantern. "And thank you again for the hair trim. Natalie—Miss Talbot admired it."

"Did she?" Charlotte asked, her voice low.

Was that a glistening in her eyes? Or, no, it must be some trick of the dim lighting from his lantern.

He nodded and made some sort of agreeable noise, and stepped backward, only to turn abruptly and stride with rapid steps in the direction of his coach.

Timmons greeted him with a wordless touch of the driving whip to his hat's brim.

"Take the coach home," Sebastian told his young valet. "I have bid Mrs. Deems stay home. We will not disturb her again. You do not have to sit with her son anymore."

Timmons sat up at attention at that. "The ship's come, sir?"

Sebastian shook his head. "Soon. I pray God it is tonight." He lofted the bundle for Timmons to see. "I have other clothes here, and I will change in the woods before I try to slip into the house. I've no alibi in place tonight, so there is no reason for you or the horses to be out."

Timmons frowned. "It'll look peculiar-like, you walking home late, m'lord."

"I am willing to chance that, rather than make the horses stand in harness for hours. I can always pretend to be drunk, if anyone questions my behavior."

Timmons still looked disinclined to commend his master's bidding, but he nodded in acceptance. "I'll be waiting up for you, m'lord," he said, so firmly that Sebastian smiled to himself in appreciation of the lad's devotion even if he had not gained the young man's approval.

The carriage rolled away, Sebastian closed off the lantern's light, and he turned to begin walking back toward the river.

A chill swept through him, telling him it would be another cold night on the cliffs—and a lonely one.

Charlotte stood watching Sebastian walk away until the night swallowed him whole, and only then did she turn and slip back into her cottage, his gift clutched in her hand.

She removed her cloak and hung it on its peg, even

though a part of her balked at Sebastian's being alone out there. If she were with him, she could act as another pair of eyes, another set of ears. She would not leave Oscar alone however. She had seen Timmons driving the coach away, so she could not press him into staying with her son. She had no choice but to yield to Sebastian's wishes . . . at least as far as she was willing. There was no reason why she could not sit outside her own door, within hearing of Oscar, but also with eyes scanning the night.

If she put a chair at the corner of her cottage, she could watch three-quarters of her own property. She would be aware of any sight or sound of troops coming from either the north or the south. She could not watch the river or its bank below, but she could provide a set of eyes to spy any approach here on the topside of the cliffs. Then she had but to scream, perhaps to pretend there had been a strange rough-looking man who had run off toward the village, away from the river. . . .

She wondered briefly if it was some kind of sin to pray that a smuggler should be successful, but she sent a prayer heavenward anyway. Still, before she donned her cloak once more, before she placed a chair outside, she would open Sebastian's gift.

The twine and paper parted easily to reveal two pairs of gloves: one of finest linen, intricately embroidered white-on-white; the other pair was of calfskin dyed a deep, rich blue. Blue, she supposed, to match her cloak. Although their color was darker than Sebastian's pea-cock blue gaze, she knew she would never be able to look at them without thinking of his eyes.

Her vision misted over as she reached for the dark blue pair and pulled them on. They did not fit perfectly, but they were a good fit and would more than suffice.

Gloves were the kind of gift a man was permitted to give a lady, and she to accept. They were not too forward, nor too inappropriately expensive, nor even un-likely. The gloves were well-made and charming in design, but not rarefied. They were not of exceptional value nor matchless workmanship, so that was not what

moved her. No, it was that Sebastian had thought to give
the gloves to her at all.

He no doubt thought of them as a kind of redress
against having trespassed into her property, her home,
her life. He could not give her back what he had taken—
and he had taken more than she would ever let him
know—but he could show that he had learned to care a
little for her, by remembering her need. It was a little
thing, to recall that she had only a single pair of gloves.
But the real gift was in the remembering; he could not
have given her a finer gift.

Charlotte pressed her gloved hands to her face, not to
force back tears but to hold in the high, wild emotions
that coursed through her. Elation clashed with despair.
Despondency collided with longing. God help her, Sebastian was not even in the room and yet she tingled with
awareness of him.

Tonight he had asked her if they were friends, and she
had answered that they were, and had meant it. But just
because they were friends did not mean that it would be
easy for her to be near him, to watch as he made a life
with Natalie Talbot.

She swallowed the anguish that filled her, clinging to
the exaltation of having such a friend to call her own.
Sebastian. She loved him. She knew it, and knew it was
implausible that she should have come to love him in so
short an acquaintance, but what an acquaintance it had
been! Had she and Jarvis ever talked so much, in all
their marriage? Had she ever shared so much of herself
with him? Had she ever been allowed to see so deeply
into a man's soul as she saw into Sebastian's?

One thing she knew for certain: with Jarvis, her heart
had never leaped into her throat. Not even on her wedding night, when she'd been nervous and hopeful and
overly attuned to Jarvis's masculinity. But tonight her
heart had leaped into her throat when she'd opened her
door to Sebastian, like a doe leaping through the brush
in response to her mate's call. Tonight she had finally
understood that she might have learned to respect and

have an affection for Jarvis—but she never would have loved him.

Love, unbidden and misplaced, had touched her at last, and she understood it either *was* or *was not*. One could not will love to bloom; one could only be so fortunate as to recognize it. And if one were truly blessed, recognize it at the right place, in the right time, and reach out with both hands to seize it.

Clearly, I am not blessed, Charlotte acknowledged to herself with a sad little interior smile.

Squaring her shoulders, she lowered the gloved hands that would not be allowed to reach out for Sebastian, and stood. She crossed into the chamber she shared with Oscar, and verified her son was asleep, contentedly sucking his thumb. With resolve, she moved to a window in the sitting room, propped it open an inch or so, then donned her cloak and picked up a chair.

She settled the chair outside, at the corner of her cottage near the window through which she would be able to hear Oscar if he cried out, and she sat.

The night and the breeze both reached out to chill her, but still she sat, her determination to do what she could for Sebastian supplying fire enough inside her. To pace was to possibly miss some small sign, some tiny sound, so she sat as the hours crept by, appreciating anew the gift of the gloves. Her eyes burned with weariness, but she kept her vigilance.

Her mantel clock struck each passing half hour, and at the striking of one o'clock she looked for some sign of Sebastian. Would he pass? It would be the easiest path to come back this way, but there were other paths he could take.

When the clock strike told her it was half past the hour, she knew he had to have gone another way. She rose stiff with cold from her chair, secured the window and door, and made her way into bed.

The next day brought rain in the morning. Charlotte and Oscar baked sweet buns flavored with citron and currants, as much for the heavenly scent they produced as for something to do, and they played with Oscar's carved wooden soldiers. At a little after noon, when the rain had ceased, they donned their walking boots and strolled to the Hyatt home, just to share the bounty of sweet buns and pass a bit of time before Charlotte was due to be driven to the Hubbards' home for supper.

"You won't be wanting the babe at your supper, now will you, Mrs. Deems?" Mrs. Hyatt protested. "There's no talking or enjoying a meal with a little one along. Leave him here with me," she insisted.

From there it was only a matter of time before the Hyatt girls insisted Oscar should stay the entire night, in case Charlotte wished to stay longer at the Hubbards' for "dancing or playing instruments or such" as Mrs. Hyatt summed up.

Charlotte gave a small frown, just about to explain that as she believed she was the only invitee there would be no music or dancing—only to bite her lip. If Oscar spent the entire evening here, Charlotte would be free to leave the side of her cottage late tonight, to act as an even better sentry for Sebastian. For that matter, Oscar would probably be safer, further from the scene of any disruption that could occur.

"Thank you, Mrs. Hyatt," she agreed.

She walked back to her cottage alone, her last glance back at Oscar showing him happily toddling after the Hyatt girls. It did not take long to change into a more formal gown and be sure her hair was smoothly up and pinned. She had elected to believe that Sebastian would send a carriage for her, as he'd said he wished to, instead of walking the three miles, so there was no need to hurry.

Timmons drove a coach right up to her door at a little less than thirty minutes before two o'clock, exactly on time to deliver her to the Hubbards'.

Sebastian had remembered.

"Ma'am." Timmons saluted her as he jumped down to hand Charlotte up.

When they arrived at the Hubbard home, Timmons went off to unharness the horses and probably take a light meal with the grooms who were employed in the stables, and Charlotte was greeted warmly by Mr. Hubbard and his sister. They both looked faintly relieved to learn that Oscar would not be joining them, although they expressed regret.

Supper was delightful, as was the company, although Charlotte found she looked at Mr. Hubbard through new eyes today. Once she had vowed to help Sebastian, right or wrong in his choice to smuggle, she could not help but see Mr. James Hubbard as something of a threat.

She drove home as the sun was setting, listening to Timmons's light chatter about how the Hubbard stables were run. It had been a perfectly lovely afternoon—but she was anxious for the night. Anxious that it be past, behind them all, that the ship would arrive and Sebastian's task finally be completed.

She frowned up at the sky, now gray fading toward black, just able to make out that the clouds raced west tonight. Sitting at her cottage, the wind direction would see to it that she would hear little of anything that might happen near the riverbank. If she sat at her cottage, she'd have little or no forewarning of approaching Revenue men, not unless the wind played the occasional trick. Just as well she need not linger at her cottage, but was free to move to a place that could offer her unwitting compatriot an advantage.

When her clock struck ten, Charlotte left her cottage, dressed in her dark cloak and gloves, the smuggler's lantern that had been gathering dust in her stable now dangling from her hand. It was lit and the panel completely down, to hide its glow.

She moved with care through the dark, listening, watching, careful not to trip. The Revenue men had a station house about a mile north on the river—she walked to the cliffs, then turned that way. She would hear riders before Sebastian could, and she would throw the lantern panel up and wildly swing the light to and fro, should she hear horses or men approaching. Sebastian would be bound to notice a lantern's glow—if her light was not obscured from his vision by the lay of the land. She would run toward him, shouting as well, veering off from approaching him only when she neared her cottage, where she would take refuge and pretend to have been abed for hours, praying that Sebastian had also taken flight.

But by half past one, if there had been Excisemen about, she had not heard any sign of them. She frowned up at the westerly wind, knowing it was possible it could have carried such sounds away from her.

Still, there was naught else she could do, not tonight. Charlotte made her way back to her home. She secured the house, stoked the fire, and left her clothes on the bedchamber floor, so eager for bed and oblivion that she could not summon the will to tend to them tonight.

She dreamed of ships sailing up and down the Severn. Sometimes she was watching them, and sometimes she was aboard them, and she had gone sailing in order to find something. She heard the sound of water slapping against the hull, loud thumps, an insistent sound, vaguely frightening. . . .

Sitting bolt upright in her bed, Charlotte came instantly awake. She realized the pounding was real, and very near at hand. Her frantic gaze found Oscar's cot through the predawn gloom, and she knew a moment's profound gratitude that he was not here to be frightened by the fearful pounding. She flung herself from the bed, and stumbled out of her room.

Charlotte stared at the wall of her sitting room, the wall from whence came all the pounding, and watched in a horrified fascination as the stucco cracked and fell away in chunks, revealing bits and pieces of the door and the jamb she knew had been hidden there: someone or something was trying to come through the secret door that led into her home from a smuggler's tunnel.

Pushing her one good chair ahead of her, Charlotte scrambled toward the crumbling stucco. She would block that door in any way she could. There was no knob under which to secure the chair, so Charlotte pushed the chair up against the crumbling stucco and reached to grab a spindly kitchen chair. This she slid in front of the old smuggler's door as well, and then reached for the kitchen table, hearing her own breath come out in ragged little pants. The small table felt so light now, so inconsequential, but she pushed it into the jumble of things before the old door anyway, even though these few things could not possibly stop whatever battered the other side.

She turned, involuntarily issuing a low moan of fear, and confirmed with utter frustration that her only other piece of furniture was her secretary, a delicate piece that was clear across the room. She stepped toward it, even as she knew it could do too little good, but she got no more than three steps when the door exploded inward behind her, scattering a hail of stucco pieces. Charlotte felt a scream bubble up inside her head, poised to erupt from her lips as she twisted back to face whatever had just broken into her home.

A man, covered with stucco bits and dust, stooped and stumbled through the short doorway, his face utterly unfamiliar. He spied her at once. "Madam, you must help me!" he cried, his voice accented, his eyes wild.

Charlotte's throat locked, frozen on the scream, and she reached out blindly, a fear reaction telling her to find some kind of weapon without ever taking her eyes from the man's face.

Only the man turned and bent, and reached back into the undersized doorway, oddly exposing himself to attack. Charlotte watched in mingled confusion and dread as the man dragged forth a burden, another man.

"Please, madam, I am beg with you," the man said in fractured English. "You must help us."

Charlotte stared, a new horror dawning in her. The other man, the one dragged in, lay very still, and his head was bloodied. She knew him at once: it was Sebastian.

Chapter 15

"What have you done to him?" Charlotte demanded of the stranger.

"I? I have done nothing!" the man cried, and now it was possible to distinguish his accent.

"You are French." It sounded like an accusation.

"Yes," the Frenchman assured her on a grunt, as he bent and attempted to drag Sebastian farther into the room. Charlotte watched him keenly for several long moments, trying to judge the situation, her heart still thundering in her chest. She was torn between wanting to drop to her knees and minister to Sebastian, and distrusting the man who had battered through her wall. She took a deep breath, and then logic told her that if the Frenchman had meant to hurt Sebastian further, he could have long since done so. She must trust that this stranger had no evil intentions hidden under this show of dragging Sebastian from the tunnel.

The man was well dressed if not elegantly so, in dark colors, obviously in hopes of being unseen in the night. He had no overcoat, which suggested either he did not plan to be out long in weather, or else he had left any coat behind in the desire to move quickly and lightly.

Her pounding heart began to return to its normal tempo, and with it came comprehension. "Sebastian told you about the tunnel and the secret door!" she stated as the realization dawned.

"Oui, madame."

Sebastian groaned. That was enough to cut through the shreds of Charlotte's caution, and she knelt beside him, searching his face for any sign of returning consciousness. The Frenchman peered down as well, and Charlotte saw that the stranger was white around the mouth; he'd had a nasty shock, she would guess.

"You are from the ship, the ship he was waiting for," Charlotte said to the Frenchman as she reached to feel at Sebastian's neck. His heartbeat pulsed strongly there, dividing her distress in half.

"*Oui*, Madam, yes." This time, the man did not use the French form "madame," using the English pronunciation—correcting himself back and forth as one does when not quite proficient in a second language. Charlotte did not doubt that her French, at which she'd never been accomplished, would sound just as back-and-forth to him.

The man also knelt at Sebastian's side, examining Sebastian's scalp with searching fingers. Charlotte had time to note the stranger was decidedly nondescript: neither handsome nor ugly, not noticeably tall or short. He had dark eyes, a nose that was slightly big for his face, and brown hair clipped short to his head—still, the only thing that made him distinctive was the odd article that strapped around his chest, running over one shoulder. The front was merely a wide strap, but the back was a pouch, complete with heavy buckle, a kind of saddlebag designed to be carried by humans. It bulged, showing it was filled.

It seemed obvious that whatever was being smuggled, it was in that pouch.

Charlotte glanced down at Sebastian, struck anew by concern when his eyes flickered, as though he struggled to regain consciousness but failed.

She hurried to her kitchen, coming back to the sitting room with a cold, wet cloth. The Frenchman took it from her hand.

"*Merci*," he said, using it to wipe the blood from Sebastian's forehead and hair, the gesture erasing even more of Charlotte's initial alarm about the invader. Sebastian made a sound, an unintelligible murmur, then lay still again.

The Frenchman sat back on his heels, looking relieved. "It is only a little wound. On a big, er . . ." He strove to find the word, but could not. He settled for making a sign on his own head that indicated a growing bump.

"A lump?" Charlotte suggested.

The Frenchman shrugged, possibly not able to confirm that was the word he sought, and bent back to removing the streaks of blood.

Sebastian groaned a second time, his eyes fluttering open and closed again. Charlotte bent to untie his cravat, discovering its black folds were tangled with the kerchief he always wore about his neck in case he needed to cover his face. She glanced up at the stranger. "Tell me what has happened," she demanded.

The Frenchman's English was fair, if a little halting when he could not think of a word. Charlotte learned in short order that the ship had indeed arrived and signaled. Sebastian had signaled in return, and both parties had begun to work their way to the riverbank.

"The men of the ship, they were already, er, making to go back to the ship in their little ship—"

"The dinghy?"

"Yes, I think they call the little ship a ding-ee," the Frenchman agreed. "Then it was only *monsieur* and I on the, er, the earth. He says to me, 'Come, I 'ave a place for you to 'ide while we wait for the other ship to take you away,' and I am 'appy to go with him."

In the French fashion, the man tended to swallow his h's, so that Charlotte had to concentrate a bit in order to make out everything he said.

"But then there is a shout," the man went on, his eyes widening in remembered alarm, "and a man, just one man, he comes and he says we must halt, and we must wait for the *gendarmerie* to come and arrest us. And *monsieur* says *non*, it is not so, not tonight, and he takes the gun and he, er . . ." The Frenchman made a gripping fist and then a downward motion with his arm.

"Did he strike him? Please tell me there were no shots from the gun!" Charlotte said in alarm.

"Hit him, that is what I mean, *oui*! He takes the other man's gun and he hits him. But the man, he hits *monsieur* as well, and *monsieur* is on his knees and there is the blood! The other man, he is, er, not awake. He is the problem no more."

"But not dead, I pray?" Charlotte held her breath.

"*Non!* Not dead."

"And *monsieur*'s face, it was covered?" She pointed to the black kerchief she'd unwound from around Sebastian's neck.

"Yes! All the time, the face it was covered."

She breathed out her relief in a sigh. Better the man had only been knocked out, not killed—and better yet that he could not have seen Sebastian's face. Tonight would be aswarm with Excisemen anyway, but had there been a death or had the man been able to identify his attacker, she had no doubt that Navy men would be added to the Customs troops searching the entire coastline for those responsible.

She rose and fetched her cloak from its peg, rolling it and using it to pillow Sebastian's head. His eyes fluttered open, but did not focus. After a long moment they closed again.

"But then we hear the horses coming, and we know more of these Excisemen, they come. *Monsieur*, he says to me, 'Armand! There is a tunnel! We must find it!'"

The man's name—apparently his Christian name—was Armand, Charlotte noted silently.

"So he gets to his feet," Armand went on, "and his face is more white than the moon, but still we look. And, as you see, we find it, this tunnel, and we come up and up and up! To here. I see the door, and it does not open, and *Monsieur* says 'You must push very hard. You must break it.' Then, *monsieur*, he is not awake, and I think 'the Exciseman has broke his head, he is dying' and I push in the door."

Charlotte looked sharply back down at Sebastian at the word "dying," but felt her stomach unclench at the evidence of her own eyes: he occasionally tried to rouse, there was not too much blood, and the cut was not deep. There was reason for concern, but she did not fear the worst.

"Did anyone see you enter the tunnel?" she questioned the Frenchman. Would Excisemen be flooding up the passageway into her home at any moment?

"*Non*, no!"

Charlotte heaved another sigh of relief—things were not good, but they could have been much worse.

"We hear the horses come, but the men, they do not see us, I am sure of this," the Frenchman expanded.

"Then there is some time," Charlotte said.

"Time, *madame*?"

She ignored the man's inquiry—she could explain to him in a bit, but for now she reached to examine Sebastian's scalp for herself. The lump was sizable, but it had swollen outward, not in on the brain. Yet more confirmation that Sebastian would most likely be all right once he regained his senses.

"I will get some blankets," she told the stranger, only to hesitate before rising to her feet. "Armand—should I call you that?"

"Oh," the Frenchman looked surprised at the idea of keeping his identity secret—or perhaps startled to realize he had already called himself by a certain name in her presence. He gave her a grin, somewhere between devilish and abashed. "Yes, 'Armand.' But that is all, eh? No, er—"

"Surnames?"

"*Oui*, surnames, if this means the name of the family. The father's name."

"It does. And I agree. I am Charlotte," she said as she rose.

He rose as well, and made her an elegant, decidedly Gallic bow. "*Madame* Charlotte, it is my pleasure to meet you. But I would have it be in a better moment, yes?"

"Yes," she agreed wholeheartedly.

She went to her room and fetched a dressing gown to cover her night rail. She also pulled on a pair of house mules, for her bare feet were chilled. Fetching two counterpanes from the chest at the end of her bed, she returned to her sitting room.

"He awakes," Armand announced, and sure enough, Sebastian's eyes were open. He was white around the mouth, but she was sure this time he saw her.

"Charlotte!" he said at the sight of her, the word slightly slurred, as if he'd had a pint too much of ale.

She knelt beside him. "Sebastian, Armand has brought you up the tunnel— "

His eyes went wide and lost their focus. "I hear 'em!" The slur in his speech increased. "We haf tuh get away. Wha—? No!"

Armand and Charlotte exchanged glances. "You are at my house, Sebastian," she said with a quiet calm she did not really quite feel. "Everything will be fine."

He said something else, but the words were as much babble as Oscar sometimes offered. His eyes rolled in his head, showing white.

"He is concussed," Charlotte concluded. She shook her head, now a little more worried than she had been before. "We must get him off this cold floor." She glanced around her small cottage, as if a sofa would magically appear—but there was nothing for it. "We must put him on my bed," she told Armand.

Armand did not argue. With his bundle still strapped to him, the Frenchman dragged Sebastian to her room, Sebastian's boots scraping along the wooden floor. Between them they managed to hoist him just high enough to get him half-sprawled on her bed.

"This cannot be helping his head," Charlotte fretted.

She crawled onto the bed and pulled, Armand pushed, and at last they had Sebastian's length under the covers and his head cushioned by a pillow. She motioned to Armand, and the two of them slipped out of the bedroom into the sitting room once more.

"The Revenue men will eventually find their unconscious fellow on the riverbank, if they have not already long since done so," she explained to Armand. She knew the Excisemen would not dismiss their fellow's injury—indeed, they would call in more men, would fan out over the water and the shore. They would stop any ship that stood a chance of having delivered goods this night, and they would search house to house to see if any smuggling activity could be detected, or anyone was out of place, not where they ought to be. She knew, for that was exactly what had happened on a summer's night when her grandpapa was caught, his wagon still fully loaded with French lace when he was overtaken by the Excisemen.

She took Armand by the sleeve and pulled him to the kitchen, where she handed him a broom and a dustbin. "The Excisemen will come here, Armand. We must hide every sign that we can of your having come here."

Armand went pale. "I cannot be taken! I would be let go when my sponsor is known, for he is very important, but I coming to England was to be the big secret! I must come and go away again, with no one to know."

"Then you had best do a thorough job of sweeping up," she commanded, turning him around and giving him a small shove toward the broken and scattered stucco pieces.

As Armand began to pick up large chunks, Charlotte returned from her room with two more folded fabrics: one was a Holland cloth, the other a pieced counterpane of white and yellow linen handed down from her grandmama.

"Put the big pieces on this," she ordered Armand, spreading out the Holland cloth on the floor.

She hurried to the kitchen, coming back now wearing an apron with two pockets, into which she had deposited iron nails and a hammer. She shook open the counterpane. "It is the most likely of my things that a woman would hang on the wall," she explained at Armand's quizzical glance.

After tacking her grandmama's pretty counterpane over the space where the secret door had had all its stucco disguising knocked to the floor, she stepped back to survey her work. "I had better secure the sides as well, so it cannot flutter," she assessed, sighing just a little at the holes she had to make in the lovely fabric.

"All I can say is, I hope whatever you are smuggling in that bundle of yours is worth all this!" she said warmly when she was content that she'd done her best to hide the door and the broken stucco sufficiently. She was too vexed to pretend at a politeness she did not feel.

"My plans? Are they important?" he said, reaching a

hand to point over his shoulder at the bundle yet strapped to him. His chest expanded and he lifted his chin. "*Oui*, it is my plans we smuggle, as you say, but it is also *myself* that is for the smuggle. If these are lost, I am the one who makes more. I am the one who knows all, here." He pointed now to his own temple. "It is I who is important, to get from the ship, from one to another. I am the smuggle for which *monsieur* waited."

"You—?" Charlotte's mouth dropped open in astonishment. It had occurred to her that the "cargo" might be slaves, but once Sebastian had assured her slaves were not involved, she had assumed the contraband being transferred was a "thing," not a human being. Not a person such as Armand, who was clearly of some significance to someone with his "plans," be they in his pouch or in his head. Obviously this man had invented a thing that required drawings or designs, or he had stolen such plans, or . . . Her imagination ran dry, for it was not important. What was important was that this man—or the knowledge he had—was coveted by others. That was the only thing that made sense of his need for this covert journey of his.

"A man of much important—"

"Importance," she corrected reflexively, as she did Oscar's odd speech patterns. She knew her eyes had gone round; she could feel herself staring at him.

"As you say. This importance man has paid for me to go to another country, where I am safe from *idiots*!" This last word was said with the French inflection and deep resentment. "So, you must help *monsieur* and I, for I know nothing of how to go to my next ship, the one that takes me away to a safe land. England is not a safe land, not for me, so I go on."

Charlotte put a hand to her forehead—what had Sebastian mixed himself up in? "You are fleeing France, through England?"

"France, yes. And her wrath."

Charlotte stared, for to flee "France's wrath" was to flee one man's reprisal.

"The Emperor of France?" she squeaked. "Napoleon Bonaparte?"

Chapter 16

Armand's expression became closed. "I say no such thing. I say only importance persons wish me punished. *Monsieur* cannot help me, so *you* must."

Was it possible? Had Sebastian somehow, for some unfathomable reason, become entangled with a Frenchman evading Napoleon's anger, or oppression, or threats, or . . .

"Tell me something, and be truthful," she said as harshly as she could, startling Armand into drawing back several inches. "If you tell me a lie, I will know it, and I will hand you over to the *gendarmerie*."

"And if I tell you the truth and you do not like it?" Armand asked, unable to mask a return to the alarm he had shown upon first breaking into her home.

Charlotte stared at him, then gave him what she demanded: the truth. "I do not know."

Some of his alarm receded. "You speak without the, er, pretending. Ask, and I will answer if I can."

"Do you or your plans represent a threat to England?"

"Threat?" he questioned, his gesture showing that he did not understand the word.

"Harm, or hurt. Will you hurt England?"

"*Non, madame!*" he cried, insulted. "I have try to give England a new weapon, one that France does not have. One they are too *stupide* to comprehend. I wish to help England, and for this wish, I am given gold and sent to a new land."

Given gold, provided with a secret passage to a "new land"—she supposed his destination must be America or New Holland. Someone with lofty influence, someone who had been offered a weapon designed by this Armand, now made it possible for this Armand to make an escape from France's wrath.

The man had turned his back on his own country . . . but that was not her concern. For tonight, her immediate concern was for Sebastian only.

"So you will help me, yes?" Armand pressed.

"I know nothing of what Seb—" No, no names; it was obvious that Armand only knew Sebastian as *"monsieur."* "—I know nothing of what *monsieur* has planned. I cannot help you with anything to do with ships or politics or—"

"Then you must hide me," Armand said, but any hauteur he had shown earlier had now slipped away, leaving him sounding alone and unsure, even frightened.

Charlotte's mouth worked as though in indecision—but there was no decision to be made here, not really. Armand might be an inventor or a thief or a spymaster, for all she knew—whatever he was, two continents vied to control him. Her own government, presumably, was attempting to get the man secretly away from France. Even if she wanted to defy what some fellow countryman had set in motion, she would not. To turn over Armand to the authorities was to surrender Sebastian as well, and that she would not do.

"Sweep!" she ordered him, reaching for the kitchen table, in order to restore the furniture in her cottage to order.

She glimpsed a grateful look that swept over the man's features, but Charlotte had no time for gratitude. "Hurry!" she told him.

Where he had swept, she followed with a dampened cloth, picking up the dusty debris the broom could not.

"Fold that cloth up and tie it like a bundle of laundry," she ordered, indicating the Holland cloth holding the larger stucco chunks.

Armand did as she said, then opened his mouth to make some comment, but she interrupted him with a shake of her head. "Anything else must wait. Now we hide you."

She knew exactly where the planks came up at the far edge of the kitchen, because she stored her potatoes and onions down in the cool space built under the floor. The small hiding place where she hid her jewels in her bedchamber had been built for just that purpose—hiding small valuables, such as jewels or money or gold. This other space had been built to store or hide trafficked goods. Was tonight the first time it would be used to hide a living being? Possibly not, since the space was big enough for at least two people sitting down, even with the potatoes and onions pushed to one side.

"It will be dark, and you must be absolutely quiet and still until I remove the planks. It may be a long while. Do you understand?"

Armand, sitting beside the bundle of stucco that was to be hidden along with him under the flooring, nodded. He sat on a small blanket from Oscar's cot, and had her cloak around his shoulders, for she had no remaining blankets to offer him.

"*Merci, madame.* Thank you," he said with apparent sincerity, but then a flicker of nervousness ran through his dark-eyed gaze. "Do not forget I am here, eh?"

She smiled her assurance, and replaced the planks.

Charlotte returned to the sitting room, stoking the fire there. Then a glance around the room assured her that if no Revenue officer thought to look behind the counterpane nailed on her wall, no one would know that anything was amiss . . . unless they ventured into her bedchamber. How could she ever explain Sebastian's presence there?

Sebastian was stirring on her bed when she looked in on him. He was restless, not quite conscious, but some rudimentary instinct was pushing him toward consciousness. That was well, in terms of the bump he'd taken—but not so good if the Revenue riders found him here and wondered why he had a bump on his head and blood on his shirt. What if in his delirium he said something incriminating?

Charlotte bit her lip, and knew what she had to do. She fetched the bottle of wine, the one they had shared on the cliffs but had not finished—was that really just two nights ago? She took out the cork she had carved down to make it fit anew, and poured wine onto a cloth. She sponged Sebastian's shirt with wine, obscuring the blood if not covering it up. Then she walked around the room, sponging wine anyplace that she thought it would not show too much, but would provide a pungent odor. She opened her dressing gown and deliberately spilled the last of the wine down the front of her night rail, gritting her teeth against the wine's cold caress. It would smell and look as if they'd been drinking for hours.

When the pounding came on her front door, as she'd known it would, she scampered at once to answer it. And just as she'd imagined they would, the Excisemen stared at her now uncovered night rail, its winestains down the front, and her bare feet. She knew she looked as though she had just come from a bed in which she had been carousing.

"Madam, there has been trouble on the river with smugglers tonight," the senior riding officer informed her stiffly. She did not know him, but she did not know many of the Excisemen who came to the service from all manner of distances, seeking employment where it was to be had.

"We must inspect your house. Our apologies," the officer rapped out. The apology was empty, for encroachment was the rule, not the exception, when one lived near the Severn and its smugglers. Normally Charlotte would not have minded much, it was simply part of being on the river. She would have felt more protected than invaded, but tonight everything had reversed.

The officer waved his men into her home, and Charlotte retreated without a word—playing the part of wearied half-drunken cottager. She swallowed, not quite sure she could play the next part that would be asked of her.

"This room," the officer inquired, pointing to the closed door of her bedchamber.

Two men moved at once to open the door, and Charlotte gave a cry of protest. "Sirs, please—"

The two men stopped short, and the one could not

stop a grin from forming. The senior riding officer came and looked over the grinning man's shoulder, then whipped around to fix Charlotte with a disgusted look. He did not call her a harlot, but it was in his gaze.

He had done as she'd hoped he would: assumed the man in her bed was her drunken lover. What else could he assume from her dishabille, from the bits of clothing she'd strewn about her floor, from the heavy scent of wine that snaked forth from the room? What must he think of her if he had noted the child's cot? Charlotte blushed scarlet—knowing it would only underscore the impression she had meant to give.

Two men moved into the room. The one looked in her chest, the other under the bed. There was no wardrobe to open and examine; there was nowhere else for a person to hide in the room. They retreated as quickly as they'd inspected.

"Who is it?" the senior riding officer asked, a movement of his head indicating the occupant of the bed.

His subordinate was so cheeky as to cast Charlotte a lewd glance. "Lord Sebastian Whitbury." He smirked.

"Wha—?" Sebastian called from the bed, struggling to lift his head. He groaned.

"It is the Revenue men, my lord," Charlotte called to him, her heart racing in alarm lest he give them away. "There has been a run of the trade tonight. They are looking for someone."

"Two men," the senior man corrected her.

Sebastian gave another low groan.

Another underling came in through the front door, and the senior riding officer turned to him. "There is hay and straw in the stable, but no sign of usage tonight," the subordinate reported. "No horses there. No droppings."

The officer turned to Charlotte, who hugged her arms to her chest, feeling cold and half-naked and mortified. His gaze swept over her, a bold calculation as to her worth as a mistress. She saw calculation shift to dismissal—how could a riding officer compete with the favors of a marquess's son?

"Thank you for your cooperation. Ma'am," he belatedly added, as if the courtesy was only present due to his good manners, not because she deserved it.

With as little ceremony as they'd shown coming in, the Excisemen retreated.

Charlotte closed the door with hands that started to shake. She slid the bolt home, and pressed her forehead against the rough wood of the door, sending up a silent prayer of thanks for deliverance, even while a full flush of embarrassment still stained her cheeks.

She waited, listening to the sound of the men's horses retreating, and waited even longer. Finally, when she felt it was safe, that they had really gone not to return tonight, she moved to take up the kitchen planks. Armand peered up at her, blinking against the renewal of light. "I am safe?" he asked.

"Oui, monsieur," she assured him.

He stood, then startled. *"Madame*, is that blood?"

Charlotte put a hand to the wine stains still wetting her night rail's bodice. "It is only wine."

Armand eyed her dishabille, but declined to comment. Instead he crawled out of the hole, helped her restore the planks, and followed Charlotte into her bedchamber. The odor of alcohol was impossible to miss. *"Mon Dieu!* Did you give *monsieur* much wine?" Armand cried.

"It was a disguise." At his puzzled look, she sought another word. "A masquerade. So the Excisemen would not know he was injured."

"Ah!" Armand said with a spreading smile. "The Exciseman, they think he is drunk!" But his smile faded, and he eyed Charlotte's night rail again. "But what else do the men think, eh?"

"What would you think?" Charlotte said tartly, the blush returning to her face.

"That I have came here and make stop the love-making."

Charlotte pursed her lips, vaguely satisfied that she had indeed achieved what she'd intended, but aware that her "reward" would be social ostracism. By tomorrow afternoon, everyone within miles would know that the widowed Mrs. Deems was caught in a lovers' tryst with the son of the owner of the largest estate manor—Sebastian Whitbury, the local rogue.

She looked to where Sebastian had grown calm on the bed, his breathing even. It would seem he had given up the struggle to regain consciousness for now. Seeing his even breathing, it was difficult to resent the path she'd chosen, the choice she'd made to save him from capture, even though she knew it would make her future even murkier than it had been before tonight.

Armand looked from Charlotte to Sebastian, and back again. "*Madame*, what do we do now? Does *Monsieur* stay in your bed all night?"

"I am afraid so," Charlotte said. She shook her head. "Any surgeon is too far away, in Bristol, even if we dared to send for one."

"So . . . ?"

"So I hope the floor is not too uncomfortable," Charlotte said, pulling the topmost counterpane from the bed and handing it to Armand. "You should sleep while you can."

The Frenchman said nothing, not even when Charlotte moved to the bed and wriggled in under the remaining covers, turning her back to Sebastian's prone form. Armand simply wrapped the counterpane around himself and his bulky pouch, and then wormed his way under the bed. It was a poor hiding place, but it was better than allowing himself to sleep exposed, she supposed.

The quiet of the evening slowly crept back into the cottage, replacing the alarms and upheavals that had rippled through her home during the darkest part of the night. Armand's journey must have been difficult, or long, or both, for in short order the even breathing of slumber could be heard from beneath the bed.

While in her bed there was a weight, at once foreign and yet familiar, the weight of a man at Charlotte's side. Not even considering the marital act, sharing a bed had been a pleasure Charlotte had not expected to enjoy upon her marriage. To her surprise, she'd found that the shared warmth was a luxury, an unexpected benefit, but even more had been the companionship that came with lying near another human being. The dark was not as deep when one had but to stretch out a hand to touch a companion . . . but in time she had also learned that a bed could be warm to sleep in, but cold all the same.

Lying awake now, a man once again at her side, with whiffs of wine rising from the night rail slowly drying against her skin, Charlotte allowed her mind to wander where it would. She even toyed with the sure notion that in the morning she'd find she was a ruined woman in the eyes of all of Severn's Well.

If I am to be ruined, then why can I not at least have the sport that precedes such ruin? she asked herself with a small rueful laugh at her own expense. Truth was, it was not difficult to imagine sharing a bed with a whole and healthy Sebastian—and not to sleep, but to make love. Somehow it was easy to think of making love with the man beside her, and in the truest sense of the words. It was much more difficult to imagine the sex act being performed from a sense of duty or obligation, not with Sebastian. Not by him.

"Natalie Talbot," Charlotte said on the smallest whisper, "you are a fortunate woman."

But Charlotte did not want to think about Miss Talbot, not here, not after all that had happened, not with Sebastian's arm abutting her own. So she let herself be lulled by the warmth Sebastian unwittingly shared with her, and let any more fanciful thoughts or recriminations wait until the morning.

Chapter 17

Charlotte awoke, eyes still closed, to the feel of a hand brushing a strand of hair from her forehead. For a moment she wanted nothing more than to give herself over to that sweet touch, but the dawn heralded the harsh light of day and the hard press of consequences, and she opened her eyes.

Sebastian lay beside her, balanced on one elbow, looking down at her where she lay half facing him.

"While I thoroughly enjoy finding myself in bed with you, Charlotte," he said, smiling ever so slightly, "I have to wonder how I got here."

"You are awake!" she said, her voice coming out as a whisper of gratitude. He was going to be all right, just as she dared to hope. Tears stung her eyes, but she blinked them away, the better to be sure of the comprehension that had returned to his peacock blue gaze.

His hand reached out again, this time to run a finger down the curve of her cheek. There remained the wisp of a smile about his mouth, and Charlotte had to swallow a strong impulse to reach up and touch her fingers to that mouth.

"You were knocked unconscious," she told him.

"I remember being struck by an Exciseman, and bleeding." He moved his hand to gingerly feel the lump on his head, sucking air in through his teeth at its tenderness.

"Armand brought you up the tunnel to me."

Sebastian frowned, but he nodded. "I vaguely recall something of that. Where is Armand?"

"Here, *monsieur*," came the reply from under the bed. Sebastian's brows disappeared under the tousled blond fringe on his forehead. Despite the awkwardness of everything, Charlotte had to laugh.

He smiled down at her, but then the smile faded and a warmth spread through his gaze. "Alas," he said on a light whisper, "we are not alone, my dear." That thought must have reminded him to glance over his shoulder at the cot where Oscar ought to be, and he half twisted for a glance. When he twisted back to Charlotte, a lifted brow asked where her child was.

"He spent the night at the Hyatts'."

"Ah." A disturbance under the bed indicated that Armand was extricating himself. Sebastian made a face. "I suppose this means we must get out of bed."

Charlotte just nodded, but before she could toss back the blankets, Sebastian leaned forward and pressed a kiss to her mouth. His lips lingered there, long enough for Charlotte to meet his gaze with her own, long enough to make a thrumming spread like warmed honey through her limbs.

He pulled away. "That was for tending to me in my battered hour of need," he said in a voice meant just for her ears. "Thank you."

She nodded her thanks, self-conscious of saying anything in return with Armand emerging right there next to her side of the bed. Besides, she was not entirely sure she'd be able to say anything coherent; all she wanted to do was throw her arms around Sebastian's neck and kiss him again. They both turned to climb from the bed, and she was sure her face must be flaming red. Both men would no doubt put this down to embarrassment, but it was at least half exhilaration as well. She knew she would remember that kiss, and the feel and look of Sebastian in her bed, for a long, long time.

As she slipped her house mules onto her feet, she saw out of the corner of her eye that although Sebastian put a hand to the wall to steady himself for a moment, he quickly recovered, shaking his head with seeming ill-effect.

He looked down at himself. "By Jove! How much blood did I give up?"

"Most of that is wine," she assured him.

"Wine?"

"The *madame*, she made the room smell of so much wine, and the Exciseman thinks you are drunk," Armand explained with an expansive gesture of approval that emerged from under the counterpane he'd draped around his shoulders.

"Excisemen?" Sebastian threw Charlotte an alarmed glance.

"They thought you were making the love with *madame*."

"What?" Sebastian cried. He must have seen verification written on her face, for he blanched. "I do not understand."

"Let us have some tea," Charlotte suggested grimly as she drew on her dressing gown. "Then I will explain."

As they sat down at her kitchen table, Armand dragged her sitting room chair over to join Sebastian and Charlotte where they sat on her two kitchen chairs. Over a pot of tea and some of the remaining sweet buns, Charlotte told of Sebastian's occasional bouts with consciousness, his outbursts, the fact that in a semi-lucid condition he could not be hidden in the secret space with Armand. Lastly, with her gaze fixed on a ribbon on her dressing gown, she explained how she had managed to make Sebastian and herself seem occupied all night at something other than smuggling.

He stared at her in dawning horror. "But . . . but your reputation! You are ruined!"

She shrugged, not even trying to lift her gaze up to meet his. "Yes, I must be." She took a deep breath and plunged on, "I will leave Severn's Well, move to . . ." Words failed her—she could not think where she might try to establish a new home for her and Oscar.

"Where? How? You have no funds with which to make another move!"

She put up her chin. "I would if I sold this cottage."

He sat back in his chair, stunned. "But it is yours free and clear. Why surrender that? Where would you go? Severn's Well at least had some connection, some feeling of 'home' for you."

"Home is where your people are," Charlotte said, pouring herself another cup of tea. "As long as I have Oscar, I have a home."

"No." Sebastian leaped up from his chair and began to pace. "No, this is wrong."

"Sit down, *monsieur*! You will make yourself ill and, er, fall into the asleep again," Armand suggested in his inventive English.

Sebastian did not sit down, but instead stooped in front of Charlotte, his insistent gaze at last capturing hers. "You cannot afford to move," he repeated.

"I will manage," Charlotte insisted, pursing her mouth to keep her lower lip from trembling. She would manage, she knew, but there was no joy in the prospect of moving yet again. Of moving far from Sebastian. Although, what would be worse? To never see him again, or to be near him while he married Miss Talbot?

He scowled, thinking. "I saw you getting off the Mail coach two days ago. Does that have something to do with your insistence on moving? You cannot want to move. After all, this will be gossiped over, yes, but we could stare anyone down. There is no need for you to remove from Severn's Well. When I marry Natalie, that will put an end to any idle rumormongering . . ."

Sebastian stopped cold, having caught the skeptical look Armand threw his way. "In a little town such as this?" Armand said, an eyebrow arched in derision. "Gossip go away? Never, *monsieur*."

Sebastian looked once more to Charlotte, perhaps hoping to see a different opinion there. Whatever he saw, his shoulders slumped.

She put her hand over one of his. "Dawn has already broken. You should go home now, before your brother learns you never came home last night."

He uttered a curse under his breath. "Not my brother so much," he said, managing a weak smile. "But Timmons! I ordered him to go to bed last night. He has missed too much sleep of late. But when he finds me gone this morning and my bed untouched—!"

Charlotte rose to her feet, thereby forcing the men to rise to their feet as well.

Sebastian stepped close enough to take up her hands, which he shook gently. "Do not fret. We will think of something. You should not have to leave your home." He frowned. "There has to be a way."

"Monsieur," Armand said on a polite little cough.

"Yes?"

"Monsieur, you have but to marry *madame.* You have, er, made of her the wicked woman, and you are to marry her, yes?"

Sebastian looked into Charlotte's face with shock— clearly, the idea had not yet occurred to him. At least he had not dismissed the notion out of hand, for it had yet to occur to him . . . but he *should* dismiss it. His heart lay elsewhere.

She shook her head vehemently. "No!" she said. "I do not want to marry."

She would rather move a hundred, a thousand miles from here than force Sebastian to marry her. She might have borne another marriage like the one she'd shared with Jarvis, but not with Sebastian. She would rather watch him wed Natalie Talbot than marry him herself and live devoid of his love. There had grown an affection between them, undeniably, and he had radiated moments of blood-stirring attraction several times—he'd even kissed her not half an hour ago—but his love?

Nothing less would do. She would not make that mistake twice. And she had no reason to think he loved her. It was not enough that she loved him. She would not trap him. He had not chosen to lie in her bed. *He* had not compromised her—she had chosen to compromise herself, so she must be the one to pay the penalty.

"You must go before you are missed," she repeated to him, hoping her expression was as devoid of emotion as she tried to make it be.

He dropped her hands, a wave of frustration clearly washing over him. "Charlotte, I—"

"Go."

He nodded, reluctantly, but then he moved to the sitting room, his glance taking in and surely divining why a counterpane hung at a certain place on her wall.

"Armand," he called to the Frenchman, who then preceded him out the door. Sebastian hesitated there, one hand on the doorjamb. "Charlotte, I will think of something. There is a solution somehow."

She nodded, trying to look more convinced than she felt, only to gasp as a coach came rumbling down the road at an unholy pace, rocks spitting from under the wheels.

Armand gave a cry and ran to the far side of her cottage, and Sebastian cursed. But then his face cleared. "Timmons!"

The young valet-coachman brought the horses to a thundering halt, scarcely securing the reins before leaping down from the coaching box. "M'lord!" the young man cried, clearly delighted to have found Sebastian. Then horror filled his face as he stared at his master's clothing. "Blood!"

"I am fine, Timmons. Does anyone know you've come for me?"

"I don't know, sir. Took the coach out in the dark, I did, when the other lads were asleep. Been out driving for an hour, as you never come home! I thought you was caught, sir, or dead."

"Not yet," Sebastian replied. "I will explain all as we hurry home. Armand!" he called, the cry bringing the Frenchman peeping around the corner of the house. Seeing that Sebastian was waving him over, the Frenchman relaxed and stepped forward.

"Get in!" Sebastian ordered Armand, moving to throw open the coach door. "We are taking you to where you can be hidden until I can arrange your safe passage to the captain who will sail you to America."

Armand nodded, Sebastian closed the coach door, and turned to climb up on the box beside Timmons.

He looked down at Charlotte, giving her a long, concerned gaze. Finally he shook his head, a gesture of frustration. "Thank you. For saving me from the Revenue men."

She did not trust herself to speak, so she merely nodded in somber acceptance.

The valet turned the horses in the wide yard before the house, and then the coach rumbled away. Charlotte watched, a curious stab—it felt ridiculously like joy—going through her when Sebastian twisted to gaze back at her. He touched his fingers to his hatless head in a salute of sorts, and Charlotte managed to produce a shaky smile for him.

She closed the door, knowing she was closing another door as well, this one on any future she might have had in Severn's Well and her snug little cottage.

All the same, to save Sebastian, she would do it again in a heartbeat.

Two hours later, Sebastian waited in Natalie Talbot's drawing room, to which he'd almost been refused admittance. He'd stared the butler down, saying in an insistent voice that the butler must be sure to take a note up to Miss Talbot.

He knew her father was not home, because he had waited down the street until he'd seen Lord Lamont roll away in his carriage. Only then had Sebastian approached the front door.

The past two hours had been full, as Sebastian had cast about in his mind for what he must do. Unfortunately all thoughts led to the conclusion that *he* must be the first to tell Natalie of the tale that was sure to reach her ears, to make it as palatable as possible for her. But, along with his tumbled thoughts, Sebastian had also had a dozen things to accomplish.

He'd taken Armand into Gideon's wine cellar, which had its own exterior door from the rear of the house. It was not a well-fitted door, and so a little light crept into the otherwise dark and dank space. They could not risk leaving Armand with a candle or a lantern, but at least he'd not have to sit in total darkness. Timmons was to return to the man soon with food and blankets.

Armand settled, Sebastian had then sneaked into the house through the kitchens, surprising Cook, who muttered under her breath, "Men! Coming home in the wee hours!"

He'd given Cook a noisy kiss on her cheek as he passed by, nearly making her drop a bowl of stirred eggs, and flew through the house and up to his room. He threw himself under his covers, only to ring for a servant. When the footman came, Sebastian hid his dressed state under the counterpane and requested a hot bath.

Timmons arrived halfway through Sebastian's bathing off the scents of wine and blood and stucco dust. The remainder of Sebastian's toilette had been spent in soothing the valet's ruffled feathers by explaining all that had happened last night.

"Cor!" had been Timmons's unhelpful response, but then a puzzled frown had settled over his young face. "But don't you have to marry Mrs. Deems now, m'lord? I mean, it won't look right and all if'n you don't."

Sebastian had closed his eyes and sighed loudly. "Normally, yes. But it is more complex than that in this matter. Not least of which is that I must call upon Miss Talbot this morning."

"Huh," said Timmons, which skeptical sound earned him a dark glance from his master. The valet must have decided Sebastian was as turned out as he could make him, for Timmons retreated at once to the small attached room where Sebastian's extra boots, brushes, and whatnots were kept.

". . . prefer the blue-eyed one over the brown-eyed girl any day," Sebastian overheard the valet muttering, but he chose to pretend he had not.

Dressed in his finest morning coat, Sebastian had then breakfasted with his unsuspecting brother and sister-in-law. He had then proceeded to walk into the village, and had waited until he saw Lord Lamont leave to go about his daily duties.

As a marquess's son, and a member of one of the largest estates in the county, Sebastian knew he could intimidate the haughtiest of butlers if he chose. Intimidate or simply charge past—whichever was going to serve his purpose of seeing Natalie.

He'd been correct; the butler had caved in to his demand that a note be sent up to Natalie. She joined him not five minutes later, proving that she for one was glad to have him call.

"Lord Sebastian!"

There was no one else here to hear her greeting. Why could she not have simply called him Sebastian? They were intimates, were they not? Something more than friends? Of course, the only people who did call him by only his Christian name were his brothers and Charlotte—and he had coerced Charlotte into doing so. He sighed as he stood to take Natalie's hands in his.

The sight of her, her black hair beautifully coifed, with a blue ribbon to match her gown winding through her locks, made the center of his chest start to burn. The burn felt very like guilt. Guilt that he had never ordered flowers sent to her. Guilt that he had slept, however involuntarily, in another woman's bed last night. Guilt for what he must explain to her today, before anyone else could carry tales to her ears. And lastly, guilt for not being able to tell her the whole truth.

He knew it was wrong. He knew he wanted Natalie to be at her very best today, to act as his life's helpmeet at this most stressful of times . . . yet he was not even going to do her the courtesy of giving her the entire truth. The thing of it was, Charlotte could have borne having the entire facts thrust upon her, but Natalie had not yet been bruised by life's inclemencies, and she was less prepared to see through the muck to the diamond underneath. Therefore, only the diamond could be presented.

"Oh, Lord Sebastian," she said, her eyes sparkling, "I am so glad you have come to call." She took back her hands, and he wondered briefly why she had, for she only folded them in her lap. Charlotte would have left her hands in his, would have seen that he was anxious to tell her something. They were only a few years apart in age, the two women, but a century apart in experience.

"I have to tell you about our supper at Heversham's home yesterday!" Natalie went on, her eyes dancing with amusement. "It was the most distasteful experience. It is not so big a house as your brother's mansion, but it is very well appointed—"

"Natalie—"

"I did not care much for the Chinese Room, but everything else was very pleasing. More than the house, however, I have to tell you about supper! I was seated to Lord Heversham's right, so I could hear every time his teeth clacked as he chewed! He has false teeth, can you imagine? I understand they are carved from ivory. I was quite horrified that they positively clacked—!"

"Natalie," he interrupted again with a small, patient smile. "There is a matter of some import—"

"This will make you laugh. Well, I was so horrified by that clacking, that I scarce could eat my own food, which was just as well because everything was soft. Like food you make for an infant! The veal was beyond tender— it had become sodden. The soup was strained, with nary so much as a whole pea to be had in it. There were potatoes, but they were boiled almost to paste—"

"I am pleased that you did not enjoy Lord Heversham's table, truly, quite pleased," he said, his relish of her distaste however far exceeded by a growing awareness that they might not have much time to discuss something of far greater gravity. "But I have something more important to discuss—"

Now Natalie interrupted him. "More important?" She gave a small frown, clearly taken aback.

"Yes, more important." His patience thinned, for they could be interrupted at any time, even by Lord Lamont returning.

"More important than cricket, I pray?" she said coolly.

Sebastian started to respond, but then he just met her gaze with his own, hearing her hurt under the comment. It was enough to divert him for a moment from his more serious topic.

"Do I always talk about myself, Natalie?" he asked on a sigh.

"Well, no," she admitted reluctantly. "But you do talk about cricket a great deal."

He did, there was no arguing that. "Do we ever talk

about you?" he asked with a growing sense of discomfort. He tried to recall any conversation between them that had gone beyond her appearance or dances or social events. They'd had so few moments alone in which to really talk. Not like the hours he'd had on the cliffs with Charlotte, where talking was the sole defense against sleep's siren call. No, that was not true. His talks with Charlotte had been more than that—they'd been stimulating, invigorating, unfettered by conventions. He'd never been in any danger of falling asleep when Charlotte engaged him in conversation.

He tried to imagine Natalie sitting on the cliffs for hours, always coming up with something to add to a discussion—even one about cricket.

"Do you find cricket tedious?" he asked her, gazing into Natalie's eyes to gauge the truth of any reply she might give him.

"Of course not." Some of her frosty demeanor retreated, and she reached to place her hand over his. He was glad for it, that she had reached out to touch him. When they married he would have to explain how important it was to him, this business of touching, of being reached out for.

Charlotte had made that same gesture recently, trying to comfort him, to tell him he was not to marry her even though his presence in her bed had ruined her reputation. The memory made him want to frown, but he suppressed the instinct, not wanting Natalie to wonder what could have made him frown.

"Well, cricket *can* be tedious sometimes," Natalie conceded.

Time was wasting; he ought to hurry on with his invented explanations, the convenient lie that he'd been found toppled in the road, fallen from his horse. Only feel the lump, here, that was proof that he'd struck a tree limb with his head. It had been Mrs. Deems who had found him and who had kindly cared for him. But an inspection of her home by the Customs men had made an innocent moment look like something it was not. More to the point: that very same innocent moment would be seen by others as a dalliance, and rumors would flourish.

He must tell Natalie that he would have to take all the money he'd hoped to take as profit—his reward, of whose source Natalie could never be honestly told—and use it to help Mrs. Deems move where gossip could not sting her for her kindness. But he and Natalie could still marry, and live with his brother until Sebastian was able to find another path and turn another profit. Their plans must change, but not so very much.

He had the story well-rehearsed . . . but, be damned, at this moment the story seemed less pressing than Natalie's opinion. By Jove, he had the woman to himself, and they would talk, really talk for once.

"Natalie, let us sit," he said, the words an order and not a request.

Natalie lifted a brow, but she moved to take a seat on a settee, and Sebastian joined her. "Tell me," he said, gazing steadily into her brown eyes, "what you like most about cricket."

"Well," she considered a moment, clearly surprised by the question. "Cricket? Well, er, I like when you get your runs, especially a six," she said with a nod of approval.

"Yes, of course, but what else? What about cricket *entertains* you?"

Natalie's brow wrinkled as she thought a moment. "I will tell you what I do *not* like. I do not like when nothing happens for ages upon ages."

"But something is always happening! You just have to be aware of it. There is strategy, and moving the players, and—" He stopped himself, realizing that these more subtle aspects of the game could not be learned in a drawing room. He would have to have her come to a game, many games, and he'd sit by her side and tell her what was occurring so she learned the shadings of the play.

He sat back on the settee, knowing a frown had settled on his features, but unable to stave it off. "If . . ." he began, feeling a little stupid, but then he felt compelled to ask anyway. "If you thought it might rain, would you still come to watch me play cricket?"

"I suppose. If it were not a downpour."

"What if it snowed?"

She gave him a quizzical look. "Well, I suppose I would tend not to go out in snow. But cricket is never played in snow, is it?"

"What if I asked you to picnic by the river with me, at midnight?"

She laughed. "Lord Sebastian! You are in a frivolous mood today!"

"But would you?"

"I suppose," she said with a small shrug of her shoulders.

He gave her what must be a very odd smile, with only the left corner of his mouth rising—it was actually the most of a smile he could summon, a twisted quirk. Just like that, he felt something spreading through his veins, not warm at all, but cool and thick and oddly sad. Was this the feeling of resignation? Of a lovely dream dissipating like chalk marks in the rain?

She had given him the wrong answer. "I suppose," she had said. She had answered lightly, easily, without realizing the question ran much deeper, without noting that the question had required any answer other than "I suppose." She had been playing a parlor game, never hearing in his voice nor seeing in his eyes that he asked so much of her.

He knew in that instant that he did not love Natalie. He found her beautiful, and graceful, and even charming, but he did not love her. He never had. What he'd once described as puppy love had proven itself to be nothing more than that: infatuation. In his life he'd had only peripheral examples of the kind of love a man ought to have for a woman, but nothing at home to teach him the depth of feeling that bonded a man and a woman's hearts together.

It had taken real love to make him know the difference.

"You have gone all pale, Lord Sebastian. Are you well?" Natalie asked, concern lacing her voice.

"No," he said, then gave a small, self-deprecating laugh. "I have had a terrible thought, Miss Talbot, and it has made me feel . . . peculiar."

Natalie was not stupid; she cocked her head just a bit at his reversion to using her surname. Oh, she was clever enough—but he did not love her. "A terrible thought?"

"I realize now that you ought to marry Lord Heversham, not me."

They stared at one another, Natalie's eyes wide in shock. "I beg your pardon?"

"No, my dear lady, I beg yours. I have led you a merry chase, and it will not suit."

"What?"

"I . . ." he hesitated a moment, then gave her as much of the truth as she would appreciate, as much of it as would salvage her pride. She was not at fault. She had committed no crime other than being a woman he could admire at a distance but could not love up close. "I am afraid I betrayed your trust last night, Miss Talbot," he went on, his voice firming as he spoke. "You will hear rumors, soon enough, that I spent the evening in the company of . . . of another lady, and in all honesty I must tell you I did so."

"Lord Sebastian!" Her eyes were wide, but to his great surprise he did not see deep hurt there. Confusion and censure, certainly, but if she felt pain it was to her pride not her heart.

He thought of how she had taken her hands from his when she could easily have left them, could have relished the touch of skin on skin, and knew he had not harmed her beyond repair, not really.

"I understand that our association cannot go forward from here," he said, rising to his feet. "Your father would never approve of me now."

"Well, I . . ." she tried to argue the point, but of course she could not.

He sketched her a bow, as elegant as he could make it, a kind of apology for both the bluntness of his professions and the termination of their affections. "My lady, you have my regrets."

"Lord Sebastian," she said, a softer calling of his name, but one tinged all the same with a comprehending resignation. She stood as well, and he could see a mingling of anger and something else in her eyes. Regret? Or relief? Had Heversham's mansion been a temptation after all? And who could blame Natalie if had been, for there she would be mistress, not merely a tolerated occupant as she would have been in his brother's home.

"I pray you marry well and happily," he said, and meant the words.

He bowed again, and turned, and without a backward glance he exited Miss Talbot's drawing room and her life, leaving her openmouthed in his wake.

For several long moments, disgrace clung to his shoulders, but with each step he took it slipped away, falling to the floor like a neglected cape. Natalie would recover and be glad, probably sooner than later, that their association had ended. But thoughts of Natalie were already retreating. His steps hurried, and then he was running, and he knew he had but one destination: he had to talk to Charlotte.

There was no question, she could have anything she wished of him. Any money he might earn as his reward, any money Gideon would give him. He would help her move to a bigger town, a grander house, a more comfortable existence, whatever she wished. She had but to ask, and he would get it for her. He would even give her his name, if he could, if she would have it . . . except it was already too late for that.

He had been blind too long. He had cost himself any opportunity to convince Charlotte that he admired her above all women. She would not enter a second marriage with doubts in her heart, and she had every reason to doubt the man who'd been "devoted" to another woman until five minutes ago.

There were no words to convince her his eyes had been unveiled, no action he could take to show her his heart had been wedged open and light allowed to flood in. . . .

Except to remain her friend. There might be some hope in time passing . . . that fragile prospect was all that was left to him. He would live near wherever she lived, that he might see her, might continue to live on the meager crumbs of optimism.

Still, even if she never took his heart, he would see that she accepted his generosity, all that he could give, because it had been his selfishness that had ruined her ability to remain in Severn's Well.

He hurried through the village and up the hill to his brother's home, intent on obtaining a carriage for the drive to Charlotte's home.

"Sebastian!" he was hailed as soon as he entered the house. "There you are."

His brother stood in the open double doors that led into the front salon, three other men flanking him: their own village's Alderman Wallace, a wealthy-looking man with too many fobs on his chain, and a man dressed in somber hues. "Sebastian!" Gideon hailed again, waving his youngest brother into the room.

"I cannot—" Sebastian began breathlessly.

"Oh, I think you can, and you will want to," Gideon assured Sebastian with an eager smile. "You will be very interested in what these gentlemen have to say about cricket."

"Cricket?" Sebastian echoed.

Chapter 18

Sebastian paced inside the quayside shack, driven half-mad at waiting for the captain of the America-bound ship to appear. The sun was leaning toward the afternoon part of the sky, beginning to cast longer shadows. Twenty minutes had already elapsed since he'd come to the quay—twenty more minutes that kept him from calling on Charlotte. Unfortunately he could not stomp about and demand the man be brought to him, for this was a furtive meeting.

So he paced, as though to echo the turmoil inside him. Fate kept interfering, keeping him from Charlotte. As each hour ticked by since he'd left Miss Talbot's home, he wondered what Charlotte must think of him, of how he had yet to return to her cottage with any resolutions or offers of support. He longed to be at her side, to let her know that she was not abandoned in the disgrace he'd brought to her door. He who loved to flirt, to wile away his days, who had spent his most recent days in idle pursuit of pleasure, balked now at any indolence or delay that kept him from showing Charlotte that he cared about her and her son's well-being.

The meeting with Alderman Wallace, the wealthy merchant by the name of Mr. Longacre, and the third man who'd been introduced as a magistrate, had stretched on far longer than Sebastian would have liked. It had proved, however, to be filled with the happiest of all offers for him. These men of authority wanted to form something new: a cricket club for the county of Gloucester.

And they wanted Sebastian to be its overseer.

"For a sum of five hundred pounds a year, you would

be expected to establish teams with regulation schedules, recruit players, and instruct where and as needed within the county. It would mean quite a bit of travel during the fair weather months," the magistrate, Mr. Polk, warned him. "So naturally we would provide a horse and gig in addition to the salary."

Sebastian had found himself grinning rather foolishly, dazzled at the very idea that he could make a living wage at the sport that he loved. "Make it a wagon for hauling supplies, and it is a deal," he said at once.

"Now, lad, you may want to think this over. There will be a great burden resting on your shoulders, since the success or failure of the Gloucester Cricket Club would be primarily made with you."

"Just as I would wish it to be," Sebastian had assured Polk, his smile widening, his palms practically itching at plans that were already forming in his mind.

There had been more terms to discuss, and meetings to be agreed to, fees to be fixed, and hopes of a future cricket oval to be considered. Sebastian had nodded and commented and agreed to think about their suggestions, and all the while could scarcely wait to tell this news to Charlotte. If she insisted on moving away, could he convince her to stay within Gloucester county?

No matter. If he must leave the county to be near her, then he would surrender this offer of employment with only a sigh of passing regret. As she had said "Home is where your people are"; and she had become his home, even if she never came to know it.

He'd just been about to hurry away from the successful meeting, leaving Gideon to salute the agreement with the three gentlemen, when Gideon had summoned him to one side with a look.

They excused themselves, stepped outside the double doors, and into an alcove. Gideon put his hands on Sebastian's shoulders. "Congratulations, little brother. I know you will make a go of this idea."

"Thank you." Sebastian could not help grinning anew.

"Now, I have something odd for you, which I will expect you to explain later because it is clear your feet are on fire to be elsewhere at the moment."

"I have lost all my subtlety," Sebastian said lightly, not caring if he had, so long as he was finally free to go to Charlotte.

Gideon reached into his coat pocket to hand Sebastian a folded missive. "It is from some ship's captain tied at Paulmuth Quay."

"I know the place." It was a tattered dock a few miles away, between Bristol and Clevedon, little used because it was in need of repair.

"A cabin boy brought the note, and said you would not be sending a reply."

Sebastian unfolded the note, seeing what he'd expected to find. "Captain Ramson, HMS *Babylonia*" was written in a spiky slanted hand.

He looked up at his brother, sensing the questions Gideon restrained from asking, and nodded. "There is in fact much I have to tell you, Gideon," he said. "But later."

Gideon made a dismissing motion with his head. "Then go."

Sebastian flashed him a quick smile, and then bounded up to his room. There he fetched a money purse, and then it was down the back stairs and out the house to the stables. It was short work to rouse a dozing Timmons, and then to pull the coach close to the outside door to Gideon's wine cellar. Armand, awakened from a daytime slumber in the gloomy wine cellar, was hustled into the coach, which Timmons set in motion at once.

Sebastian handed the Frenchman the money purse. "You have had to travel very lightly, *monsieur*," he said. "You will require money to establish yourself in America. You sail on the *Babylonia*. You are not listed on her manifest. No one knows you are aboard but her captain and crew, and they are paid well enough not to remember ever seeing you. Her purser can change this to American money for you."

"Merci beaucoup," Armand had said over a bow of thanks from where he sat. "Your prince, he gives Ar-

mand into the hands of a good man, yes? You, *monsieur*."

Sebastian had nodded in recognition of the compliment.

Now he felt like throttling someone. Where was Captain Ramson? What was the delay? There should be none. Sebastian had sent a missive, to which the man had replied with one of his own, which was the signal that all was ready. So why this tarrying?

"I hope the plans you have in that pouch of yours are worth all this bother," Sebastian growled at Armand.

"*Madame,* she says to me much the same thing."

"Did she?" Sebastian paused, his anger dissipating. Truth was, if anyone was inconvenienced—not to say harmed—by Armand and the steps Sebastian had taken to get the man unnoted and unseen to America, it was Charlotte.

What had she thought when he had not seen the obvious at once, that he ought to offer her marriage since she'd been compromised on his behalf? He'd been too set on pursuing the flight of fancy named Miss Talbot, too fixated on reaching out toward imagined happiness to see that the real thing stood before him. What indeed must she have thought of him, that his first response toward her difficulty had not been the chivalrous one?

She had thought he could not love her, as Jarvis Deems had not. Small wonder she had refused the offer he had only belatedly thought to offer her.

"So what are these precious plans of yours anyway?" he snarled at Armand.

To his surprise, Armand was not loath at all to share the plans, for he slipped the pouch over his head and unbuckled it. He pulled out a folded oilcloth, which was spread open to reveal a large piece of parchment, folded several times over. He unfolded the paper with care, revealing a drawing. "*Voilà!*" Armand exclaimed. "The machine for the making of war."

Sebastian moved closer to the Frenchman's side and peered down at the drawing. There was a lightly sketched human shape imposed over a more defined drawing of a vehicle with two wheels in tandem, one front and one back. It had a frame that supported the wheels one behind the other. The sketched figure was seated on a long padded seat, the legs hanging on either side of the frame to touch the ground. There was a bar that intersected the vehicle's body several inches in front of the figure, to which the figure's hands held.

"What is it?" Sebastian asked, utterly baffled.

"Your English importance men have named it a War Wheeler."

"War Wheeler?"

Armand smiled, the inventor tutoring the apprentice. "It takes the place of the horse in battle. A man makes it go by touching his feet to the earth. The man does not grow tired too soon, not like marching, and the vehicle, she needs no food or water. She is very, er, not take much money."

"Inexpensive. Not costly," Sebastian supplied.

"*Oui*, not costly. And here"—he pointed proudly at a metal tube affixed to the frame that supported the wheels—"a spear is put, and then the man can spear another man in battle."

Sebastian frowned at the drawing. "How does the contraption turn?"

"You lean, like so." Armand leaned from side to side.

"Would it not be better to have one of the wheels be able to turn, like the front wheels of a phaeton, for easier maneuvering?"

Armand's lip curled into a sneer. "You are like the leaders of France, always saying 'this could be better' and 'horses can go more far than can a man, who must eat and drink more if his horse does not do the work for him.' You have no understanding of the greatness of this idea. This War Wheeler, it cannot die, like the horse can."

"But the wheels can break, as they do on a carriage. And a horse can be trained to attack, giving a man yet another weapon—"

Armand made a disgusted noise. "You ask the questions, like your prince. He does not know if this is 'quite the idea I had hoped for,'" Armand mimicked with disdain.

"But surely you see that a horse can jump a fence or a hedge. You would have to carry this . . . this apparatus over on your own back, if you could get over the hedge at all! How much does it weigh?"

Armand snapped up his drawing, crisply folding it. "All of you—! You all think only 'this is different, so it must be bad.' You have no understanding, no vision! I will not discuss this with you." His accent grew thicker with his agitation. "No, *monsieur,* I will not! I will not discuss my genius with a *stupide* man who does not even see love under his nose!"

"Love?" Sebastian put a hand to his forehead, confused by the shift in the conversation.

"*Oui, monsieur,* the love of *Madame* Charlotte. You do not see it, so I know you are *stupide* man."

"I scarcely know Charlotte," Sebastian said, but the protest was hollow. He had not known her long, but all the same he felt he knew her well. "How could she possibly be in love with me, or I with her? You are mistaken, *monsieur.*"

"Oh yes, I am mistaken. Just as I am mistaken with my War Wheeler, *oui.*" Armand rolled his eyes, thoroughly out of patience with his host.

A knock interrupted any further discussion. Captain Ramson entered, saying, "My apologies, gentlemen. We were waiting for reports from our posted men as to whether there had been any Customs men or unfamiliar faces about. But all is clear. Still"—he turned to Armand—"if you would be so kind as to don this domino, sir?"

Armand donned the domino, pulling the hood well over his head. The pouch on his back gave him a hunchbacked appearance. Sebastian thought he looked more noticeable dressed this way in broad daylight than not, but his charge over the Frenchman was coming to an end, so it was not his concern. He shook the captain's hand, who said, "I will alert the proper authorities as to your completion of this matter."

Sebastian nodded in thanks, then offered a second nod to Armand, who still bristled at the insult to his work, but who nodded back.

As Armand walked away in the captain's wake, Sebastian found himself hoping the Prince Regent had not chosen to have these War Wheelers replace horses—the idea was absurd. Laughable, even. All the same, he would mention the vehicle to Gideon before his brother returned to London for the sitting of Parliament. Forearmed with a warning, Gideon would no doubt choose to vote against such a contraption should the matter ever come up in the House of Lords.

Sebastian watched from the shack as Armand was safely escorted aboard the *Babylonia* with no alarms raised. As soon as the ship set her sails and drifted away from the aging quay, he left the shack and found his coach.

"Mrs. Deems's," he instructed Timmons.

Just saying her name gave him a flutter in his very center. All those times he had flirted and played and been challenged by her, and he'd never thought to look at her through fresh eyes.

No, that was not true. A few times he'd been swayed toward her, reaching out for something intangibly wonderful, something irresistible. Just this morning he had kissed her while she lay beside him—and God knew where things might have gone from there if the Frenchman had not been playing chaperone under the bed.

He ached, deep in his soul. He ought to feel jubilant that he had seen his duty through, that a promised reward of ten thousand pounds was to be his—presuming the Prince of Wales was better about paying private debt than he was his public ones. Certainly Sebastian ought to be floating on clouds at the offer he'd received to be the overseer of a new cricket club.

These things, however, were just that: things. Their value to him now was only in knowing they made it possible for him to do everything he could in recompense to Charlotte.

Charlotte . . . Armand had said there was *love*

there. . . . Had Armand seen Sebastian's attraction to Charlotte? Had he sensed that Sebastian's regard had slipped into something greater, something even finer than friendship? Had he seen what Sebastian had refused to let himself see for far too long? Or had Armand sensed some such notion from *Charlotte* . . . toward Sebastian?

He shook his head, reminding himself with a sober frown that Armand had thought his invention a worthy design—which was evidence enough that the man was not the most sensible of persons.

Sebastian put his head back against the squabs of his coach and moaned in confusion. On one hand the world had suddenly decided to hand him so much—but it seemed the world did not give without also taking away. It was not losing Natalie that he thought of; walking away from her had carried far too little sting.

But the idea of losing Charlotte—! He would not do it. Not unless Charlotte herself bid him leave her be, that she wanted no part of his friendship. He would hate to go out of her life, but he would if she asked him to, but *only* if she asked him to. It would never be his own choice.

He stared morosely at the floor of his coach, as if he could find his heart somewhere down around his boots.

When Timmons stopped before Charlotte's cottage, Sebastian's breathing caught in his lungs out of simple raw nerves, but there was nothing for it. He had to face her decisions, whatever they were, sometime.

" 'Bastian!" Oscar called out from where he looked out the window from a chair.

Charlotte dropped a just-washed dish, not even noticing if it broke as she turned to hurry to the window to watch wide-eyed and heart pounding as he climbed down from the coach.

She was half surprised he had come back to her home, now so much later. Hours had passed since he'd left her cottage this morning, hours in which she supposed rumors of her ruin had been rampaging through their small community. When he did not come, hour after hour, she'd begun to wonder if he'd realized the alternate solution he sought did not exist. She had but two choices: marry him, or move. She'd refused the former . . . and she'd begun to wonder if she would be doing the latter entirely on her own, with nary another word from him.

But that had been difficult to believe, that he'd never come back. Sebastian was many things, but he was neither coward nor churl. He might withdraw his friendship, but he would not abandon her entirely. Therefore, she'd been left to wonder what could his long absence mean? That he'd publicly aligned himself with Miss Talbot and dared not approach Charlotte on the same day? That his brother, out of embarrassment or snobbery, had forbidden him to "take the widow as a mistress"? That solving her problems would involve Sebastian's attention, monies, and servants, but not his own person directly?

But he was here, he'd come back. Just the sight of him was enough to make her mouth tremble and her hands shake.

Charlotte wiped her unsteady hands dry, and turned from the window in time to spy the unbroken dish. She moved to pick it up, as if putting the room in order might also order her thoughts, but she had no luck there. Just as she drew off her apron, Sebastian's knock sounded on the door. She forced herself to walk calmly and open it to him.

He looked very fine, his dark coat beautifully cut, his buff breeches well-fitted. His boots were polished, a fine high crown hat in his hand, and his beautiful hair was artfully tousled.

"Sebastian," she greeted him. If he looked, he'd be able to see that her hands were shaking, but at least her voice did not betray her.

" 'Bastian!" Oscar cried out again, scrambling off his chair. He ran to Sebastian, stopping short and looking up at the man towering over him. He put up his arms, clearly signaling that he wished to be picked up.

Charlotte opened her mouth to tell Oscar that no gentleman in his fine clothes wished to pick up grubby-fingered little boys, but before she could, Sebastian bent down and scooped Oscar up.

"Good day, Oscar," Sebastian greeted the boy.

"G'day, 'Bastian," Oscar replied.

Charlotte could not say why, but something in the exchange broke through the tension of the moment, and suddenly a semblance of sense returned to her, and she thought to step back and allow Sebastian into the house.

"Tea?" she questioned, even managing to find a fleeting smile for his benefit. After all, what was the worst he could say to her but what she already knew, that she'd have to leave Severn's Well?

"I like my tea with sugar," he answered her.

Sebastian sat at her table and bounced a giggling Oscar on his crossed leg while Charlotte prepared the pot. When she brought cups and saucers to the table, he put Oscar down, assured the boy they'd do more "bouncies" later, and turned to her while Oscar toddled into the bedroom in pursuit of his carved soldiers.

"Well now, Charlotte," Sebastian said, and Charlotte felt her mouth tremble into something close to a smile at how normal and *Sebastian* he sounded. A semblance of normality had settled between them as she'd tended to the everyday task of making tea, and Charlotte was grateful for it. The moment had lost its acuteness, allowing her nerves, which had been tightening all day, to relax a bit. Perhaps she and Sebastian could remain friends after all—albeit not friends who touched or spent long evenings together.

"Your son seems to be content to play in the bedchamber," Sebastian noted. "I am glad, for we must talk."

Charlotte nodded.

"And I confess that while I was enjoying your son's squeals a great deal—" Sebastian said, perhaps delaying the talk they must have. It made Charlotte smile just a little to think that he must not be entirely comfortable with this reunion either.

"Liar," she said, taking a light tone, trying to make this interview easier on both of them.

"I was not lying." Sebastian looked affronted for a

moment, but then he let a slight smile rise to his lips.
"Well, a little. I like your son, but I have little doubt
constant squeals would pale after a while. It is a good
thing that he does not squeal all the time."

She conceded that with a little nod of her head as she
poured them each a steaming cup of tea. "I have to
agree. And imagine the noise in this little cottage if there
were more than just Oscar about."

He fell silent, his mouth pursing. She had expected
him to smile back, but the look he gave her was utterly
somber. She watched him in some fascination, aware he
was thinking deeply, measuring, coming to conclusions.
Was he thinking how he could best tell her bad news?

She watched as several emotions washed over his face,
a little startled that he let them show to her so freely.
First came consternation—easy to imagine why, if he'd
finally concluded she really only had the one option if
she did not wish her son to grow up under a cloud of
disapproving gossip: that of leaving Severn's Well.

Then came unhappiness—and the very sight of his lowered brows and twisted mouth afforded her a lightning
hot flash of acute satisfaction, knowing he was unhappy
to think of her going. He cared for her, at least in some
small way—the proof was right there on his face.

Last came something more difficult to define: a tightening of his jaw and shoulders, followed a long moment
later by the smoothing of his posture and his features,
and the slow lifting of his gaze to meet hers.

He stared into her eyes for another long moment—a
minute or perhaps even more, and then he reached out
to touch her hand.

He might as well have kissed her mouth, so intimate
did his touch feel. His fingers closed around her wrist,
gently, not a gesture to bind her but to hold her, to bid
her stay, or perhaps even to come closer. She moved her
own hand, and she saw the beginning of disappointment
in his gaze, the sting of rejection, so she was quick to
turn her hand over, to grip his wrist as he did hers, a
gentle binding of her own.

The disappointment faded from his blue eyes, replaced

by something deeper. His fingers tightened, not to hurt but to pull her forward, so that Charlotte half-sprawled across the table, willingly, her head tilted back and her face turned up to his.

He pressed a kiss to her lips, not gentle, and she kissed him back, wanting this, wanting it even if it was a farewell kiss. She must have this, or regret it the rest of her days. A thrill chased down to her toes and back up to her lips, a sensation she'd never known, one she would cherish always. It was one thing to kiss a man, and another altogether to kiss the man that you loved. She'd known there would be a difference, but she'd not expected how devastated it would make her feel.

Slowly their mouths came apart, and Charlotte sank back into her chair, aware her legs had gone unsteady. She ought to have turned her eyes away, ought to have shied away from the intensity of his gaze, to have felt embarrassed or flustered by such a steady regard, but instead she felt her lips part as if ready to kiss him all over again, and a slow, deep rhythm began to pound in her blood as she kept her gaze locked with his.

"That's the thing of it, Charlotte," he said, his voice a little uneven, his tone intense. "I can. I can imagine this cottage filled with more children. A sister and a brother for Oscar. Our children. Yours and mine."

Charlotte felt her lips move, but no sound came forth until she tried again, and this time it was the merest whisper. "Sebastian?"

His intense gaze did not waver, did not give any hint of doubt or teasing or funning. "I came here with some vague notion of making things right, and then I looked into your face, and suddenly it all made perfect sense. Kissing . . . well, it only confirms it."

"What made sense?" Charlotte managed something a little above a whisper.

"Why do I not love Miss Talbot."

Charlotte felt her heart leap. "You do not?"

"I do not."

Sweet heaven, she believed him, from the steadiness of his gaze if for no other reason.

"Do you want to know how I know I do not love her?" he asked.

She nodded, breathless.

"I will only tell you if you accept that I am speaking the absolute truth."

"I am to believe," she managed to get out, "that you are incapable of lying at this moment?" The faintest smile touched her mouth.

"Yes."

She felt her smile fade and she looked even more deeply into his eyes, then slowly nodded. "Tell me why you know you do not love Miss Talbot."

He did not hesitate. "Because I love you."

She could have offered a quip, or cried, or protested he could not know his own mind, which had so recently been devoted to another . . . but instead she merely took a deep breath, then hiccoughed.

"Do not misunderstand me," he cautioned. "Do not think I am making you an offer simply because I 'must.' That I have compromised you, however unwittingly, and am now being a decent fellow and throwing myself on a matrimonial sword in order to make an honest woman out of you."

Charlotte could only stare at him, absorbing every word he said. She raised a hand to her mouth, vaguely noticing that she had begun to shake again. She was glad Oscar played contentedly in her bedroom, for he might not understand that a woman could tremble from joy as easily as from despair.

"But I am not a decent fellow, you know that. Since you do know that, I hope you have the good sense to believe what else I have to say. I want to marry you, Charlotte. Not because I have to, not because I should, but because I want to."

Something passed between them, an understanding deeper than words, so profound and real and tangible that a sigh escaped Sebastian's lips and he sat back, a dancing light now dawning in his eyes. Something crossed over his features, a look Charlotte had seen in other athletic men, an acknowledgment of triumph wrapped up with humility and gratitude and satisfaction and glory. Charlotte knew he had declared himself from the very depths of his heart, and had seen something in her own response that confirmed him victorious.

"Your promise to Miss Talbot?" Charlotte managed to sputter.

He leaned toward her, a look of playful outrage dawning over his face, fear and dread having been replaced by exultation. "I asked Miss Talbot if she would come watch me play cricket even if it snowed. Do you know what she said?"

"What?"

"She said 'I suppose,'"—he raised his voice an octave—"'if you tied me to a tree.' And when I asked her what her favorite part of cricket was, she said 'When the ball goes over the net.'"

"Net—?" Charlotte gave a laugh, a laugh as victorious as the dancing light in his gaze. "Oh, Sebastian, you made that up!"

"I did, but the words she said do not matter." His humor remained, but it did not disguise his earnestness. "It only matters that she and I would never suit. But—" He pushed their neglected cups of tea to one side, reaching across the table for her hands, this time taking both into his own. He was a man who liked touching, and his hands on hers now were strong and warm and creating a new sense of triumph in her, a proprietary joy that it was her home to which he had come today, her hands he had reached out to take. "But, Charlotte, how could she and I suit? She is nothing like you, and you are the one I love, the one I want to marry."

"We have only known each other—"

"Do not tell me we have only known each other a week," he said, shaking his head even as he grinned at her. "Do not tell me it is too soon, that I could not possibly love you. All these things are so evident, so clear—but I do not believe them anyway. I am asking you not to believe them either."

"Sebastian!" she said, her voice catching.

"I know you have every reason to doubt me. I am

young. I am foolish. I am impetuous." He laughed. "Until today I had no employment."

"Today?"

He told her of the offer to oversee the cricket club. "It is only five hundred pounds a year, but that is more than enough to live on in the country. And there is the ten thousand pounds the Prince Regent has promised." He glanced toward the bedroom where Oscar played, then back at Charlotte. "Your son—our son—would be well taken care of, and he would be able to go to school. Eton, if you like."

"Not so far away as that," Charlotte said. Her head was spinning.

Sebastian visibly brightened. "Can I ascertain from your wish for Oscar to go 'not so far away as that' that you wish to remain in Gloucester county? If you marry me and we live here, I can accept this offer I have been made."

"Of course you must accept the offer!" she cried.

"I want to, but it all depends on where you wish to live. If you will not marry me, well"—his voice faltered a moment until he swallowed thickly—"well, even if we do not live together, I want to be where you and Oscar are."

"Oh," Charlotte said, but she must have said it with a great deal of meaning, for Sebastian flashed her a broad smile.

His smile fell away, though, and he stood, still holding her hands in his. He frowned down at the table, then went down on one knee. He looked into her face, looking vulnerable in a way she'd not seen before. "You have not said you love me, nor that you will marry me, you know."

"I love you, Sebastian."

His hands tightened on hers, and her heart leaped again in answer to the intensity of his gaze, the exultation and hunger he did not try to hide from her. "And you will marry me?"

She took a deep breath, and let it out. He had to know about her past, first, or there could be no marriage, no real bond between them. "I cannot, not until you know everything about me."

"Ah. Your secret." He shook his head. "I do not care what it is."

"I care."

"Then tell me."

Charlotte looked down at her lap, aware of her hands still caught in his, aware he had gone down on one knee to bid her to marry him. Would he drop her hands and turn away if he knew she had stolen from her own son?

"You hesitate. Very well, let me go first and tell you my secret. The person who engaged me to smuggle Armand from one ship to another was Admiral Lowell," he said without further pause.

"*Admiral Lowell?*" He was only one of the most famous admirals to set sail, and now a member of the Privy Council.

"He knows of my brother, Benjamin, who was in the navy at one time. When they needed a favor—"

"They?"

Again he did not hesitate. " 'They' meaning Admiral Lowell and the Prince of Wales."

"Oh," Charlotte said, feeling as though someone had squeezed the air out of her lungs. Sebastian's task had been commissioned by the Prince Regent?

"When they needed a favor that encompassed the Severn River they thought of Benjamin's family, since we reside here. Gideon, as the marquess, was not approachable for such a delicate matter. Benjamin lives in Kent now, of course. But the youngest Whitbury brother was here and available, and more than willing to earn a generous fee."

Sebastian gave her a level look. "As I told you once before, this was my only attempt at smuggling, never to be repeated. Let us be clear on one other point, however, that I did not do it for the glory of England, but to fill my pockets. And now, my love, you have to admit that I have been very honest with you. I have even broken my vow not to tell anyone who employed me. I would not have done so except to convince you there are no secrets between us. So you owe me yours."

Charlotte felt her face flame red, but it was not with embarrassment or shock. It was a pure, raw reaction that came from believing who had employed him, believing he spoke only words he *wanted* to say to her. No half-truths, no politeness, no secrets. He said he loved her, and she believed him . . . but he had yet to hear her own secret.

"Oh my," she said, the faint words the opposite of the tumult sweeping through her. She believed him . . . and he believed her a good, honest, decent woman. What would his offer be if he knew what she had been doing, about the jewels she had stolen from under the solicitor's nose?

"Very well," she said through numb lips.

He quirked his head just a bit. "This is, I think, something more than the secret you told me of your grandpapa the smuggler." He frowned. "It has something to do with your going on the Mail coach the other day," he predicted.

"It does."

He let go of her hands, turned his chair around, and folded his arms atop the chairback. "Tell me," he said.

Chapter 19

She told him about the tin box stashed under her bed-chamber floor. How she took the Mail coach occasionally to Bristol and pawned the jewels, one by one, living off their proceeds. How Jarvis had forced her hand. How she had lied to the solicitor.

"But, worst of all, I am stealing from Oscar," she said. "The jewels are his, by law and by right."

Sebastian stood, and took her hands to pull her to her feet. She braced herself for his withdrawal, his renunciation of his offer.

"Perhaps they are Oscar's by law," Sebastian said, surprising Charlotte by pulling her into his arms. He hugged her to his chest, his arms around her, holding her, making her want to melt into his embrace. "But they are most certainly not his by right. By right your husband would have left you something on which to live."

"I am a thief," Charlotte said, no longer able to stave off tears as she allowed her arms to wrap around his waist.

"Well, you did steal my heart," Sebastian agreed. Charlotte gave a sob, which she immediately stifled. He squeezed her tighter. "Charlotte, you can be very slow-topped for a clever woman!" he chided gently. "If you do not believe me that you only did what you must, then ask Oscar when he is five-and-twenty. See if he minds that you kept him sheltered, and clothed, and fed."

She buried her face against the snowy linen of his shirt-front. "It sounds so much nicer put that way. But it was still wrong."

"Oh no," he said in the lightest of mock horror. He

reached between them to lift her chin, to raise her blue eyes to meet his own. "However can we make the madness stop? Oh, I have an idea. Why do you not marry the nice man who will give you a home along with his heart, and then you can keep the remainder of your jewels against the day that your son tells you to cease being ridiculous and keep them?"

She laughed, a blubbery sound. "You do not mind? That I am a thief?"

"*Have been* a thief, you mean. Just as I have been a smuggler. But perhaps I should ask, do you mind? Does my one act of smuggling disgust you?"

"Of course not."

"And am I less capable of indifference to your past than you are to mine?"

She gave a sudden, teary laugh. "Is it possible?" she asked him, wondering idly how awful she must look since she was halfway between crying and laughing.

"To love so soon, so quickly, and so well?"

"Yes. Is it possible?"

"I do not know," he said with raw honesty in his eyes and his voice. "But we will never know if we do not at least try. I know we have had a poor beginning, in many ways—"

She shook her head. "No! I cannot agree with that. Our beginning was the night you rescued Oscar, and there was nothing poor about that."

A slow smile spread across his face. "I stand corrected. But then what impediment is there? Dearest Charlotte, will you never give me an answer? I took a risk that night. Will you take one today? Will you agree to marry me?"

She wanted to close her eyes as though in prayer, but she needed to see the invitation in his own, to believe in what he said, without holding back, without fear.

"I will," she whispered.

"Thank God," he said, and might have said something else except that Charlotte went up on her toes and kissed him full on the mouth, her arms tangling around his neck.

He did not protest, however, instead tightening his arms around her again and holding her close.

A tug on Charlotte's gown interrupted a series of kisses that had gone on rather a long time. Charlotte took half a step back, picked up the puzzled-looking Oscar, and smiled with a sudden sense of shyness up at Sebastian once more.

"Oscar," Sebastian acknowledged her son a bit breathlessly. "Good man. Well done. You interrupted something that was in danger of spiraling into behavior most unbecoming in a betrothed couple." He glanced ever so briefly toward Charlotte's bedchamber door.

She could not meet the dancing light in his gaze, but neither could she keep a shy laugh from bubbling up to her lips.

"Just recall," Sebastian informed Oscar, reaching for his hat, "that once your mama and I are married, this sort of interference can only be occasional."

Oscar gave Sebastian a smile, and then everyone was laughing.

Chapter 20

"How goes the cricket club these days?" Charlotte's sister-in-law, Elizabeth, asked.

Charlotte looked up from her new nephew, who was cradled in her arms, to smile at Elizabeth. "It is still so new. Some people do not care for it. They say it is a waste of young men's time and energy."

"Which I suppose it is. But young men have the time and energy to expend, and better to spend it on cricket than in drink or those other 'sports' that young men tend to favor," Elizabeth assessed. "But I suspect it will be accepted in time. I know several game disputes have been settled per the Gloucester Cricket Club rulebook."

Charlotte grinned, for the newly printed rulebook was one of Sebastian's innovations as Overseer. She would have to tell him that even Elizabeth, who was less in society these days since Nicholas was born, had heard word of it.

She and Oscar, and Sebastian if he was not about on business, came to the Whitbury mansion every Sunday for church and a meal afterward. Their own home, given to them as a wedding gift by Gideon, was only five miles away. Gideon had called it "a mere hunting box," but it might better be described as a manor house with its fourteen rooms and separate kitchen.

"Better that it be occupied and cared for," Gideon had said, "than sitting empty and declining." It kept Sebastian busy, between his jaunts about the county as the cricket club Overseer, and provided an income that far outstripped the one he earned at his latter employment. Charlotte was still adjusting to the bounty that had come into her life, but had quickly delighted in being able to share that bounty in weekly calls upon the tenants who worked the land. But Sunday was a day for family. Charlotte had grown quite fond of her new sister-and brother-in-law.

Now she looked up from her nephew, who seemed likely to have the curious light eyes of his father the marquess, to spy a very large dog named Titan happily rolling in the field grass. She looked beyond the mutt that gave Oscar "pony" rides, and found her husband of three months also in the middle of the field at his brother's estate. As usual.

He was showing Oscar how to hold a cricket bat, a small-size one he had carved especially for Oscar, and Oscar was laughing. Her heart did a flip for the simple joy of seeing how the two of them had attached to one another.

When Oscar decided to sit and pull each petal off a series of daisies, Sebastian wandered over to his wife's side, throwing his length down beside her where she sat. Elizabeth had retrieved her son and gone to join Gideon, who was chatting with one of the estate gardeners about plans for an herb garden.

"Have you told Elizabeth?" Sebastian asked.

"Not yet," Charlotte said.

"She will begin to suspect you are expecting when I start to carve another small bat."

Charlotte gave a small laugh. "What if the baby is a girl?"

Sebastian gave her a scandalized glance. "What? Do you think *any* child of mine, male or female, will be neglected in being taught the art of cricket?"

"I forgot for a moment whom I was speaking with, Master Overseer," Charlotte said on a grin.

"Quite right, you did."

"I will tell Elizabeth and Gideon before we leave for home."

"They will be thrilled." Sebastian sat up and gathered up her hand. "As am I."

"As am I," Charlotte said with deep feeling, squeezing

Sebastian's hand, glad he was a man who liked to touch and be touched, delighted to find where Jarvis had been cold Sebastian was all warmth and embraces and lingering glances. "To think I once feared that Oscar would have no siblings."

"No fears now, eh?" Sebastian said, and Charlotte smiled again as she watched him fish in his waistcoat pocket, clearly intent on showing her something. "Here you are then," he said. Charlotte reached with her other hand, her palm open, and he dropped a golden object there.

"Grandmama's locket!" Charlotte gasped.

"The last of the missing jewels," Sebastian affirmed. "They have all been retrieved now, my love. Should any solicitor ever ask to see them, you can produce them all. You have no more secrets that need keeping."

"How did you ever find it?" she asked, although she knew he'd been using some of the reward money he'd earned from the Prince Regent to finance a quiet search. Still, it was a small miracle that everything had been recovered.

"If you offer twice what it is worth, it is amazing what can be 'found,' " Sebastian said, trying to look rueful but not succeeding. He'd already long since convinced her it was worth every penny of his reward if he could restore her peace of mind along with her jewels.

"And," Charlotte added, so filled with contentment that it was easy to match her husband's light tone, "things worth finding must be looked for in the oddest places." She slanted Sebastian a glance. "Such as on cliffs."

"Or in smugglers' cottages," Sebastian pointed out.

"Or on the cricket field."

"Or in fields of wildflowers," Sebastian said, but their game of words ran out then, turning instead into a game of touches and kisses as they lay back on the sun-warmed grasses and explored anew the joy of having found one another.